ALSO BY HELENA HALME

A FREE STORY!

The Day We Met is set at Uppsala University in Sweden where Alicia is studying English. When a migraine is threatening to ruin her day, the last thing she expects is to meet the man of her dreams.

Liam, a British doctor is in Uppsala attending a medical conference when a beautiful leggy blond chooses to sit at the same table as him in the busy student canteen. She's not the first woman Liam has ever been attracted to, but there's something beguiling about this young student and he cannot take his eyes off her.

This short prequel story is not published and only available to members of my Readers' Group.

Go to helenahalme.com to sign up to my Readers' Group and get your free, exclusive, story now!

THE ISLAND AFFAIR

CAN ONE SUMMER MEND A BROKEN HEART?

HELENA HALME

COPYRIGHT

With humble gratitude I dedicate this book to the Englishman who keeps my body and soul together.

THE ISLAND AFFAIR

CAN ONE SUMMER MEND A BROKEN HEART?

Alicia wakes up with a fuzzy head. The curtains to the bay window in the bedroom have been closed, and she hears muffled voices downstairs. She puts her hand on her body and discovers she's wearing a pink dressing gown over the oversized T-shirt she sleeps in. The clock by the bed shows 3.25am. On the small bedside table, she sees a half-empty glass of water and a packet of pills she's never seen before.

Then she remembers, and a horror rises in the pit of her stomach. She gets out of bed and crosses the landing to Stefan's bedroom. The familiar musty smell of her teenage son, her nearly grown-up son, her beautiful boy, hits her as soon as she opens the door, searching the dark room for the bed in the middle of the space. Wanting to see signs of the lanky shape, she looks for a narrow foot peeking out from under the familiar blue and white cover with the cockerel logo of Spurs football club. She prays for the sight of a mop of blond hair on the pillow above the bedcovers. Carefully, slowly, as if still in a dream, she walks over the threshold of the room. When she sees the bed is neatly made up and empty, she falls on her knees and lets out a cry.

She hears rapid steps behind her and feels Liam's hands on her shoulders. He's squeezing her hard, too hard. She can feel tears running down her face and realizes she is weeping. She's making noises she doesn't recognize, animal sounds like a wolf's howling.

ONE

Alicia is standing looking at the vast display of bottles in the ship's tax-free shop when the deck beneath her suddenly shifts and she almost loses her balance. The ferry must be out in the open sea between the islands and Sweden. Liam has gone to sit in one of the 'sleeping chairs'. He's taken a seasickness tablet and feels drowsy. This is the routine they have fallen into over the years, and mostly he is fine, as long as he stays still and keeps his eyes on the horizon. Luckily the quiet compartment has vast windows overlooking the sea.

The Viking Line ferry passes through the small islands between Stockholm and the coast before sailing through the open sea to the Åland archipelago. Usually conditions are calm, but sometimes there's a high wind and the sea is so choppy for an hour or so that the staff close the bars and restaurants.

Alicia tries to listen for any announcement above the clinking sounds of the bottles, but she can't hear anything. Again the ship moves abruptly, and Alicia loses her balance. She suddenly finds herself looking into a pair of piercingly blue eyes.

She had noticed the tall blond man walking along the aisles when she entered the shop. He was difficult to ignore in his trendy jeans, sailor shoes and soft suede jacket. He had an expensive-looking tan and ruffled hair. He's even taller than Liam, Alicia thought, but she didn't spot him standing next to her until she bumped into him.

He takes hold of her arms. His gaze is so direct and suggestive that Alicia gasps.

'Sorry,' she says and the man smiles. The intensely azure eyes and the slightly open mouth surrounded by laughter lines make her instinctively grin too. The sensation on her mouth feels strange; she doesn't remember when she last felt the urge to smile.

Alicia feels the man's strong hands keenly on her elbows. She senses the heat rise into her neck and face. She looks away, embarrassed.

When did she last blush?

'Don't be, I enjoyed it,' the man says, and his smile grows wider at her discomfort.

She straightens up, and the man's hands fall away from her. For a mad moment, Alicia wishes he would put them back and hold her, but she shrugs such thoughts away and gives a short, flustered, laugh.

The man stretches his hand out. 'Patrick Hilden,' he says. He has a very Swedish accent, from Stockholm, Alicia thinks. She tastes the name on her lips.

'Alicia O'Connell.' His hand lingers around Alicia's fingers.

'You're not an islander, are you?' he says.

'Is it that obvious?' Alicia manages to say. She doesn't know how. She's finding it difficult to speak. She's breathless, as if her lungs have been emptied of air.

'It takes one to know one,' the man continues to smile shamelessly into Alicia's eyes.

'I moved with my mum to Åland when I was a baby, but then went away to university and never returned,' Alicia says. She doesn't know why she feels she wants to tell this man her life story.

'Ah, that makes sense. All the best ones leave,' Patrick says.

'And you, you are obviously not from Åland either?'

He laughs. 'Originally from northern Sweden but I now live in Stockholm. One of the unlucky ones.'

Alicia returns the man's laugh. Everybody on the island hates the arrogant *Stockholmare*.

After what seems like minutes, Patrick lets go of Alicia's hand but he's still standing close to her, and his scent of expensive leather and something else, a manly tang, envelops her. She knows she ought to take a step back, but she can't move. She lifts her eyes toward his face and those eyes again.

'You don't sound like a *Norrbotten* Swede,' Alicia says, and then, seeing the man's raised eyebrows, adds laughing awkwardly, 'Sorry, I didn't mean to be rude.' Alicia has forgotten about the many sensibilities surrounding the Scandinavian countries. She's so used to what one can and cannot say about accents in the UK, but she suddenly feels clueless about the similar issues here. She's been living away from home for too long.

The boat shifts again, and Patrick puts his hand out in case Alicia loses her balance.

But this time she's prepared and steadies herself by placing her hand on the edge of the drinks display. 'Not much of a sailor, am I?'

Patrick laughs into her eyes. 'You're over for a holiday?'

'Yes,' Alicia replies simply. His scent and presence are intoxicating. She isn't hearing or seeing anything else but this tall, blue-eyed stranger. It's as if he's mesmerized her, and the old ship's clanging sounds and smells of diesel and paint have disappeared.

'Here you are!' Alicia is woken from her hypnotized state by an almost equally tall and elegant woman, who is striding toward them, speaking loudly in an Åland accent. When she sees Alicia, she looks her up and down and then turns to Patrick. 'Look, they're about to close the shop. There's a storm apparently, so we need to get a move on. Did you find the champagne?'

'This is Alicia O'Connell,' Patrick says, ignoring her urgent question and stretching his arm toward Alicia. He turns to Alicia and says, still smiling, 'And this very rude woman is my wife, Mia.'

The woman looks at Alicia more closely. 'It's you!' Her voice is very shrill and Alicia has a sudden desire to cover her ears with her hands, but instead she smiles. She feels Mia's arms pulling her into a tight embrace.

'Hello, it's been a long time,' Alicia replies from inside the woman's hug. The thin, but muscular arms are holding her tightly.

'So sorry I didn't recognize you!' she says, releasing Alicia.

'You know each other?' Patrick says, his eyebrows raised.

'We went to school together!' Mia shrieks. 'But we have to get on. Alicia, are you going to be on the islands over Midsummer? You must come to our party! Give me your email, will you?'

'Hmm,' Alicia says, not knowing what to reply. She glances over at Patrick, but his face betrays no emotion. He looks bored more than anything else now.

'Oh, don't worry, I've got your mum's address. You must all come. I'll send you the details!'

She drags her husband away. Patrick turns and looks at Alicia. With his right hand, he tips an invisible cap as if in a salute. Alicia stands there with a stupid smile on her face. She watches Mia speak to Patrick rapidly, like a machine gun. Patrick's shoulders are wide and she can see blond hairs curl up at his neck and a tiny, brown patch of skin above his shirt collar. She imagines stroking it, running her fingers along his neck and into his thick hair.

What's happening to me?

TWO

Liam wakes with a start. He checks his watch. He's only been asleep for a matter of minutes— half an hour at most. He wipes his mouth with his thumb; his lips and the side of his cheek are dry. He's paranoid about falling asleep in public and drooling, but all seems to be fine. And then he remembers where he is, on a ferry to the islands, and what has happened. Each time this occurs, each time he lets the knowledge slip from his mind, it's as if a cannon ball hits him in the guts when he remembers. The pain of the realization is intense, and for a moment he struggles to breathe. His heart is beating fast and he closes his eyes again, telling himself that breathing is as natural as living.

Living!

He knows this is just a minor panic attack, a reaction to the death of his son and part of the grieving process. These attacks will lessen and then hopefully disappear. That is what his colleagues at St Mary's Hospital tell him. When it happened the first time, a month or so after the accident, he thought it was his heart and had welcomed the panic and the pain. It would have served him right to die, to follow his son to an early grave. Besides, it would have been a relief.

But to his surprise, after a while his breathing had returned to normal. He remembers how disappointed he had felt, lying in the dark in his bed, next to Alicia, who was gently snoring. She had been on heavy sedatives then, on pills that he had prescribed.

'Acceptance of the facts is the first step,' his psychologist and colleague Constance Bell—a fair-haired older woman—had said. He'd given little credence to her practice before the accident.

'In time you'll be able to celebrate your son's life rather than grieve his death.' Connie, as everyone called her, gave him a half-smile, lifting the corners of her thin lips just a fraction on either side, and nodded her head. That movement meant it was the end of the session. Liam knew the woman was also seeing Alicia, and got the uneasy feeling she was on her side in all of it. He knew that professionally she wasn't taking sides, but after a few sessions, he had detected a coldness in her manner. Now he wonders if, when they're back in London, he should ask to see a different grief counsellor, but he knows changing now would only raise eyebrows in the hospital where they both practice.

Forcing her eyes away from the broad back of the blue-eyed man, Patrick, and her old schoolfriend Mia, Alicia sees Liam walking up and down the aisles. He's carrying a basket and Alicia sees a packet of cigarettes in the bottom. Marlboro Lights. After the accident he started to smoke again.

What is he doing here, especially when there's a storm brewing?

Alicia waves to him several times, and calls his name, soliciting stares from the people around her, until he eventually sees Alicia and walks slowly up to her.

'They're closing the shop,' he says.

Alicia remembers why she is here. Hilda, Alicia's mother, has asked her to bring wine, two bottles of white and two of red, to be precise. 'Something nice,' she had added on the phone, as if Alicia would buy some worthless plonk as a welcome present, or alternatively, as if she was completely unknowledgeable about wine.

'I know,' she says to Liam, and picks up four bottles at random and puts them in Liam's basket.

'We've been invited to a party,' she says over her shoulder, walking toward the tills.

'You hungry?' Liam asks as they leave the ship's tax-free shop. As they pass the loos, a woman comes out, and the familiar smell of the ferry—a combination of drains, diesel oil and paint—hits Alicia's nostrils. For a moment, she feels a wave of nausea overwhelm her. Perhaps she's suddenly developed sea sickness too?

But she nods to Liam. She wants to follow the old routines on this journey. Veering away from what they always did would be to betray Stefan's memory. Alicia feels his presence strongly now, and she doesn't want to let go of him.

Every summer, Alicia, Liam and Stefan would fly from London to Stockholm and then onto Åland, a group of islands between Finland and Sweden.

Alicia's home.

Usually, Alicia's mother picks them up from the airport and drives them to the *Ålandsfärjan* ferry port in Kapellskär. But this year, Hilda didn't come to meet them in Arlanda. Alicia knows she's scared and wants to postpone the moment when she has to acknowledge Stefan's absence. Instead, she and Liam take a train to *T-Centralen* in Stockholm and a bus to the harbor.

During the hour-long bus journey, Alicia withdrew into her memories of the many times they'd taken this trip together. When Stefan was a baby, they would rent a car, and she'd fuss over the unfamiliar Swedish car seat. How did it work? Was it safe? Alicia would ask all the questions while Liam calmly looked at the instructions and eventually strapped—the usually crying—Stefan into the seat. Alicia looked over at Liam's profile. She was sitting on the aisle seat in the bus, while Liam was asleep, his head resting on his folded jumper by the window. She loved him then; she thought she could never do without him.

In the past, when the seas were heavy Liam got very seasick and had to sit and stare at the horizon close to the bathrooms while Alicia, her mother and Stefan ate and drank in the restaurant, talking about what had happened during the months, or sometimes a full year, since they'd last seen each other. During the meal they admired the breathtakingly beautiful archipelago with its many islands, while Hilda stared besottedly at her grandson, commenting on his taller frame, new haircut or smart jacket.

As the ship picked its way through the small channels, Alicia and Stefan would gawp at the large seaside villas, with their intricate woodwork, built decades ago on the larger islands, or the tiny red houses, with sparkling white window frames, perching on top of small rocky outcrops.

'Can we live there?' Stefan would ask each year, pointing to a particularly beautiful villa, with a boathouse below it and a long jetty jutting out to sea. Even when he was older, they went through this routine, picking out a place they would like to own.

'We already have a cottage on the islands,' Alicia replied.

One year—Alicia cannot remember how old he was —her son said, 'When I'm a grown-up, I'm going to buy that one,' pointing at one particularly grand villa just outside Stockholm.

They had laughed at his naivety—the villas cost a fortune and were rarely even for sale—and Stefan had cried, his dreams crushed by the stupid adults.

'You sure you want to go to the restaurant? It was Stefan who ...' Liam now says, gazing at Alicia, his dark green eyes trying to figure out what is going on in her head. She knows she's shutting him out, pushing him away, but she is too tired to soothe Liam's grief. All her energy is spent on trying to keep herself composed. Trying not to slump down and cry in the middle of the passage, among the holidaymakers, who are laughing, happy at the prospect of a long break on the islands.

Liam is standing in front of her and they are blocking the other passengers, some of whom tut and say *'Ursäkta'*, the Swedish for 'Sorry' in a loud voice.

'You OK?' Liam says. He reaches his hand out, about to touch Alicia's arm, but she moves away just in time and Liam's hand flops down.

Alicia looks at Liam. He is definitely a bit green around the gills.

'How are *you* feeling?' she manages to say, even putting an emphasis on the 'you' to show that she cares, even though she doesn't register any kind of feeling for her husband.

'I'm fine—let's risk it. What else is there to do?' Liam says, pulling his mouth into an attempted smile. Alicia looks at her husband. The lines around his eyes have grown deeper in the past few months, and his skin looks pale and sallow. He's got his feet planted wide, but he is ever so slightly stooped, perhaps because he's holding the plastic bag from the tax-free shop. He'll feel better once they enter the Åland archipelago, Alicia thinks, and walks in front of Liam.

Even though Liam knows the layout of the ferry intimately after all these years, Alicia still feels she is the local, and he the foreigner. When the deck below her shifts again, she takes hold of the bannister of the central staircase leading up to the restaurant. She glances behind her and sees that Liam is steady, holding the wall to keep his balance. She nods to him and he follows her up the stairs. As they make their way to the restaurant and are shown to the end of a long table by a large, oval porthole, she remembers how she and Stefan would devour the buffet lunch of gravlax, herring, meatballs in gravy and rye bread and eat too much. She and her son had the same tastes; they both missed proper Finnish food in London. Her lovely, serious boy, who seemed to understand the sacrifice Alicia had made to live away from the islands. He loved the sea, the sauna, the silence of a nightless night at Midsummer when the only sounds were the faint cries of the birds, flying low above the seashore.

Alicia swallows a lump in her throat, trying to control herself. Not that she could cry anymore. There are no tears left, just the pain in her chest, the lump that won't go away however much she cries, or tries to calm down. She makes an effort to concentrate on the familiar, but still stunning, view of the dark wooded islands resting like tufts of carpet on the teal-colored sea. They are entering the calmer seas, thank goodness.

THREE

Hilda has another new car; a red low-slung BMW. Liam's feet almost hug his chin as he settles himself on the back seat. He had insisted Alicia sit next to her mother in the front so that they could chat away in Swedish. It's safer that way. Liam never enjoyed being driven by his mother-in-law. He knows the journey from the ferry port in the capital Mariehamn to his father-in-law's farm in Sjoland takes only 15 minutes—unless the swing bridge over the canal is open—but anything could happen even during the short journey. Hilda's driving is as erratic as her character. If she has to lean back to talk to her daughter, her concentration would suffer even more. Besides, Liam has never learned the language they speak on the islands, a version of Swedish that sounds like Finnish but isn't.

After nearly twenty years of holidaying on the islands, he can understand a little of the Swedish conversation, but Finnish is still incomprehensible to him. Alicia keeps telling him how lucky he is that she and her mother speak

Swedish to each other. Alicia never got to learn her mother tongue, because she was just a baby when Hilda moved to the islands.

Liam thinks about Stefan and how fluent he'd been in Swedish, and how much effort Alicia had put into his bilingualism. Although she disliked the Swedes for some curious reason only known to her, for years she had sent Stefan to language lessons at the Swedish Church in Marylebone. When Stefan was fifteen, he'd gone on a week-long confirmation camp in Åland and had fallen in love for the first time. Liam remembers picking his son up from the station in Mariehamn, watching the teenagers spill out from a bus, their heavy bags slung over their shoulders.

Stefan was holding hands with a slim girl with straw-blond hair and bright eyes. Liam could well understand his son's infatuation with her; she had a pale complexion yet was tanned. Her fair eyelashes fluttered as she shook Liam's hand and introduced herself as 'Frida'. Of course, that romance hadn't lasted, but Stefan said they were still friends. Liam had seen her again the previous summer, when the group from the confirmation camp had met up for a drink in Mariehamn. Liam remembers how grown up they had all looked when he'd dropped Stefan off at Torggatan. He'd watched the group of teenagers greet his son with hugs and high-fives through the rear-view mirror as he drove away.

Liam wonders if Stefan's friends have been told. He hopes so, for Alicia's sake. With another pang of guilt, he remembers how Stefan had begun talking about getting a moped; he'd begged and begged to be allowed to ride on the one belonging to Alicia's stepfather, and at last Liam had agreed. Of course, both Alicia and Hilda were against it, so he'd colluded with Uffe to allow Stefan to ride around the farm, and then take a trip on his own into Mariehamn on a day when his mother and grandmother were shopping in Stockholm.

But Liam knew regrets were useless. He made himself concentrate on the road. He would at least try to prevent an accident while in the car with his mother-in-law, and get safely to the farm.

Uffe stands outside the large wood-clad house that he was born in over 65 years ago and watches his stepdaughter and her husband get out of Hilda's car. He decides to let Liam carry the bags; he is young and strong, whereas Uffe's own back has been in spasms all morning. Although he now has enough workers on his farm to do the heavy lifting, he still likes to get involved and has been knee-deep in mud all day. He should have stayed in the fields, overseeing the first crop of potatoes being lifted onto the lorry, but he knows what Hilda's reaction to his absence at the visitors' arrival would be. At a few minutes past five, he hastily got into his Subaru and drove the couple of kilometers home along the road. He had just changed his shirt in the bedroom, when he saw the BMW turn into the drive through the window.

Uffe waves when he sees Alicia walking up to him. Suddenly noticing how dirty his hands are, he places them quickly behind his back.

'Uffe,' his stepdaughter says and buries her head in his

chest. Uffe hugs her hard and feels a tightening in his chest as he thinks about the handsome lad, his grandson. Or step-grandson to be precise. (Uffe has never considered Alicia anything but his daughter even if he didn't officially father her.) It's incomprehensible that the young lad would no longer be coming here; that he no longer exists.

Of course, Uffe and Hilda went to the funeral. They stayed in Alicia and Liam's silent house in London and tried to help as much as they could. Alicia seemed distant then, asleep most of the time. Uffe only hugged her once during their two-night stay in the small house in a pleasant suburb. Even when they left, the day after the funeral, Alicia stayed in bed while Liam ordered a taxi to take them to Heathrow. It had been foggy during their stay, and they didn't see the sun once, even though the grass in the nearby park was a lush green, which Uffe marveled at. The landscape in London was so vibrant compared to the gray and brown at home, making a mockery of the reason they had been visiting Alicia.

He and Hilda had spent a lot more time together than they usually did on their visits to London. Normally he'd be stuck with Liam, trying to communicate with his schoolboy English that he'd long since forgotten. While Alicia and her mother shopped in the fancy stores in the West End, Liam usually took Uffe to the pub, or once to see a football match with Stefan. Stefan was a keen supporter, and Uffe had been surprised at the passion he'd displayed when his club, the name of which Uffe now forgets, scored—or missed—a goal. Usually the boy was quiet, a bit like his mother: a thinker.

After Stefan's death, Uffe had been concerned about his stepdaughter; he saw the pills she was taking, but Hilda told him in no uncertain terms that Liam was a doctor and knew how to medicate his own wife. Uffe wasn't so sure. As he now watched his son-in-law struggle with the bags, smiling at Hilda, while glancing furtively back at him, looking for assistance, the older man wondered what it was about Liam that he so disliked. There was just something shifty about his dark eyes, and his unnaturally thick hair. It was as if when he spoke to Alicia, or to Hilda and Uffe, he wasn't fully there, as if he didn't *want* to be there. Uffe had thought that it was something to do with his profession; how could a man deal with death all day without losing his faith in life along the way?

'Would you like a sauna before dinner?' Hilda says as they stand awkwardly in the newly decorated hall. Two years previously, on the advice of their young, female architect, the old steep stairs, which had been in the house since it was built in the 1920s, had been removed and replaced by a set of modern wide steps in light wood. The boxed design with a small landing made the hall look so much cleaner and bigger, even though the new stairs took up more space than the old narrow staircase had. They made Hilda finally feel at home in this, her in-laws, house.

Hilda sees Liam look at Alicia before responding to her query and almost imperceptibly shake his head, but her daughter ignores him and says, smiling, 'Yes please. You'll come with me, won't you, *Mamma*?'

Whenever her daughter uses the Swedish term for 'Mother,' Hilda feels tears well up inside. This has started happening more and more, getting sentimental over silly little things. She must pull herself together, for her daughter's sake, Hilda thinks and nods. She goes into the downstairs bathroom to fill a basket with towels and toiletries. In the large kitchen, which has also been refurbished, she takes a few cans of cold beer from the large American-style fridge.

'Would you like a *Lonkero*?' she asks, turning around to address her daughter.

Alicia is in the middle of what seems like a heated conversation with Liam on the other side of the kitchen island, where Hilda has a collection of fresh herbs neatly arranged under a low white lamp. Between the plants and the light, she can see Liam shaking his head at Alicia. His lips are in a straight line and his hands are crossed over his chest. Hilda walks around the kitchen island and stands in front of her daughter. 'Everything alright?' she says, feeling her throat constrict, making her voice sound tight and hostile.

Liam looks down at her; he is such a tall young man, or is it that she has shrunk, as happens to so many older women? She straightens her back and extends herself, realizing with relief that she had kicked off her heels when they entered the house and is now in her stockinged feet, whereas both Alicia and Liam are still wearing their outdoor shoes.

'No problem,' Alicia says, putting her arm around Hilda's shoulders. She attempts a smile but all that she manages is a straightening of her mouth. 'Will Uffe want a sauna?' Alicia continues.

Uffe has disappeared. Hilda suspects he's gone into the old milking parlour, which he converted (badly, in Hilda's opinion) into a little farm office just after his mother died. He does all his paperwork there, although how he manages when he doesn't even have a computer, Hilda never understands. Mostly, she suspects, he sits there, reading the paper and listening to the radio. It's his escape from her nagging, she knows. But she doesn't mind, not really. It's good to be rid of his clutter in the house. She avoids the 'office' as much as she can, only glancing in when she goes into the small utility room next door, where there's a large freezer and the washing machine.

'Oh, I'm sure he will,' Hilda says, turning to her son-in-law, 'but it's no problem if you don't want one. Uffe is quite used to going to the sauna on his own.'

FOUR

Liam realizes for the first time how much he hates this sauna ritual. He feels awkward having to slip his clothes off in the small dressing room, trying to avoid looking as the naked body of the older man is slowly revealed in front of him. Uffe may be in good shape for his age, if you ignore his pot belly, which seems to grow larger each year, but he still feels awkward with him. But to say 'No' to the first-night sauna would upset everyone, as Alicia said between tight lips to him in the kitchen earlier. Liam doesn't really understand why; all he can think is that it's like refusing a cup of tea when you are guests in the UK. Which, by the way, he is never offered in Åland.

Liam sighs and sits down on the slatted bench.

Uffe is bent over, leaning on his knees, looking out of the small window, at a slice of the sea and the beautiful, cloudless sky above.

I'm definitely refusing a dip in the freezing water.

As the heat seeps into his skin, a sudden image of

large full breasts comes into Liam's mind, and he sees her smile, that naughty, raunchy smile Ewa has when she's on top of him. He feels guilt about his son all the time, and now about Ewa, but he's not sure how he would have coped for the past six months without her. Being with the soft-skinned nurse, her body so different from his wife's slim, athletic figure, has given Liam his only respite from grief. He knows he should stop the affair, and that to anyone on the outside, his actions look unforgiveable, to say the least. But he can't help himself. When he is better, when Connie's sessions begin to work, and his mind is clearer, not full of guilt about the moped, then he will stop seeing her.

Liam is rudely brought back to the present when Uffe, before he has time to protest, throws water on the hot stones and a stinging steam hits Liam's face. It catches in his throat and he struggles to breathe, so he ducks, and now the heat is spreading over his shoulders, back, thighs and eventually his legs. How the locals think this torture is pleasurable, he will never understand.

'Hot, hot, hot,' Uffe says in English and gives a short laugh, throwing more water on the stones. His watery eyes, now almost gray, matching the thin wisps of hair that are now damp and stuck to his skull, gaze at Liam. It's as if the old man knows what his son-in-law has been thinking about.

Liam turns his face away from the old man's scrutiny. Sweat drips from his temples into his eyes, stinging them too. Turning back to Uffe, he wipes the corners with his thumbs, and tries to smile at him, but only manages a grimace. It's their joke and the only words that pass between the men during their annual sauna sessions. Liam has often tried to speak to Uffe, but Uffe's English is nonexistent and although he nods enthusiastically, Liam suspects he doesn't understand a word of what he says. Over the years, the two men have settled on a silence that in Liam's mind is all but comfortable. They manage to communicate with nods and gestures, like now, when Uffe gets up and moves his head in the direction of the sea to indicate that it's time for a swim. Liam knows from past years that the sea will be bitterly cold this early in the summer, and he wonders what the old man would say—or rather do—if he refused to participate in the ritual. But he doesn't, and the two men walk the few yards toward the jetty. Liam is barefoot and remembers too late the advice Ewa gave him about ticks and Lyme's disease. 'They perch on the blades of grass and just wait to hop on you.'

'Like you,' Liam had said, taking hold of Ewa's waist.

They'd been standing in the basement landing of St Mary's East wing, outside the Chapel, a place they often used if they needed some privacy at work. Ewa was his theater nurse, and Liam had been on his way home, having just finished seeing his private patients. It was nearly 10pm, he'd been running late all day and was exhausted. But he wanted to say goodbye to Ewa. He knew she expected it, and for the first time he felt he would miss her during the two-week holiday with Alicia and her family. He'd seen her more than the usual one evening a week (Wednesdays after his private clinic), and not just for sex, even though that was the main reason Liam couldn't keep away. The sex with Ewa was satisfying. It made Liam forget. Alicia hadn't let him into her bed since Stefan's accident, and even before that their love-making had been—to say the least—sporadic.

'Lyme's disease is very dangerous, you know,' Ewa had said, stroking Liam's cheek.

They were in an embrace, Liam trying to get close to her, to take a piece of her with him to Åland. He kissed her, not caring if someone might open the door to the corridor and see them there. The people using the small room set aside for grieving family and friends of patients, would mostly likely not know Liam, and even if they did, tonight he didn't care.

'I do know, and I will be careful, I promise,' Liam said. 'What time do you finish?' he added, nuzzling her neck, taking in the scent of sandalwood and sweet lipstick.

'Midnight,' Ewa sighed, arching her back and pressing her breasts against Liam's chest.

He knew her neck was her most erogenous zone, and just a few kisses or caresses would be too tempting for her. He thought briefly about his consulting room; it would be empty now and if they were quick, and careful, they could use it again. He wondered if the other consultants had finished their appointments. He decided to take the risk. He'd tell the other nurses he'd forgotten something. Ewa could take the stairs and slip into the room unnoticed, if she was lucky.

'Is this your long break?' Liam said into her eyes, his voice hoarse, his erection hardening in his pants.

'You're impossible,' Ewa laughed, throwing her head back and making her delicious curls shake.

· · ·

The sea, as Liam feared, is extremely cold, and he manages just a few strokes in the water. Uffe on the other hand, swims expertly further away, to the other side of the line of reeds in front of the wooden jetty. Liam gives the old man a wave and walks briskly back to the sauna, holding the towel he's taken to cover himself. He sits on the porch and watches a family of mallards approach the jetty from further along the shore. It's past seven o'clock but the sun is unnaturally high in the sky, bright in a near cloudless sky. There's no wind, and the surface of the sea beyond the band of reeds is still. It is beautiful here, Liam thinks as he watches the mother mallard, ahead of her family of four, take a sharp turn on seeing Uffe's head bob up and down on his way back to the jetty. The pale blue sky, broken only by the cottonwool strips of white clouds, and the three dark green islands on the horizon—one large, two smaller—contrast breathtakingly against the deep marine color of the water. Liam thinks again about Ewa and wishes he could bring her here. But that would never be possible. Liam inspects his feet and toes for ticks and decides that what he needs to do is be braver.

FIVE

Alicia feels pleasantly tired. She's had far more to drink than usual. In the sauna she had two cans of *Lonkero*, the gin drink she'd liked when she was underage in the park in Mariehamn, and later when visiting the islands from Uppsala, where she'd gone to university. It was the drink of her youth. Her mother always remembered to buy some when Alicia was back home. Although sweet, the *Lonkero* tasted delicious after the sauna, as she and her mother sat outside on the porch, watching the calm sea. Alicia had also had wine during the excellent meal her mother had prepared. They had eaten venison, shot by Uffe the previous fall, with lingonberries, a creamy mushroom sauce and new potatoes grown by Uffe. Alicia ate heartily, more than she had since. *Since.* She could see Liam look at her approvingly; he was always telling her she was too thin.

Now up in the attic bedroom that Hilda always prepared for them, Alicia fights back tears when she thinks how much Stefan would have loved the perfectly cooked game prepared by his grandmother, bloody in the middle just as he liked it. Instead, Alicia forces a smile, undresses in the narrow en-suite bathroom, and thinks about Uffe's description of Liam in the sauna. How he was like a baby deer, with his thick hair turning curly and his large eyes fixed on Uffe in horror as he poured more water on the stones.

Alicia translated what her stepfather had said, wanting Liam to laugh too. It was an annual joke of theirs, how Liam hated the sauna but suffered it in silence. Usually he took the Mickey out of himself and got drunk on the vodka schnapps Uffe poured for the two men, but tonight he didn't join in. All through dinner Liam was quiet, hardly saying a word even to Alicia, or Hilda, who always made an effort to speak English to him. *He is hurting*, Alicia thinks. *Or, was he missing her?*

Liam is in bed reading the *The Telegraph* on his iPad. He tries to get himself comfortable on the two lumpy pillows, but fails. What is it about these Nordic types that they can't make proper pillows? They were either as thin as anything or lumpy as hell. Once again he curses himself for not stuffing his Canadian goose pillow into the suit-case. Now he has to look forward to two weeks of bad sleep; just what he needs before going back to his hectic schedule at the hospital.

Alicia slips in beside him. She's wearing a long T-shirt, and her legs look thin and muscular beneath it.

A moment after she's settled down to read, slowly turning the pages of her book, Liam hears a low buzzing noise. He tries to ignore the mosquito, hoping Alicia will get up and kill it. She is a local after all, and expert at it. The mozzy does a low fly-pass over Alicia's nose, but she waves a hand absentmindedly and continues reading.

'You're not going to kill it?' Liam says in disbelief.

Alicia puts down her book and looks at him. 'No.'

There's silence while Liam tries to get back to an article about Brexit. Liam is enraged; all the lies, like the increased funding for the NHS, touted by the Brexiteers during the campaign make him furious. The knowledge that the health service will struggle without the easily available workforce from Europe, or the funding for medical research, makes him fearful for the future. Liam knows he's had too much beer and wine, and that he is probably a bit drunk, but the sense that his life is going in the wrong directing seems suddenly terribly clear to him. His country is going to the dogs; he's lost his wonderful son; his wife is now a cold, skinny woman whom he doesn't love anymore, and he is on holiday on some islands in the middle of the Baltic, where he doesn't want to be, with her.

There, he's said it.

The quiet is broken by the sound of more insects, the sole mosquito has been joined by his friends. Liam throws down his iPad on the bed and climbs indiscriminately across his wife's body. The bed is situated against one wall in the attic bedroom, under the sloping roof. He gets up so abruptly that he bangs his head against a thick beam.

'Fuck!' he exclaims.

Alicia stifles a laugh. Liam looks at his wife in disbelief. Her face is hidden by the book with a bright blue and yellow cover. One of her romance books, he thinks. What is the matter with the woman? Is she drunk? Alicia knows that he suffers badly from mosquito bites; more than anyone else in the family. Even Stefan had a built-in immunity to them, but Liam gets huge swollen, itchy patches on his skin each time one of the little devils gets to him. Liam turns on the main light in the bedroom and stares at the ceiling, holding a rolled-up magazine he's picked up from the round table by the bed. But now there's no sign of the mosquitoes and there is a silence in the room.

'*Oj*, that light is very bright!' Alicia says, lowering her book and glaring at him.

The use of the Swedish '*Oj,*' which he understands means something close to 'Hey', somehow annoys him. Whenever Liam hears Alicia speak her own language, she sounds like a teenager. A stroppy teenager at that.

Liam turns out the light and returns to bed, being careful not to bang his head again when he climbs over Alicia.

Alicia gives a loud sigh, and Liam suppresses his growing anger.

There's silence again and Liam manages to read two sentences of the article. Then two loud buzzing noises fill the room, and Liam feels a sting in his arm.

'Fucking hell!' he says. 'Now look what's happened, I've been bitten!'

'And how exactly is that my fault?' Alicia says. She's lowered the book and is staring at Liam with those dark eyes. There's a dangerous-sounding calm to her voice, but Liam ignores it. He's had enough. There's blood on his hand where he managed to kill the mosquito, but he knows he'll have a painful and itchy bite on his arm tomorrow. The sting will most probably be inside his skin, which means a more prolonged healing process.

'We wouldn't be here if you hadn't insisted. We could have gone to France, or Italy, or ...'

'Really? And not see my mother and Uffe? You would deny me time with my family now, especially now!' Alicia has raised her voice.

'You could have come on your own!'

Alicia is quiet for a moment and then turns to Liam. 'That would have suited you, wouldn't it?'

Liam looks at his wife's unmade, worn-out face. Her eyes are still the same color of blue they were when they met, but they now have dark circles around them. It was those pale eyes, like shallow lakes, Liam had fallen in love with in Uppsala, at the Swedish university he'd visited as a research fellow. Alicia had been a second-year student, cool and collected for her young age.

'What do you mean?' he now says, looking squarely at her.

'So you can fuck your little nurse while I'm out of the way.' Alicia says the words in a low hiss, so quietly that Liam doesn't think he's heard her right. Her face shows no emotion whatsoever, but her eyes regard Liam coldly. All the warmth from her youth gone.

The buzzing of another mosquito breaks the silence, and Alicia, calmly closing her book, turns around and kills the insect with the palm of her hand against the white wall behind her head.

'Why couldn't you have done that before?' Liam says, trying to smile, to make a joke of it.

Alicia picks up a tissue from a box beside the bed and wipes her hand. She gazes at him with hard eyes, which make Liam turn his head away.

A silence fills the room.

'So you know?' Liam says quietly, looking at the white ceiling between the dark wood beams. He moves his eyes to the foot of the bed where they had folded the dark red quilt that Hilda had proudly shown Alicia. Liam understood it was a new purchase to be admired.

'Yes,' Alicia says. Her voice is low but there's no feeling in it.

'How long?'

'Does it matter?'

'No.'

SIX

'I want a baby.'

The words escape from her mouth before Alicia realizes she's going to say them.

Liam gets up and leans uncomfortably against the wall. He turns toward her.

'What did you say?'

Now she's finally plucked up the courage to tell him, because of the *Lonkero* and wine, and because she knows he must feel guilty about the affair. She must carry on. She also rises from the bed, and picks up a red cushion from the floor to place behind her head. She knows tomorrow morning she'll not be this brave. She takes hold of Liam's arm, but he pulls it away.

'Ouch, that's where the mozzy got me!'

'Sorry,' Alicia says. She sits with her hands in her lap, and continues, 'I'm relatively young, and I know if I begin eating healthily and looking after myself again, I'd be able to ...'

'Stop!' Liam raises his voice. He is staring at Alicia with an incredulous expression in his eyes.

Tears are running down Alicia's cheeks now, but she doesn't want to give up. The thought of having a baby, a new Stefan, has been haunting her for weeks now. It started when she was in the local Waitrose. She'd seen a mother, well into her forties, with gray hair, fuss with her child in a buggy. Alicia, who was laden with bags and trying to leave the shop, couldn't get past them. When the woman turned around, Alicia saw the child, perhaps three or four months old, with a mop of blond hair and blue eyes, just like Stefan. She stood there and gasped, letting the mother and baby slowly move away, out of the shop.

At home, she stood in front of the mirror and remembered what it was like to be pregnant, waiting for the miracle that was a baby to be born. She had loved the feeling of life growing inside her. Even toward the end of her term, when her back ached and she had to pee every five minutes, the baby pressing on her bladder and seemingly kicking her innards to smithereens, she was more satisfied with her life than she had ever been before, or since.

She had never forgotten the elation when little Stefan, so beautiful with his handsome, perfect asymmetric face, little toes and hands, and wide, innocent eyes, had been placed in her arms. She could do it again; she could even have more than one child before it was too late.

'I'm only 38 years old, and nowadays women go on to have children well onto their forties,' she says, wiping her eyes.

'Alicia, we don't share a bed anymore,' Liam says quietly.

'But we could.'

'You want to share a bed with me just in order to have a baby?' Liam has grabbed hold of Alicia's shoulders. He fixes his eyes on hers.

Alicia can't read him. Is he angry with her? Or has he been thinking the same? Or is he no longer in love with her?

'You've fallen in love with your little nurse? Is she going to give you more babies, now is she?'

'You cannot replace a child with another. Stefan was ...' Liam lets his hands drop and looks down at them, seemingly unable to go on.

'How can you say that?' Now Alicia is shouting, not caring if Hilda and Uffe hear them.

'Shh!' Liam says and this infuriates her even more. It's her mother and stepfather who live in the house. If she wishes them to hear, it has nothing to do with Liam.

'Stefan was my life! Nothing, or no one,' Alicia gives Liam a stare, making sure he understands exactly what she means. 'No one can ever replace him.'

'Don't I know it!' Liam says and clambers out of bed, over Alicia. He begins to pace the small space, taking two or three steps toward the door and two steps back again. 'I was nobody to you after Stefan was born.'

Alicia stares at her husband. This man, who is so wise, so competent and has been fucking another woman behind her back, has the temerity to be angry with her?

'You were jealous of your own son?'

Liam sits down on the bed. He places his hands,

palms up on the white sheet and spreads his fingers out. She can hear him take slow breaths in and out. *He's trying to compose himself.*

'Of course not. I just knew how close you two were and sometimes I felt a bit left out.' He lifts his eyes toward Alicia. They are now full of sadness. Alicia doesn't know what to say, how to respond. She's still angry, and confused. What is Liam trying to say to her?

'Can you understand that?' Liam adds.

Alicia nods, her fury abating.

They are both quiet for a moment. Alicia can hear the old grandfather clock that Uffe insists on keeping in the lounge in spite of Hilda's repeated pleas to have it removed strike one. She checks her phone and sees it is indeed an hour past midnight. Which makes it eleven o'clock in the UK. Still, it's late.

'Couldn't we start again?' Alicia asks.

Liam looks at her. His eyes are so sad that she feels suddenly bereft. I've lost him, she thinks.

'It's late,' Liam says and lies down on the bed, with his back to Alicia.

It's too late, he means.

After the row, lying awake next to Liam, who eventually falls asleep after tossing and turning for what seems like hours, she waits for a feeling of loss, or anger, or something, but there is nothing. What is her marriage compared to the death of her son anyway? If Liam is not prepared to have a baby with her, then he doesn't love her anymore. Besides, she cried over Liam enough when she found out about the affair from one of their so-called friends—Susan, a do-gooder who runs a charity cashmere stall at St Mary's hospital, where Liam has his private practice.

Four months ago, on a cold February day, Susan telephoned Alicia and asked to see her for coffee because she had 'something very important' to tell her. Alicia didn't have a clue what the older woman wanted; they'd only become friends because Susan's late husband had worked with Liam at the hospital. Feeling sorry for her after the sudden loss of his friend and colleague to an aggressive form of pancreatic cancer, Liam had convinced Alicia to invite Susan for dinner. Alicia felt guilty for not liking the woman. They had nothing in common. Susan was about 15 years older than Alicia, and was staunchly conservative. She always made a point of asking Alicia about her 'home country', making sure it was understood that Alicia was foreign and didn't belong in Britain. Alicia now suspected she had voted for Brexit. With her cashmere cardigans and pearls, and two children graduated from Oxford, she had the air of being better than Alicia. The dinner had been three years ago, at a time when Stefan's Oxbridge ambitions had been mere dreams, mere possibilities hinted at by his school.

Alicia had met Susan for the occasional coffee since then ('You don't drink tea, do you, dear?' she had said), always at the behest of the older woman. Alicia had even bought a cashmere poncho from her stall; at £105, it wasn't cheap, but Susan had said the purchase was 'a steal.'

The day she told her about Liam, they were at

Richoux in St John's Wood, where they always met. The coffee was expensive, but Susan always said she couldn't drink coffee anywhere else. Besides, she said, she only used buses to get into town, because she couldn't abide the underground anymore.

Alicia suspected that contrary to what she liked people to believe, Susan was short of funds, because each time they went for coffee, Alicia somehow ended up paying the check. But she didn't mind that much. In spite of her airs and graces, Alicia was certain Susan was lonely. Her two brilliant children, now grown up, rarely visited her, and she didn't seem to have any other family around. That must be why she was so involved in the St Mary's charities, Alicia had once said to Liam, and he'd nodded, although Alicia could tell he'd not heard a word.

Once they were seated at a table at the back of the café, Susan cocked her head to one side, corrected her gray-blond hairdo and placed her wrinkly manicured hand over Alicia's.

'Now, I'm so sorry for what I am about to tell you.'

She looked kindly at Alicia. Her eyes, which looked as though they'd been heavily made up in a darkened room, had traces of dried mascara under her eyelashes, and eyeliner spread heavily over the upper eyelids.

'What is it?' Alicia was puzzled; usually during their meetings Susan tried to sell her tickets to a charity auction, or once a comedy night, raising funds for the hospital. On several occasions she'd used the excuse of 'something important' to a have coffee with Alicia, only to push her into attending another benefit gala.

'I'm sure it's just a passing fling. Robert had one of

those, you know. I did nothing, it was a nurse, just like with your Liam, and it soon passed over. Men are like that you know ...'

Alicia suddenly felt bile rise in her throat, and she thought she might bring up the skinny latte she'd just gulped down. She swallowed hard and leaned over to look at the older woman. 'What are you telling me, Susan?'

'Oh ...' It was as if the old woman had forgotten where she was.

After several tries, Susan had finally told her that she'd seen Liam kiss a nurse in the stairwell at St Mary's.

Alicia had been stunned. They'd just celebrated their 18th wedding anniversary in the spring, and although their love-making wasn't as passionate, or as frequent as it had been in the first few years of their relationship, they still did it. And she thought they both enjoyed it.

'I hope I did the right thing telling you?' Susan had said, her eyes full of concern.

'That's fine,' Alicia had managed to say. 'Sorry,' she said, and she left without paying, rushing out of the café and onto the street. It had started raining while they'd been inside, and Alicia got soaked on her way to the car, which was parked a few streets away. She got inside her VW Golf, and sat looking at the dashboard clock, listening to the heavy drops fall onto the windscreen.

She thought back to how Liam behaved with her; had he changed recently? He was always so busy, what with his surgeries going on until late in the evening.

'Oh my god,' Alicia yelped out loud.

Of course, all those late nights! For some time now he'd come home and go straight upstairs to shower instead of flopping down on the sofa next to her, as he used to do. When had that started? Alicia tried to think hard, but she couldn't remember. She started the engine and drove home to Crouch End. Inside the house, she rushed up the stairs and went into Liam's bedroom. His wardrobe looked tidily arranged, with suits, jackets, trousers and shirts neatly organized into sections. Alicia began with the suit pockets. She found train tickets, a few receipts for coffee and meals and a printed sheet for two cinema tickets. She looked at the date, January 23rd 2018, and the name of the film, *A Woman's Life*. Alicia turned the piece of folded paper over in her hands. The film had shown at the Everyman on Baker Street. She'd heard of the movie, and had wanted to see it herself, but knew Liam wouldn't have wanted to see an historical French film. It wasn't his thing.

Alicia carried on looking through Liam's wardrobe for further evidence of his infidelity. (If the cinema tickets were any evidence.) Of course, he could have bought them for Alicia and himself, and then forgotten about the tickets in his jacket pocket. She felt calm, unusually so, and wondered if she was in some kind of shock. It wasn't until she was looking through Liam's sock draw by his bed that she began to feel faint. At the bottom of the drawer she found a key, an ordinary key with a fob to a security gate. It was the keyring that confirmed Susan's account. It was pink leather and, heart-shaped. Alicia recognized it as an expensive one from Smythson. It had a tiny engraving in gold lettering: 'To my love, Ewa x.'

Alicia had sat down on Liam's bed and cried.

SEVEN

When Alicia comes downstairs the next morning she finds her mother fussing over Liam and his breakfast in the kitchen, just as she used to fuss over Stefan. The surge of pain hits Alicia's chest so hard that she has to hold onto the bannister to steady herself.

'Morning,' Alicia's mother says and comes to hug her daughter. Liam doesn't look up. He is reading something on his iPad, all the while eating cereal out of a bowl. Alicia sees it's the kind he likes, Swedish granola that her mother gets in especially for him.

Alicia goes to sit on a stool in the corner of the new kitchen, diagonally opposite Liam, and begins to chat to Hilda about her clothes shop in town, and about Uffe's potato crop. Her stepfather has left early to supervise the work, her mother tells Alicia, as she pours her a cup of strong coffee. As she sips it, Alicia begins to feel better. From the kitchen window, which overlooks an apple orchard, fields, and the sea beyond, she sees it's a sunny day. The rays glitter on the surface of the water. The kitchen is in the corner of the old house, which is surrounded by fields sloping down to the shore and the sauna cottage. She can just make out the roof and chimney pot.

Uffe owns all the land as far as the eye can see, and for some reason, especially today, this thought of complete privacy, being cut off from the world outside, comforts Alicia. There's another red wood-clad cottage at the edge of the field, where Stefan once stayed with a friend he brought along for the holiday, and another one further down, painted pale yellow. There's a third cottage along the shore, beyond the sauna and the jetty.

Alicia knows Uffe built all the simple square structures himself when his parents were still alive, and his father took care of the farm. He rents the properties out to holidaymakers via the Viking Line ferry company, and has done for thirty years or more.

'Do you have any guests this year?' Alicia asks her mother.

Hilda shakes her head. She's mixing flour with eggs and milk; she's making Liam and Stefan's favorite, oven-baked pancakes. 'The red and the yellow cottages are taken up by farm laborers.'

'Oh?'

She looks at the red cottage again, and sees a window is open. Outside, a striped towel and something looking like a pair of swimming trunks are hanging on a washing line fixed between two birch trees. She's saddened by the fact that she won't be able to wander around the cottages; sometimes she helps Uffe on changeover day, when one set of guests are leaving and another arriving. They clear out the rubbish, sort out sacks of empty beer and vodka bottles, plastic mugs, and crisp packets and take the bags on Uffe's tractor to the dump at the edge of one of the fields.

'Can I talk to you for a minute?' Liam says suddenly. His English sounds wrong here somehow. But he's looking at Alicia, so she nods and gets up.

'Sure.'

Hilda lifts her head and gives Alicia a searching look.

'It's OK,' she says to her mother in Swedish, and follows Liam up the stairs to their bedroom in the attic.

Liam stands with his feet apart in the middle of the small room, on the only spot where he has enough space to stretch out to his full height without knocking his head on the beams on either side.

'I've booked a flight from Stockholm to London for tomorrow.' Liam has his arms crossed over his chest and is looking down at his feet.

Alicia gazes at his face and thinks he looks tired. Neither of them got much sleep after the row last night. They aren't used to sleeping in the same bed anymore, but on holiday they usually manage OK. Nothing about this trip is normal, Alicia knows that. Suddenly she realizes that to her it isn't like a break, but a coming home.

'I might stay on a bit longer than the two weeks,' she says.

Liam lifts his head and now Alicia sees anger in his face. His mouth is in a straight line and his eyes dark. 'So this is it then?'

'Says you! I'm not the one who's cheated,' Alicia says, trying to keep her voice low. 'I want us to start again!'

Knowing her mother, she is certain Hilda will be downstairs in the hall, or even on the stairs, trying to listen to their conversation. Luckily, it's two floors up to the attic, and she isn't sure how much Hilda will understand. She doesn't want her to know why Liam is leaving.

Not yet.

She knows how much it would enrage both Hilda and Uffe to learn of Liam's affair; she can't cope with their emotions now.

She adds in a lower tone, 'I want us to have a baby.'

Liam's face crumbles, and he sits down on the bed. 'I'm not a bad man,' he says. 'I just think that when we are hardly speaking, sleeping in separate beds, having a baby is crazy. Besides, I can't do it. I can't take the risk of losing another child.'

His shoulders shake and he covers his face with his hands.

Alicia has never seen her husband cry. Not even during the awful weeks after the accident, or at the funeral. Her memory of those times is hazy, and she is grateful for Liam for taking care of her then, making sure she was medicated just the right amount, so that she could cope with the pain, but not so much that she would become dependent on the pills. Perhaps while she was out cold, he cried alone? She could imagine him at the pine kitchen table in the home in Crouch End, with his head in his hands, but she couldn't imagine any tears. Of course, he might have cried in the arms of Ewa, the Polish nurse. Did he cry while he made love to her, the woman with a beautiful figure and dark curls? Did he break down during her night shifts, no doubt arranged to coincide with Liam's evening surgeries at St Mary's?

Alicia had begun monitoring his movements after the discovery of the keyring, and there was a definite pattern: each Wednesday he would come home late, around midnight, sometimes even one or two in the morning. Alicia could hear the shower being turned on in the bathroom that had been Stefan's—and he would then turn in. The next morning he'd invariably be in a good mood. It was the tenderness with which he kissed Alicia on the cheek when leaving the house that hurt her most. Did he really need the infidelity, the sex with another woman, a woman so different from Alicia, with voluptuous curves, to deal with his grief? Alicia decided he did, so she just accepted this new arrangement. She was not enough for him, so what could she do? If she stopped the affair by making a scene, he'd only find someone else.

After Stefan had gone, nothing seemed to matter anyway. Until the thought of another baby entered her mind. She doesn't know how many times she had tried to talk to Liam about it at home. The time had never seemed to be right. Their individual grief got in the way, Alicia had told herself each time she failed to utter the words she had been brave enough to let pass her lips last night.

Being here, at home with her mother and Uffe, she felt more secure, safe. Even with the memories, the awful gaping hole Stefan had left behind, she is calmer here in Åland than she has been for the past six months in London.

Alicia knows she should go over and sit next to her husband, to comfort him but she isn't able to move. She doesn't seem to have any sympathy left for him.

'I am grateful for everything you did for me after... you know, after.'

Liam looks up at Alicia and nods. His face is drawn, sad. His eyes have red rims and his eyelashes are wet. His whole demeanor is so different from the confident man Alicia knows, and she's suddenly taken aback, forgetting her own pain, or the sense of betrayal she has carried with her for so many months. Even the new, fresh, pain of his refusal to give her another baby.

'Are you OK?' she says and sits next to him.

Liam puts his head on Alicia's shoulder. She places her arms around him and makes soothing sounds. 'It's OK, just let it go.' She hugs him and they rock together on the low bed. Slowly Liam's tears dry up and he straightens his back. He takes hold of Alicia's hands and says, 'You know you are a wonderful woman. And I am sorry.'

'I know.' Alicia looks at Liam's eyes. 'How did it happen? And why?'

Now Liam hangs his head. 'I don't know. I guess you and I weren't, you know, even talking properly and I needed ...'

Alicia thinks back and tries to remember when Liam began sleeping in the guest bedroom. It must be two, three years ago? At first it was because of his late-night surgeries; he'd often stay afterwards to finish the paper-work, and instead of waking Alicia, who liked to be in bed by 10pm, he'd sleep in the guest bedroom. Slowly the occasional night became a permanent arrangement. It's something they'd joke about; they even convinced themselves that sex was better when it wasn't part of a routine.

What a lie that was.

Alicia can remember clearly when they last made passionate love. It was on the August Bank holiday, when Stefan was at a sleepover with some friends. They'd finished a whole bottle of prosecco during a picnic on Hampstead Heath. It was a hot weekend, the last heatwave of the summer, and Liam had been kissing Alicia and covertly touching her breasts and bottom as they lay on a blanket underneath a vast elm. Alicia wore her favorite hot-weather dress: a floaty maxi with tiny flowers on it and a halter-neck fastening. It hugged her slim body and showed off her small breasts. They'd been like teenagers, willing the bus to take them home quicker so that they could devour each other. That weekend they'd made love three times, but as soon as Stefan came home, and the working week began, Liam had returned to the guest bedroom and the passion faded.

'How long has it been going on?' Alicia now asks.

Liam looks at Alicia with alarm.

'Don't worry, I'm not going to do anything. I just want to know.' Alicia is surprised at her own calmness. She knows it's better this way. She doesn't have any feelings left for anyone, she will never love anyone again after Stefan, so it is better that Liam has found someone else. The fact that he hasn't made love to her because he was having sex with the nurse makes Alicia feel better somehow. It isn't her fault their life is coming to an end; it's his.

'Five months.'

Alicia can't help but gasp at Liam's words. 'So it started almost right after ...'

'It isn't as simple as that.'

'No.' Alicia tries to suppress her anger. She stands up and asks, 'What time is your flight from Stockholm tomorrow?'

EIGHT

Early on Sunday morning Liam and Alicia stand facing each other in the kitchen. Liam's luggage is packed and ready by the front door. He glances through the open door at the large grandfather clock, which dominates the back wall of the lounge.

'What time did you say the bridge opens?'

'On the hour and at half past,' Alicia says. She's in her usual spot, perching on a stool next to the window overlooking the fields and the sea. The coffee machine on the other side of the kitchen is making gurgling sounds. Alicia knows Liam is fully aware of the timetable of the canal that runs between Mariehamn and Sjoland, where Uffe's house is, but he's being his English self—making pointless conversation to drown out the silence between them.

The small ferry port isn't busy when Alicia and Liam arrive there twenty minutes later.

Alicia decides to drive him in Hilda's car; it would look odd if she asked her mother to go. The night before,

Hilda offered to come along, but Alicia managed to convince her that she wasn't needed.

As usual, they are far too early. The check-in hasn't even opened and the only two desks in the tiny departure hall are empty. Alicia really just wants to leave Liam there, but she feels duty-bound to stay in case something goes wrong with his booking, unlikely though that is. Everyone speaks English, of course, but it doesn't seem right to abandon Liam at an empty ferry terminal.

'Let me know when you get there,' Alicia says and sits down on one of the plastic chairs fixed against the long wall of the waiting hall.

Liam gives her a quick glance, there's surprise in his eyes, but adds, 'Sure.'

Suddenly a door at the far end opens and Alicia sees a familiar, tall shape enter the terminal. Patrick walks confidently in, taking long strides toward the two check-in cubicles and looks up at a screen above them. He checks his phone and turns around to gaze at the large space. His eyes meet Alicia's and his face opens into a smile. In a few moments the man with the blue eyes is standing in front of them.

'We must stop meeting like this,' Patrick says in Swedish.

'Hi,' Alicia says and gives a little laugh. She cannot but return the man's infectious smile.

'Not leaving already?' he says, his gaze moving from Alicia to Liam and back again.

'Sorry, you didn't meet the other day, did you?' Alicia says, switching to English. She assumes Patrick speaks the language and sees that the man nods. She is breathless again.

What is it with this guy that makes her feel like a teenager?

'This is Liam,' she says and then, hesitating just for a moment, adds, 'My husband.'

'Pleased to meet you.' Patrick stretches his hand toward Liam. His face is open, the smile still hovering around his lips.

Liam gets up and the two men shake hands, but while Patrick looks relaxed, saying 'Good morning' in a slightly sing-songy, accented English to her husband, Alicia can see Liam's movements are guarded. With his lips in a straight line, he nods.

'You too.'

There is an awkward silence, magnified by the emptiness of the vast hall.

'Um, I'm collecting some more guests for our party,' Patrick says. He's speaking to Alicia, who realizes she didn't say why they were here.

'Liam has to go back early due to ... to his work,' Alicia says, trying to sound convincing. She smiles at Patrick. 'But I'm sure my mum and her husband would love to come.'

'And you too, I hope?' Patrick says. His intensely blue eyes are boring into Alicia and she feels herself blush under the man's gaze.

'Yes. I'd love to,' Alicia says, moving her face away from Patrick.

There is a sudden crackle of a tannoy and the arrival of the overnight sailing from Stockholm is announced.

'That's me. Well, nice to meet you. Sorry you have to

leave the islands so early. Perhaps see you later this summer?' Patrick says to Liam, and then, turning to Alicia, says in Swedish, 'I'll remind Mia to send your mother the invitation.'

With a wave, he moves toward the other end of the terminal, where a few people are already arriving from the customs hall.

'Party?' Liam says. He's looking at Alicia with a different expression from the one he had before.

'Yeah, his wife, Mia,' Alicia nods at Patrick, who is standing facing the arrivals section, his feet apart and his arms crossed over his suede jacket. 'Mia's dad basically owns Åland. They have a massive house and they like to hold parties. I met them on the ferry coming over and they invited us to their Midsummer bash.'

'And you forgot to tell me about that?'

Alicia looks at Liam.

Is he jealous?

'I forgot about it myself, to be honest,' Alicia replies.

At that point, there is an announcement, in three languages, for passengers to board the *Ålandsfärjan* ferry. They get up and walk together toward the check-in cubicles, one staffed by a woman with pitch-black hair and pale skin.

Liam turns to Alicia. 'Well, this is me.' He's looking down at his phone, the boarding card displayed on its screen, waiting behind two other passengers. He's got the black canvas rucksack that Alicia gave him one Christmas, years ago, slung over his right shoulder.

'Have a good trip,' Alicia says. Suddenly she feels

dizzy, and short of breath. Out of habit, she takes hold of Liam's arm to steady herself.

'You OK?' Liam says and grabs her elbow.

Alicia nods, but Liam steps out of the line, still holding her.

'Where does it hurt?'

Alicia wants to laugh. *Where doesn't it hurt?* She's aware of Patrick, who is just leaving with an older couple. He lifts his arm and waves to her, and she nods in reply.

The check-in woman in the glass cubicle is staring at them and listening to their every word. 'I'm OK. I just felt a bit dizzy,' she says and tries to smile. 'I'll be fine.'

Liam gives her his professional doctor's gaze. This was how their relationship began; he advised her about the headaches. She was a student at Uppsala University, studying English and journalism, and he was attending a seminar. They happened to sit at the same table in the cafeteria one wintry afternoon and Liam remarked on the weather. He wasn't used to seeing so much snow, and Alicia said how the cold weather always gave her migraines.

'Do you want me to examine you?' Liam had joked during the evening they spent together, his eyes creasing up at the corners and his full mouth stretched in a delicious smile. Under his direct gaze, Alicia blushed, and lowered her eyes. She was only a student then, and this Englishman was so obviously more experienced, and older than her. But there was something enchanting about his dark eyes and direct flirtation. So Alicia had agreed to a consultation. They had already spent the day together, and they had kissed.

Liam had gazed at Alicia, gently lifting her eyelids to look into her eyes. He then took her pulse and finally listened to her chest with an ear pressed against her breasts. Their proximity ended in another passionate kiss. Then pulling away from her, suddenly serious, Liam said, 'I have to be careful. This could be professional suicide, having relations with a patient.'

'Oh, sorry,' Alicia said, believing him.

Liam laughed, 'You are adorable!'

Liam has that same concern in his eyes now, but without the laughter.

'I'm fine, honestly,' Alicia says, freeing herself from Liam's grip. 'You'll miss the ferry!'

Liam stands facing her for a moment, and then, with a sadness in his face, nods and turns away. Alicia watches him show his boarding pass to the dark-haired woman, walk briskly toward a set of stairs and disappear. He doesn't turn to wave, but Alicia waits until she sees him re-emerge on the high glazed walkway. He looks down at her, stopping for a moment. They look at each other and each lifts a hand in a half-wave at exactly the same time. Liam nods and boards the ferry.

NINE

Liam arrives at the house in Crouch End late at night. It's empty and dark. He's taken a cab from Heathrow, a luxury he decides he needs in the circumstances. Before turning in, he stands outside Stefan's empty bedroom. He can't cry, but when he sees his late son's Spurs duvet cover, a pain fills his chest, making it difficult to breathe. There's a scent in the room, his son's masculine teenage tang, which he has forgotten about until now. Perhaps he didn't notice it before? He wishes he could hold Alicia now. He would like to share his discovery of their son's spirit still alive in their house. He stares at the bedroom, taking in details of Stefan's messy desk, which neither of them has had the heart to tidy. His school rucksack is lying on the floor exactly as he left it, as are two pairs of trainers. Liam can't take any more; he closes the door quietly and goes to their bedroom, the room in which Alicia has slept on her own for the last six months. Or was it a year? Two?

He moves quickly into the room and lies on the bed.

Unlike Stefan's room, Alicia's is tidy, with a freshly made bed covered in cream cushions. He catches Alicia's perfume of lavender. He covers his face with one of her pillows and takes a deep breath in. He lies like this, breathing in and out, remembering the contours of Alicia's body, remembering her touch on him. He cannot recall when he has missed her so much.

There's a vintage white dressing table, on which a few bottles are placed attractively. A couple of pieces of jewellery hang from the side of the carved wooden mirror. Liam gets off the bed and sits on the stool with the cream satin cover and touches one of the glass beads. He tries to think when he last saw her wear them. At a charity dinner for the hospital perhaps? Yes, that was it. With shame, he remembers that Ewa was also there, and that they had smiled at each other across the room. Sharing a secret, both visualizing their last love-making. Except it wasn't love. Liam now feels ashamed at the seedy affair. But he was so lonely during those long nights and evenings at the hospital after Stefan's accident. He needed someone to comfort him. He was so empty. He *is* so empty. He catches his own, tired face in the mirror.

How about you stop thinking about yourself for a moment?

All through the long journey from Mariehamn, the extended wait at Stockholm airport, he'd pictured Alicia's face when he left her. She seemed so worried, with dark patches around her eyes. Still, she looked beautiful with her large pale eyes gazing at him. He remembers when he first saw her in Sweden, a young student with long legs and blond hair. Those deep emerald eyes were the first thing to attract him. She was so trusting, almost naive, and he'd reveled in showing her the world. Or his world in England. And look at where he took her? He gave her a son, then took him away, abandoning her to the grief that neither of them has any idea how to handle. He knows he's to blame for Stefan's death whatever his colleague, the grief counsellor, says. Alicia was against it from the start but he thought he knew better. His son needed his independence, and the moped gave him that. Liam puts his head into his hands. What a stupid, stupid man he is.

Alicia blames him too, he knows this. And rightly so. She was immediately so closed in, as if her grief was larger than his. But Liam knows he should have been more understanding. To lose a child for a father is terrible, but for a mother it is unimaginable.

Liam takes his phone out of his back pocket and sends Alicia a short message to let her know that he's arrived in London safely. He waits for a moment, then looks at his watch. It's already past 2am in Åland. Alicia is most probably asleep.

The image of that man, Patrick, at the ferry terminal flashes through his brain. Was he flirting with Alicia? He's married, she said, but that doesn't mean anything, as Liam, to his shame, knows all too well.

Liam undresses and decides to stay in their marital bedroom rather than go back to the spare bedroom. It seems less lonely in the double bed where Alicia usually sleeps. When he lies down he realizes how tired he is. Before sleep takes over, he resolves to fix his marriage. Perhaps a few weeks apart is just what they both need?

TEN

The next morning, a Monday, Hilda drives Alicia to Mariehamn with her. It's the day after Liam's sudden departure, which Alicia explained as a crisis at work. To conjure up an illness of a fellow surgeon at the hospital was Liam's idea. Both Hilda and Uffe exchanged glances and when Hilda and Alicia were in the kitchen washing up after supper on Saturday night Hilda asked her straight up if they'd had a row. Was that why Liam was leaving, she'd asked.

'Of course not,' Alicia said, not looking at her mother and continuing to load the dishwasher. For once, Hilda hadn't pursued the matter.

When Alicia asked if it was alright for her to sleep in the sauna cottage, once again Hilda raised her eyebrows but agreed. 'I need a bit of time alone, to think,' Alicia said, and Hilda nodded.

'You can stay as long as you need,' she said and hugged Alicia.

On Sunday night, Alicia received a message from Liam saying, *'Arrived safely, take care. Liam x'*

She looked at the *'x'*. After all these years of marriage, the man still confused her. Hadn't they more or less agreed to separate? You don't send kisses to the woman you are cheating on, don't want to have a baby with, and want to leave, do you?

Alicia decided not to reply, and deleted the message.

The town of Mariehamn is the largest center on the islands, and Alicia remembers how, as a child, she'd thought the central park between Storagatan and Norra Esplanaden the most beautiful place on earth. Now the vast trees had grown, making the central path look majestic, the dappled sunshine reaching between the leaves of the tall elms. When her mother turns into Torggatan and parks the car in a spot reserved for her just outside the shop on Nygatan, Alicia sighs.

'Are you alright, my dear?' Hilda says and places her hand on her daughter's shoulder. Alicia wants to let herself cry then, for Stefan, for the unborn baby she will never have and for her marriage, which is most probably now over. But a knock on the passenger seat window stops her. A man's face, with friendly blue eyes, framed with blond, sunburnt hair, is looking at them through the window. Patrick! Alicia can feel her heart beat a little faster.

'Oh, I forgot,' Hilda says and rushes to get out of the car.

'This is Patrick,' Alicia's mother says when the two

women are on the pavement, under the bright sunlight. She takes the man's hand.

'And this is my daughter,' Hilda adds. 'She's also a journalist, from London,' she says, and Alicia sees how she stands a little straighter. Alicia can't help but smile; her mother's evident pride in her daughter's fledgling career as a freelance journalist is endearing. If she only knew how little her articles earn these days, Hilda would advise her to change professions. She doesn't dare look at Patrick.

'How interesting,' Patrick says. Alicia lifts her eyes toward him and notices the blue eyes and the laughter lines around them. Seeing him again, she guesses his age to be around the mid-thirties, perhaps less. Younger than she is, at any rate.

'Yes, we've already met,' Alicia says and takes Patrick's hand. His long fingers touch hers and send currents through her body. Both let go quickly, as if they had burned each other. Alicia turns toward her mother.

Hilda's eyes open wide, 'Oh, really?' she says.

Alicia is glad she decided to wear one of her more flattering dresses this morning. It is a bright, sunny morning, with the promise of a warm summer's day to come.

'This is Mia's husband,' Alicia says to her mother. 'You remember Mia from school? Mia Eriksson?' she adds pointedly. 'Or has she taken your last name?' she asks facing Patrick again.

'No,' he says. The smile has disappeared from his lips and he looks even more embarrassed than Alicia feels.

'Aah,' Hilda says, 'Yes of course, lovely Mia!' she's grasped the significance of the last name, even though

Alicia is certain she doesn't remember Mia from school. She was a couple of years below Alicia and they were never friends, but the school in Mariehamn was so small, everyone knew everyone else.

Mia's father owns the largest newspaper on the islands, a major shipping company and a fair amount of property. As well as much more she's certain she doesn't know about. All she's heard is that Mia's father's nickname on the islands is Mr Åland.

Although flustered, Alicia cannot help but be flattered by the covert glances Patrick keeps throwing her as Hilda opens up the shop and directs him and Alicia to the back room, where Hilda has a small office. It's just a cubicle, really, divided from the shop by a pink velvet curtain, matching the drapes across two smaller fitting rooms on the other side of the shop. Alicia knows that when it's busy, Hilda allows customers to use her office to try on the clothes, and to that end, she has a full-length mirror on the far wall. Her mother fills a kettle from a tap in the small sink in the corner of the room and asks if they want coffee, as if both of them are her guests.

'No, that's OK, I've just had breakfast,' Patrick says, and he smiles at Hilda, who says with disappointment in her voice, 'Oh, OK, I'll just make the shop ready to open and we can chat about the article.' She disappears into the main room and Alicia can see lights being switched on and hear Hilda open up the till.

'This is a coincidence, a second pleasant one,' Patrick says. Once again, he's dressed like someone from Östermalm in Stockholm, the area where the upper-class Swedes reside. Today he's sporting a pair of fashionably ripped jeans and a crisp white cotton shirt under the soft suede jacket.

'You a journalist?' Alicia asks.

Sitting opposite each other in the small room, their knees are nearly touching. Hers are bare, and she can see the tanned skin of his legs, and a few stray blond hairs, through the rips in his jeans. This is ridiculous, Alicia tells herself. I am married, at least for now, and so is he. What's more, this is probably all in my imagination. He's just being nice in a very Scandinavian way. But the man's gaze is so direct, and intense, that Alicia has to lower her eyes; is he flirting with her?

'Yeah, I work for *Journalen*. Your mum convinced me to write about her shop. She had a break-in here last week.' His smile disappears, and his eyes look even more fetching with a serious face. I must stop this, Alicia thinks.

'Oh, I didn't know about it. Was anything stolen?'

'Yes. Apparently, they emptied the till. That's all I know, so far.'

'Of course,' Alicia laughs, embarrassed. He's here to find out more about the incident.

'So you're Hilda's daughter?' Patrick asks. He is so tall that Alicia has to look up at him. She can see his taut muscles underneath the white shirt as he leans his upper body toward her. The shirt is open at the neck, revealing a triangle of bronzed skin.

Alicia manages to nod before her mother reappears.

'Right, Alicia, if you wouldn't mind staying on just for half an hour or so, while we chat? You remember how the till works, right?' Alicia's mother stands by the opening to the office, holding back the velvet curtain.

Alicia notices how very smart—and young—her mother looks in her linen trouser suit over a sleeveless silk shirt. Alicia herself is wearing one of her simple Marimekko summer dresses, and just to please her mother, her smart tan sandals with a small wedge heel, which (according to Hilda) make her legs look long and shapely.

'No problem.' Alicia gets up and turns to leave, but as she does so, she stumbles in the damned shoes, and accidentally brushes her shoulder against Patrick. They both give an embarrassed laugh. Alicia can't look at Patrick. The touch of his body against her sends a prickling sensation down her spine. A sensation Alicia knows all too well.

'Thanks, I must stop falling into you,' Alicia says before she knows what she's doing.

What am I saying!

'No problem,' Patrick says again, grinning.

Alicia knows her mother is watching the two of them, but she doesn't dare look at Hilda. Blushing at the sight of Patrick's smiling face so close to her, she walks out into the shop, feeling his eyes burning on her backside. She finds herself hoping her bum doesn't look too saggy. *Talk about making a fool of yourself*, Alicia thinks as she sits behind the till, and sees her mother close the pink curtain behind her.

ELEVEN

For the hour or so that Alicia sits alone at the till, watching the sun rise high in the sky, not one customer comes inside the shop. She sees a few people visit the bank, on the corner of their street and the pedestrian section, diagonally opposite the shop, but there are very few tourists about. It's a Monday morning after all, and the summer season isn't quite here yet. Most tourists arrive for Midsummer, which is four days away. Those few tourists already on the islands must still be asleep, Alicia thinks. It's only just past ten, and to Alicia the center of Mariehamn looks positively deserted. She's got so used to the busyness of London, where even at 4am on a Friday, when she and Liam took the cab to the airport, there had been people about, rushing to work, or home from a night out—or a rave. Did people still go to raves, Alicia wonders, as she listens to the voices from behind the curtain, and the occasional laughter, her mother's trill and Patrick's low, manly tone. Alicia can imagine how her mother's coquettish behavior embarrasses and flatters at the same time. She remembers how Stefan blushed the first time one of her friends from the Pilates class she used to attend became all flirty with him. Stefan had a huge growth spurt during his 14th summer, gaining broad shoulders, just like his father. His jawline became suddenly square, and a few strands of fluffy hair began to sprout from his chin. His new maleness had a strange effect on some women, especially those who didn't know him well. Like her Pilates friends. They'd smile at him, cocking their heads and shifting their bodies. It made Alicia laugh; how shameless they were.

'Meet my son,' she'd say and all at once, the women would become embarrassed, crossing their arms over their chests and rushing out of the door.

Alicia brushes the thoughts of Stefan away; she mustn't brood. This is, after all why she is here, to try to relax.

To avoid her mind wondering, Alicia moves the mouse on the desk and the computer comes to life. She sees her mother's sales report is open. She doesn't want to look, but she can't help herself as she scans the numbers on the screen. She is a financial journalist after all. She's shocked by the lack of sales recorded during the previous week. Only a handful of items were sold the week before that. Quickly she scrolls through the report and sees that since the New Year the shop has barely made 500 Euros a month. The rent on the premises must be that much at least, so how was Hilda able to pay the woman who comes in a few days a week? There must be the heating bill, and electricity, insurance, plus the money Hilda presumably pays herself. Alicia looks through her mother's files and finds a spreadsheet showing the shop's incoming and outgoing expenses. She notices that expenses peak about four times a year when Hilda restocks the shop. The sales look pitifully low compared to the purchases, and as she suspects the rent of the shop is nearly 1,000 Euros per month. But the shop seems to show a profit at the end of the period regardless, and she sees that the simple cashflow Hilda has prepared on a separate tab confirms this; she is over 1,000 Euros in the black. How is that possible when the costs so obviously exceed the income?

Suddenly Alicia hears sounds of movement, and the curtain is pulled to one side. She quickly closes the spreadsheets and lets go of the mouse.

Hilda walks out first, keeping the curtain back for the reporter to walk through. When they reach the till, Alicia's mother thanks Patrick. The man shakes hands with Hilda and turns to Alicia, placing his hand in hers, 'Nice to meet you again. Are you staying on the islands for the whole summer?'

He has long thin fingers and she notices a few pale hairs growing on the back of his hand.

'Not sure,' she says.

'But you'll come to the Midsummer party?'

'Party?' Hilda says, looking from Patrick to Alicia and back again.

Patrick coughs, then adds, 'You haven't got the invite yet? I must remind Mia to send it to you today.'

'That sounds lovely!' Hilda says, her eyes sparkling.

'Unless you have already made arrangements for celebrating Midsummer?' Patrick says, sounding hopeful.

Alicia looks down at her shoes, trying to remove the smile from her face.

'No, no, nothing that couldn't be unarranged!' Hilda says so keenly that it makes Alicia wince.

'Perhaps we'll meet again soon, then,' Patrick says, ignoring Hilda and looking at Alicia for a fraction of a second too long. He drops her hand and takes hold of Hilda's. 'I'll see you both this weekend.'

TWELVE

Alicia meets her mother for lunch at Indigo, one of the new breed of café/restaurant that have sprung up in the town in the past few years. In summer, the place has an outdoor patio area with wooden benches and large canvas umbrellas. The day has turned out windy, so although the sun is out, the umbrellas are down, and flapping noisily against their poles. When Alicia enters the little courtyard, where the tables are set at one end, Hilda is already sitting down with a large glass of white wine.

'Do you want one?' she asks as soon as Alicia sits down next to her.

Alicia has spent the morning wandering around Mariehamn, checking out her old haunts in the little town. Several of her schoolfriends still live on the islands, but over the years she's lost touch with all of them, not least because when she's here, most of them are on holiday, spending their long summer breaks in the surrounding archipelago. Now she wouldn't dream of getting in touch with any of them; she doesn't want to explain about Stefan.

Or about Liam.

Not yet.

She hasn't touched her Facebook feed since Stefan's accident. She is considering closing her account altogether. There are too many memories there; too many pictures of Stefan and many of him with her, her son with his beautiful, young face and lean body. Alicia shakes her head; she must stop torturing herself. Stefan is gone; as the grief counsellor told her, she must just try to remember the good times and be grateful for the years she had with her son. She was trying to do just that when she stopped for a coffee at Svarta Katten, a café in a little wood-clad townhouse with mismatching old furniture and the best *Ålands pannakaka* in town. It had been Stefan's favorite. Alicia decided against the semolina-filled clafoutis-type cake and sat in a corner reading a book bought from the bookshop at the far end of Torggatan. It is a novel set on the islands, by a recent Finlandia prize-winning author. Alicia decided that she needed to improve her Swedish, and what better way to do it than to read a novel about Åland in the original language?

Alicia now places the book on the table and leans back against the curved wooden bench of the restaurant. She watches the tourists milling around the local artisan shop opposite–a pottery and glassblower's with various cups, plates and glasses displayed on a table outside. She has several pieces by the same artist at home, colorful glassware that she'd carefully wrapped and transported in her hand-luggage back to London. She decides she ought to buy a couple of new coffee mugs for the sauna cottage as a treat for herself.

'It's only Monday, and aren't you going to drive later?' she says absentmindedly to her mother. The words come out louder and more critically than she had intended.

'Oh, not for hours yet. By then the alcohol will have evaporated to nothing. Besides, you're on holiday!' Hilda smiles and lifts up her glass.

Alicia notices that the smile is somewhat strained, so she nods and asks the waiter, who at just that moment stops in front of their table, for a glass of what her mother is drinking. The waiter is a lanky blond boy, with a long white linen apron over his worn-out jeans that makes him loom even larger over the two women. His serious eyes survey Alicia, 'And food, do you want to order food?'

'In a minute, thank you, Nils.'

Hilda gazes at the boy as he leaves them. He says something to his colleague, a pretty girl with a streak of green in her hair, which makes her laugh. He pours Alicia's glass of wine at the bar.

'They just want to take your money in this place. So rude!' Hilda is speaking too loudly, enough for the boy and girl to hear.

When Nils comes back, Hilda orders the Caesar salad, and Alicia does the same.

Their food arrives. Without looking at either of them, or speaking, the waiter places the bowls down harshly, and a bit of Alicia's lettuce falls onto the table.

'Excuse me!" Hilda says loudly, and stares at the boy.

'Oh, sorry,' he says in a way that shows he's not in the least sorry.

'That's Margaret's son, you know,' Hilda whispers when the boy is out of earshot.

Alicia doesn't know who Margaret is, or she has forgotten, so she sighs and begins to eat. A row with a waiter is the last thing she needs. She gazes at her mother, who is keeping a close eye on the two youngsters, who are still laughing and joking together.

'Wasn't that a nice young man?' Hilda says suddenly.

Alicia looks back at the waiter, who's standing very close to the girl. They look like they are together. The place is almost empty; only a few other tables are occupied.

'Yes, very nice,' she replies.

'No, I don't mean that little rascal! I was talking about Patrick!'

'Oh.'

'His father-in-law owns *Ålandsbladet*.'

'Yes, I know.'

'I bet he could get you a job if you wanted,' Hilda says as she finally begins to pick at her salad.

Alicia stares at her mother, 'What do you mean?'

'On *Ålandsbladet*.'

Has Alicia heard her mother right? 'I live in London, why would I want a job here?'

Hilda's gaze doesn't leave Alicia's face as she carefully places her fork at the side of the large bowl.

'Now, don't be mad, but I got the feeling Liam didn't leave because of work.'

. . .

To change the subject, Alicia asks about what Patrick told her.

'Somebody broke into the shop?'

Hilda doesn't look at Alicia, but just waves her hand, which is holding a fork. 'Oh that. Just some kids.'

'But they emptied the till?'

'Yes,' her mother replies.

'Was much taken?'

Now Hilda lifts her eyes. 'Well, it's early in the summer season, so the takings were only just under a hundred Euros. But I might have told Patrick the sum was a bit bigger.' Hilda gives Alicia a guilty smile. 'Any publicity is good publicity.'

'Oh *mamma*!' Alicia is shocked, but she's more worried about the future of mother's business.

'Don't tell Patrick, whatever you do!' Hilda says and grins at Alicia.

'We're not friends, you know. I just happened to see him and Mia on the ferry. And then yesterday, when I was dropping Liam off at the terminal, he was meeting some guests coming to their party.'

At the mention of the Eriksson's Midsummer bash, Hilda's eyes light up and Alicia realizes she's lost the opportunity to ask her more about the shop's finances. It's nothing to do with me anyway, Alicia thinks, and she listens to her mother go on about what they should both wear and how it's too late to find anything unique.

'You need something nice too,' Hilda says and winks at her daughter. 'I saw how that young man looked at you!'

Alicia's cheeks begin to burn at the thought of

Patrick's touch on her palm as he said goodbye that morning.

'Mum!' Alicia says. 'I'm married and so is he!' Alicia turns her head away.

Hilda is quiet for a moment. She must have seen the color on Alicia's face change, but, unusually, she doesn't comment on her daughter's embarrassment. Lowering her voice and placing her hand on Alicia's, she says, 'I know, darling. But a little flirtation never harmed anyone. It might be just what you need.' Alicia turns her eyes toward her mother.

Hilda peers at Alicia over her empty salad bowl. 'And being wanted by someone else might just bring that husband of yours running back to the islands too.'

THIRTEEN

When Hilda and Alicia get back to the house in Sjoland a few hours later, they find Uffe at home. He's speaking in an urgent tone on the phone, and when Alicia's mother shouts her usual, 'Hellooo' to the house in general, as if everyone inside the house is deaf, Uffe puts his hand up, his palm open in a gesture for her to be quiet.

'What's happened?' Hilda says in a whisper, her eyes wide. She walks to the other side of the kitchen where their landline, with a long cord, is fixed to the wall.

Uffe turns his back on Hilda and nods, dismissing her and listening to the person on the phone. Finally, he places the receiver back on its hook and sighs heavily, shaking his head. Alicia sees that he's close to tears.

'What is it?' both Alicia and Hilda ask in unison.

'One of the boys, you know the Romanians, had an accident.'

'Oh, them.' Hilda says, and begins to unload the shopping bags.

On the way home, they stopped at the grocery store to get more provisions, even though Alicia couldn't see how her mother could possibly fit anything more into the already packed fridge. But she knew better than to protest.

'We do have to eat. Uffe will have the leftovers,' her mother would say whenever Alicia protested about the amount of food Hilda bought. Hilda would look hurt, and an incident like this could trigger a mood change, which Alicia wanted to avoid at all costs. She now thinks that Hilda is shopping as if she had three more mouths to feed, not one. Has she forgotten that Stefan isn't here, would never again be here, and that Liam left the day before?

Uffe sits down on one of the kitchen chairs and lifts her eyes up to Alicia, 'He's only seventeen.' Uffe looks very gray, with his usually red cheeks drained of color and his eyes pale and watery.

Alicia sits opposite him, while Hilda stops unloading the bags for a moment and turns to gaze at her husband.

'I was on the tractor and the boys were lifting the potatoes. The guy, the one who speaks Swedish, told me that the row had been done. I had to reverse to get more room to turn around, and the boy was behind me. I didn't know he was there!'

'Is he alright?' A dread fills Alicia's gut. Her heart is beating so hard that she has to concentrate on breathing in and out. She thinks she might faint.

'His leg, oh my God, his leg.' Uffe stops for a moment, and runs his palm over his face. 'It went under the wheel, and the first thing I knew was a scream and the guy, the

Swedish-speaker, waving his arms madly at me. I looked back from the cabin and saw his body lying there.'

Alicia stares at Uffe, then turns to look at her mother. Tears begin to run down her face. 'No!' she screams.

Hearing her yell, Uffe looks up and takes hold of her wrists. 'He has broken his leg, but he's OK. I was just told on the telephone.'

Alicia frees her arms, sits down and puts a hand to her mouth but she can't stop sobbing.

Uffe is still standing in front of Alicia. 'He's fine,' he repeats a little more quietly.

Hilda comes over and hugs her. 'There, there,' her mother says soothingly.

She lays her head on her mother's lap, inhaling her familiar smell of cooking and perfume. If only she was still a child, still living here in Åland, before she'd given birth and lost a son. From under her mother's arms, which are covering her head, she hears Hilda scold Uffe.

'Look what you've done! You need to think before you speak!'

'But I was upset, it was horrible ...'

'Shush, that's enough from you.'

Hilda lets go of Alicia and hands her a tissue from her pocket. 'I'm sorry you had to hear that. But the boy is OK!'

'Yes,' Alicia manages to say. She blows her nose on the worn-out tissue. She's still concentrating on breathing in and out. The images she carries in her head about the accident have come vividly into her mind. Of Stefan's body lying mangled, covered in blood, his helmet that both she and Liam made him promise to wear, to one side, and his moped, still running and producing oily smoke, lying on its side further away. The policewoman told Liam that Stefan had hit a wall, for no apparent reason, and that he had alcohol in his blood. He'd not strapped his helmet on properly, or had possibly not worn it at all. They couldn't tell. They said it was lucky that when he'd hit the wall between Camden Lock and Chalk Farm Road, no one had been walking on the pavement and no other vehicles were on the road. It had been 9pm, so it was a miracle no one else was hurt. The police couldn't tell Liam why Stefan had slipped; they assumed it was black ice. That November night had been cold and the temperature had dropped to -3°C. Alicia asked Liam over and over whether a lorry, or one of those big 4x4 vehicles, could have nudged him and caused him to lose his balance.

'They have CCTV,' Liam had said, and when Alicia asked if he'd seen it, Liam nodded, with his head hanging, gazing down at the kitchen table, not looking at her. Alicia thought she wanted to see the film too, but Liam persuaded her she shouldn't.

FOURTEEN

Frida parks her bicycle in front of the low-slung red-brick building. She feels clumsy getting off the bar. She is so fat now that people have started giving her sideways glances. She sighs; she needs to think about the future, but not now.

She glances at her phone but there is no reply from him.

It's a beautiful evening, with just a slight wind rattling the empty flagpoles in front of the old people's home. The grass in the front garden has just been cut and gives off the scent of summer. She hears the horns of the ferries in the distance and glances at her watch. Six o'clock exactly. The ships going from the islands to Finland and Sweden are never late.

Frida hopes she can take her mother out to the small garden at the back to have coffee with the butter buns she's bought from *Iwa's Konditori* on Torggatan. The old woman gave them to her half-price because she'd known

Sirpa when she was younger and working at *Hotel Arkipelag*. And because Frida lied and said that it was her mother's birthday. It's the end of the month and her funds are running low, mainly because the bastards at the newspaper pay her so little. Besides, Frida is doing Iwa Nygren a favor by buying up the leftovers.

Holding onto the paper bag containing the buns, Frida hesitates for a moment outside the glass doors to *De Gamlas Hem*. Or *Oasis* as it is called now. Which is a bloody joke as far as Frida is concerned. Almost as much of a joke as calling the dementia ward where her mother is, *Solsidan*. The Sunnyside! Frida often wonders if some smart ass had decided it would be funny to name a loony bin for the elderly after the popular Swedish comedy about well-heeled *Stockholmare*, or if it was just a lame coincidence.

She is tired after a day spent researching useless facts about dog tourism to the islands. A Swedish woman has opened a pet hotel in Mariehamn and one of the permanent reporters got Frida to do all the legwork for a feature about the new business. The place would last three months max, Frida knows this, so it was pointless for the newspaper to spend so much time and effort on the article. Correction, it is pointless for *her*, Frida to spend time trying to find out how many dogs visit Åland each year. Now Frida's eyes ache and her brain is fried because of all the useless information she has filled it with. All she wants to do after fixing her eyes on the screen of an office pc for eight hours was to go home, fire up her own brand-new Mac and do her own research.

But that would have to wait. First, she had to see her mum. She just hopes she recognizes her today, or failing that, at least is calm and quiet. Perhaps the butter buns will put her in a good mood.

FIFTEEN

'We must stop meeting like this,' Patrick says. He's wearing the same soft suede jacket, this time over a white polo shirt, with the collar up over his neck. His dark brown leather messenger bag is slung across his broad chest.

Alicia is standing in the open-plan office of *Ålands-bladet* with a woman from personnel, Birgit Sundstrand. She's just been interviewed for a job at the paper, and to her great amazement, has been offered a post as a part-time reporter. The gray-haired woman with half-moon glasses was so impressed by her CV, and especially her work at the *Financial Times*, that she immediately asked Alicia when she could start.

'Today, if you wish!' Alicia replied and the woman smiled, revealing pale yellow teeth with red lipstick marks all over them. Alicia wanted to tell her about the smears, but the woman stood up to shake Alicia's hand before she had a chance.

'I'll email a contract this afternoon. Come and meet everyone!'

The job title, 'Financial Correspondent', is rather grand. It's been open for a while now, Birgit told her, 'waiting for the perfect candidate.' Alicia is still in shock; she only popped into the offices of the one and only newspaper on the islands to see if they had anything for her, anything at all. She has decided to stay on the islands for the summer, perhaps until the end of August, and she needs something to get her out of Hilda and Uffe's way. Besides, she knows her mother will soon start to say how Patrick, and Mia's father, Mr Åland, could get a her a position somewhere in their vast empire. But she wants to get a job on her own merits.

Today, she really didn't think her visit to the paper's offices would get her anywhere. She simply wanted to be able to tell her mother that she had tried. She imagined that a promise to look at her ideas would be the most they would offer, and perhaps the possibility of printing a few articles in the future. Alicia didn't in her wildest dreams imagine she would get a job—even a part-time post.

'You can decide on your hours yourself, all we require is that you turn in an article each week, and a feature once a month. All subjects have to be passed by the editor. I'll introduce you to him now.' Birgit spoke rapidly while walking down the steps. At the bottom of the stairs, at a set of glass doors, she stopped and turned to face Alicia, 'Is that alright?'

Alicia nodded, 'Yes, of course.' She was still trying to get used to the idea of working on *Ålandsbladet* but tried not to show it. She wanted to come across as dynamic and enthusiastic, two of the adjectives she uses to describe herself in her CV, even though she can't remember when she last fulfilled either of those traits.

'Oh, you've met?' Birgit now says. Addressing Patrick, she adds, 'What are you doing here?'

'That's a nice welcome,' Patrick says to the woman while his eyes are on Alicia, who tries hard to keep her professional composure. There's a definite atmosphere between her and the Swedish reporter.

'I was interviewing Alicia's mother last week. About the break-in.' Patrick moves his eyes from Alicia to Birgit.

'Ah, OK,' Birgit says, looking at Patrick and Alicia in turn.

'So why are you here?' Patrick says.

'I ...'

'She's our new Financial Correspondent. Part-time,' Birgit interrupts her, straining her neck toward the end of the large room, which is filled with desks divided by bright blue partition screens. Most of the work stations are unoccupied, Alicia notices, but following Birgit's gaze, she sees an office in the far corner of the room, separated from the main open-plan room by a glass partition. Inside there's a large desk and a couple of tall house plants. A high-backed leather chair is pushed away from the desk, empty.

'I wanted you to meet the editor, but he seems to have popped out.' Birgit glances at her watch, making Alicia do the same. It's 11.15am. Alicia realizes she's been with the personnel manager for just over 30 minutes and she is already a fully-fledged employee of the company.

'Well, well. Congratulations,' Patrick says and reaches

his hand out to Alicia. She takes it and once again his touch sends currents through her body.

Pull yourself together.

Patrick sits himself on the edge of a desk, and nods toward the glass box at the end of the room. 'Came to see the old man but he's disappeared.'

Birgit's half-moon glasses move toward Patrick, and suddenly her face brightens.

'Alicia, why don't you tag along with Patrick? He can tell you more about this place at the same time You don't mind, do you, Patrick?'

He looks at the personnel manager, and then smiles at Alicia, revealing his white teeth.

'It'll be my pleasure.'

'What are you working on?' Alicia asks Patrick as soon as they step outside the modern building and the bright sunshine hits their faces. 'Apart from a little break-in at my mother's shop.'

They are standing on the pavement outside the *Ålandsbladet* offices. Patrick rests his hands on his hips, the strap of the leather bag cutting into his wide chest.

'I'm off to lunch.' Patrick says, not answering Alicia's question. 'You want to join me?'

Alicia stares at the man in front of her. He's attractive, she can't pretend otherwise. His blond hair and blue, flirtatious eyes are difficult to look at without smiling.

Alicia tries not to smile in appreciation and keeps her eyes serious.

'Ah, I'm sorry. I didn't realize. When Birgit said I should come along with you I imagined you were going to cover a story.'

Patrick gives a little laugh. 'I don't work here!'

As if she should know the joke, the wide smile stays on his lips. She is standing so close to him that she notices he has cut himself shaving that morning. A tiny speck of blood sits on his chin. Alicia catches herself imagining what his blood tastes like. She licks her lips.

'So, how about it?' Patrick says and Alicia is startled. Has he read her mind?

'Lunch?' Patrick says. 'The Italian by the marketplace is nice.'

'Ah,' Alicia says. 'I'm not sure ...' She makes a show of looking at her watch.

Patrick runs his hand through his hair. 'Look, why don't we have a bite to eat and I can tell you how things work in that madhouse?' He nods with his head toward the building they'd just left.

'I'm not officially employed by the paper, but it's part of the family business, and I occasionally give them a helping hand when I'm here in the summer.'

Alicia doesn't really have a choice. She tells herself: she's just been handed the perfect job, and told by the person who's employed her to go with this man.

'OK,' she says.

Patrick nods and chin points toward the Sitkoff shopping center. They walk through the covered mall, passing a hamburger place where a few youngsters are laughing and jostling with each other, waiting for their unhealthy lunches to be prepared. Alicia thinks of Stefan. Is this where he too spent his time when he took Uffe's moped into town from Sjoland?

Patrick leads the way out of the arcade, past an outdoor café where tourists are having coffees or nursing pints of lager. Everyone is laughing, the sun shining into their faces, their bodies relaxed in a holiday mode.

The sunny Torggatan is much busier, with children running away from their mothers and couples in shorts and summer dresses strolling along the street, looking into shop windows. It's still low season, a few days before Midsummer, but already the ferries are bringing day-trippers from Sweden and Finland to the little island town. Alicia glances across the street, where her mother's boutique is situated. Clothes that Hilda has placed on a rail outside, on the pavement, flutter in the breeze. Alicia quickens her step; she doesn't want to talk to her mother, or for her mother to see her with Patrick. She'd only make a fuss about the job, and the Swedish reporter.

'Do you like Italian food? Have you been to the one in *torg kiosken*?'

'Yeah, that sounds good.' Alicia isn't at all hungry, but she wants to talk to Patrick about the newspaper and her new job. Or that's what she tells herself. She knows that she is immensely attracted to this man. But she also knows he's married. As is she.

They make their way toward the Market Square, where a handful of strawberry sellers and people offering local handicrafts have stalls. As they walk, Alicia is aware that they have matched their steps. Patrick's hand hovers behind her, close to the small of her back, guiding her through the street as if she is a tourist. She can feel the heat of his body next to hers, but tries to ignore the effect his closeness is having.

The restaurant, called Nonna Rina, is bustling. It seems everyone in Mariehamn is here. Suddenly Alicia remembers coming here with Liam and Stefan. Her son was eleven at the time, and he wolfed down a bowl of pasta salad. It was overcast, and cold, the skies above threatening rain. They'd debated whether to wait for a table inside the small café, but Stefan was hungry so they'd opted to eat outdoors. She remembers how they watched the Rockoff festival set-up nearby on the Market Square, and how they debated whether Stefan should be allowed to go there with his island friends. Alicia remembers deciding he was too young to go on his own. Instead, she and Liam had taken turns to accompany their son, much to his embarrassment, over the few days of the festival.

They were always so careful with him, but it had been of no use. Alicia took a deep breath to release the pressure on her chest. This was how Connie had told her to deal with the grief, which so often came out of nowhere, crushing her lungs, making it difficult for her to breathe.

'Just take air in through your nose and release it slowly out of your mouth,' she said.

'You OK?' Patrick asks. They are standing in a line, waiting to be seated.

Alicia nods. She doesn't want to discuss her son with this man she hardly knows. Chances are he already knows about it—her mother isn't the most discreet of people. Alicia guesses she would have told him about Stefan during her interview with Patrick. Or he might have heard about the accident through the wide circle of people Uffe and Hilda know on the islands. Everyone knows everyone else's business here in the small island communities.

SIXTEEN

'I'm sorry about your son.' Patrick's eyes are steady on Alicia. She stares back at him, not knowing what to say. There is an awkward silence between them.

They are now sitting at the table, having paid for their food at the till. The Italian owner of the café brings them two bowls of salad. Patrick seems to know the dark-haired man and the two joke about a football game that Alicia has no interest in. Instead she nods to the man and raises the corners of her lips into a smile.

'Federico, please meet Alicia, a new reporter at *Ålandsbladet*,' Patrick says.

Alicia manages to make some small talk about how lovely Mariehamn is.

'She's a local, though,' Patrick says. His eyes are still on Alicia.

Federico raises his eyebrows and is about to ask Alicia to explain when a woman behind the counter attracts his attention and he excuses himself.

'Federico knows everybody in town,' Patrick says. 'In the summer we play in a five-aside together. He supports AC Milan and I Barcelona.'

'Hmm,' Alicia is munching on a corner of a crispy iceberg lettuce leaf. She isn't really hungry; it's barely 12 o'clock. She's forgotten how early they eat lunch on the islands.

'I'm sorry about before,' Patrick says after they have both finished their food in silence.

Alicia gazes at Patrick's weather-worn face. She wonders if he is or has been a heavy smoker. The lines on his face didn't take away from the rugged attractiveness of the man, but rather added to it.

'It's OK,' she says, and adds, 'Do you have kids?'

Patrick nods, 'Two girls, eight and ten.'

Alicia nods.

'When Sara was three, she had meningitis. We nearly lost her.'

Alicia lifts her eyes and looks at Patrick. His eyes are sad when he begins to tell the story, 'She had a temperature and we thought she just had a cold. It was in the middle of July and we were at the summer place. We had some people over and we'd been drinking. When we went to bed at about 2am, I looked into the girls' bedroom and felt Sara's forehead. She was burning up. I called to Mia and we phoned the doctor. We woke him up, and he told us to look for a rash ... there were red spots all over her body. How I hadn't noticed them when we put the girls into bed, I don't know. We'd both had too much to drink to drive but had no choice. By that stage we both felt pretty sober, though. We decided Mia should stay with Sara's younger sister, Frederica, and that I would drive to the hospital, where the doctor had agreed to meet us. It was the longest night of my life. She was unconscious when I lifted her out of bed and didn't come around until the next day.'

While he's talking, the noise of the café and the people having lunch disappears. Alicia sees how difficult reliving the awful night is for Patrick, and what nearly losing his daughter means to him.

'I'm sorry,' she says.

Patrick is quiet for a moment. 'Don't be. She was OK in the end. Not like ...'

Alicia takes a slow breath in and out. She is not going to cry.

'I'm so sorry,' Patrick says and leans in a little to bring his face closer to Alicia.

She wants to touch him, she wants to put her head on his shoulder. She wishes he'd lean in even closer and kiss her.

What's got into her?

Instead, she gets herself up and says, trying to keep her voice level, 'Would you like a coffee?'

'Anyway,' I'm sorry, it must be hard for you,' Patrick says when Alicia comes back with two cups of hot, black coffee.

Alicia gazes at Patrick's blue eyes and nods. The café is still bustling and two tourists from Sweden are speaking loudly at the counter, demanding gluten-free pizzas and soya milk lattes. Federico lifts his shoulders with his arms stretched out, giving the two a southern European shrug.

Patrick and Alicia follow the ruckus until the two thin women wearing sports clothes and bum bags storm out past their table, incensed that the Italian café didn't have what they wanted.

Their eyes meet and Alicia finds herself returning Patrick's smile. The mood has lifted between them.

'I feel I should say sorry,' Patrick says, laughing.

'You can't be held responsible for the behavior of all the people of your country of birth,' Alicia replies between giggles.

'The whole country? You really don't like Swedes, do you?'

Alicia puts her hand to her mouth to stop her now uncontrollable giggling.

What is going on? She's again behaving like a teenager in this man's company.

Patrick reaches over and puts his hand on hers. 'It's OK, I'm not particularly enamored with you *Ålänningar*. My in-laws can be quite annoying at times.'

Alicia's giggling finally stops and she looks down at Patrick's bony fingers over her own.

Patrick quickly removes his hand, and coughs into it instead.

'I think I need to get back to the office,' Alicia says, getting up. They walk along Torggatan in silence, and only speak once they're back at *Ålandsbladet*.

'Right,' Patrick says and sweeps his hand over the empty open-plan space. 'This is it!'

'Any idea where my desk might be?' Alicia says

Patrick shows her to a space that he says has been vacant for a while and gets the pc working for her. He runs through the intranet, letting her use his access settings, and says it might be best if she reads through the various sections of the paper to see the style of the writing. He briefly runs through who does what.

'You seem to know an awful lot about this place for someone who doesn't work here.' Alicia remarks.

Patrick smiles into her eyes again, 'Well, I'm married to the family, what can I say?'

They have their heads close together over the screen when they hear a door slam.

An older man with totally white hair walks through the door. He has a sizeable belly and wears a gray shirt with worn-out jeans and sandals with stripey socks.

'Harri, meet our newest reporter,' Patrick says, straightening his back.

'This is our editor, Harri Noutiainen,' Patrick says, turning to Alicia.

'Ah, yes, I heard about you.' Harri doesn't take Alicia's outstretched hand, and after an awkward moment, she lets it fall and stands there in silence while the editor peers at her from under his bushy eyebrows. In fact, the three of them stand in silence for what to Alicia seems like several long minutes. Eventually Harri declares, 'I hear you can write about money matters. You worked at the *Financial Times*?'

'Well yes ...' Alicia begins, but Harri interrupts her and says, 'Good, that's agreed then. I look forward to reading your pieces.'

Without waiting for a reply, he turns away and makes his way to the glass-paneled office in the corner of the large space.

SEVENTEEN

Alicia yawns as she opens the door to the offices of *Ålandsbladet*. She couldn't get back to sleep after waking at 4am to full daylight and twittering birds, and now, just before nine, she feels as if she's been awake for half a day already. She decides to just drop off her contract and leave at lunchtime—the job is supposed to be part-time after all.

She sees Birgit come up the stairs and hands her the piece of paper.

'I'm afraid Harri is out today,' the personnel woman says.

'I met him yesterday,' Alicia replies.

'Oh, right,' Birgit says and smiles. There's no lipstick on her teeth this morning. 'But you should come to the editorial meeting on Wednesday morning after Midsummer. I'll send the IT guy to you this morning. He can get you a username, passwords, access to our cloud and that sort of thing.'

'I think Patrick sorted most of that out for me yesterday,' Alicia says

The woman pulls the papers against her chest and starts to walk away. 'You're all set then. Have a good day.' She disappears out of the door.

Alicia nods and smiles at the two other people in the office, a young man and a woman, busy at their desks. She gets similar nods back but neither comes over to say hello. Birgit should have introduced me, Alicia thinks.

Patrick is nowhere to be seen, and why would he be? He was only there the day before to speak with the editor, she reminds herself. She's not sure if she is relieved or disappointed by his absence. It's an odd arrangement, she thinks, but then remembers how things are organized on the islands. Everything is more informal. It's who you know that matters.

Alicia sits down at the desk allotted to her at the entrance to the room. For something to do, she scrolls down her emails. She manages to open her own Webmail inbox and sees there's a message from Liam.

'Dear Alicia,
I just wanted to let you know I got home OK.
Love,
Liam x'

Alicia deletes the message without replying. What is the matter with the man? He acts as if everything is the same as before. He sent her a message on WhatsApp to say he'd arrived home on Sunday, and now this. Alicia wonders if he is now staying with Ewa, if he is in her arms at this very moment. She sees that it's just half past nine, which would make it 7.30 in the UK. He wouldn't still be in bed, if he follows his old routine. He'll now be on his morning run, but would that be in Crouch End or somewhere else, where Ewa lives? Alicia sighs. It's none of her business anymore.

She scans the other emails. There are adverts, messages from companies in London she no longer has any interest in. Alicia closes the page and begins to read the online paper. It's updated twice a day, once in the morning and once around 5pm in the afternoon, Patrick told her the day before. There is nothing interesting there. Alicia wonders how the paper can afford to employ her.

Frida's heart skips a little when she sees the new woman enter the office. What is Stefan's mum doing here at *Ålandsbladet*? With her head down, concealed by the screen that separates her desk from the one opposite, Frida pricks her ears and listens to the conversation between Birgit and Stefan's mum. Pretending to be engrossed with whatever is on her screen, and with her right hand resting on the mouse, Frida takes in the information, trying not to panic. She lifts her eyes slowly up over the screen and toward the end of the room, but neither woman is looking at her. She takes the opportunity to observe Stefan's mum closely. She has the same lanky build as Stefan, and the same tilt of the head when she listens to Birgit. Suddenly Frida feels a pain in her gut again, like she's been stabbed. Her heart is now racing and she has to put her hands under her thighs to stop them from shaking.

It's OK, she doesn't know you.

Frida has seen Stefan's mum from a distance once before, when he'd borrowed his step-grandpa's moped. She was with him when he picked up his mobile, which he'd forgotten at his grandparent's place. Frida was standing by the moped on the side of the road while Stefan ran back to the house. He asked her to come in but Frida didn't want to meet the old folks. She remembers seeing the relief on his face, although he'd tried to hide it, shrugging his wide shoulders and running his long fingers through his blond, shoulder-length hair. He jogged to the house and when he re-emerged from the front door, carrying his mobile, a woman whom he later said was his 'overcurious' mother stepped out behind him. She peered at Frida standing by the road, and Frida turned her back just in time, so that the woman couldn't tell whether she was a boy or a girl. With her short-cropped hair, Dr Martens, leather jacket and loose, ripped jeans, she often passed for a guy. She didn't mind what people thought.

Quickly, Frida now types 'Alicia O'Connell' and the *Financial Times* into the picture search on Google. Her fears are confirmed. The smiling image of the woman now sitting down at one of the free work stations is the one on the screen in front of her. She closes the page down and decides to take the bull by the horns.

EIGHTEEN

'Hi,' Alicia lifts her head and sees a young woman, with short cropped hair, colored pale gray and blue, standing by her desk, with her arm stretched.

'I'm Frida,' she says.

Alicia gets up and takes the hand. It seems a very formal greeting from someone so young. Frida doesn't look any older than Stefan, but her handshake is surprisingly strong.

'I'm the summer intern,' she says and she lifts one side of her mouth into a grin. 'So basically I do everything around here.' Her face is now in a full smile.

'Right,' Alicia says.

'And my mother is an ABBA fan, hence the name.' The girl looks down and kicks the floor with her left boot.

'It's a nice name,' Alicia says.

'Whatever. You smoke?'

'No.'

'OK, well, I'll show you around anyway, yeah?'

'Now?' Alicia asks and glances around the open-plan office and the editor's cubicle at the far end. What more was there to show her?

Frida shifts in her clumpy boots but doesn't say anything. Alicia feels sorry for the girl. She's only trying to be friendly, she thinks and gets up.

'That'll be lovely, thank you,' she says and gives the girl a smile.

Frida takes Alicia out of the office and points at the door to the bathrooms on the landing. 'There's a shower in there if you ever need it,' she says and grins at Alicia. Then she turns back into the main office and leads Alicia to a door on the right. It's a coffee room with a kitchenette and a round table covered in a bright green Marimekko cloth. There are chairs all around the table. At the far end of the narrow space a tall window reaching down to the floor overlooks the Eastern Harbor.

'That's nice,' Alicia says and nods toward the view of the sailing boats rocking in the wind. The sun is high in the sky, its rays reflecting on the rippling surface of the sea.

Frida follows Alicia's gaze. 'Yeah, nice to see the Russian Mafia boats every day.' Her tone has changed, and the smile has disappeared from her lips.

'What do you mean?' Alicia asks. She gazes at the young woman who's wearing a white T-shirt and a pair of tight ripped jeans, revealing slices of the, almost luminous, white skin of her thighs. On her feet she wears a pair of black, heavy Dr Marten's, which look too hot for the warm summer weather. The temperature had already reached 20°C when Alicia left the sauna cottage that morning and got into the car with her mum.

'Oh, nothing, it's a joke.' Frida is standing by the small kitchen area, her face turned away from Alicia. 'Would you like some coffee? I'm making a pot.'

'Yes please.'

While Frida fills the percolator with coffee from a packet she's retrieved from a cupboard above the sink, Alicia admires the scene of the harbor through the tall window. There are a couple of expensive-looking yachts among the many sailing boats.

The East Harbor gets busier each day coming up to Midsummer, when the high season starts. At its peak, there will be no free spots on the jetties. The sailing club, *Club Marin*, which has a restaurant, saunas and restrooms for the yachties will be bustling with families. Alicia regrets that she didn't take Stefan sailing. Neither she nor Liam were particularly interested in boats, she thinks, as she watches Frida turn to look at the view. The coffee percolator has started dripping water loudly into the glass pot.

'You don't like Russians?' Alicia asks.

The girl whips her head around and her eyes are dark with hatred. 'They're bastards, every one of them.'

Alicia is startled by the girl's hostility. Growing up on the islands, which are part of Finland, no one had liked Russians, or Soviet citizens, as they had been some twenty years ago. But there was never this kind of animosity toward the people themselves, only toward those in power. Like Putin, now rumored to own land on the islands.

The girl's demeanor suddenly changes, and a grin returns to her face.

'How do you take your coffee?'

'Oh, black please,' Alicia says, still slightly shocked by the sudden changes in the young woman's mood.

Frida places a mug on the tablecloth in front of Alicia and sits down opposite her. Alicia sees she has tattoos on the inside of her wrist.

'That must have hurt,' she says, nodding to the small image of an angel carved onto the pale skin. It's obvious they need to change the subject.

'Nah, not really,' Frida says, glancing inside her own arm. She lifts her eyes toward Alicia. 'It's in memory of someone very sweet. I believe he's an angel now.'

Alicia stares back at Frida. How does she know that is exactly how Alicia thinks about her own son. Has Frida also lost someone dear to her? The question, 'Who?' hangs in the air, but for some reason Alicia is too afraid to ask.

'Well, I'd better get back to work,' Alicia says instead, and gets up.

'It was nice to meet you and thank you for the coffee,' she says over her shoulder to the girl, who is not looking at her, but staring out of the window. She doesn't reply and Alicia hesitates for a moment by the door. She cannot put her finger on it, but Alicia has a strange feeling that Frida was talking about Stefan, her Stefan, but surely that couldn't be? To stop the train of thought, Alicia throws another glance at the luxury Russian yachts. The East Harbor has more of them each year, flying their wide striped white, blue and red flags. But so what? All they do is bring tourist cash into the small economy, surely?

NINETEEN

'Have you seen this?' Hilda has printed a sheet from her computer and is waving it in front of Alicia. She's sitting on her favorite stool in the corner of the kitchen, waiting for her mother. They're planning to cook dinner together and Hilda has been upstairs changing out of her work clothes. Alicia takes the piece of paper from her mother. Her heart skips a beat when she sees it's from Mia—Patrick's Mia.

'Patrick is true to his word then,' she says, trying to sound nonchalant.

'Of course he is!' Hilda snatches the paper out of Alicia's hands and turns toward the front door, where Uffe has just appeared.

'Have you heard, Uffe, we're invited to the Eriksson's Midsummer party!'

Uffe glances at Alicia and smiles, 'Well, aren't we going up in the world.'

'Oh, my,' Hilda says, her eyes fixed on the piece of paper. 'It was sent on Saturday, that's three days ago and we haven't RSVP'd. That could be seen as rude, you know.'

Alicia rolls her eyes at Hilda, 'Mum, how come you haven't seen the email before?'

Hilda waves her hand over her freshly coiffured blond bob. 'Oh, I don't check my emails more than once a week, if that! It's usually all adverts or messages from people I don't like.'

Alicia has to suppress a smile. She's about to ask how come she doesn't get her emails on her brand-new iPhone, but she doesn't want to get into a long conversation about how the internet does or doesn't work on Hilda's mobile. It's all organized a bit differently in Finland, and she's no expert herself. A few years ago she made the mistake of trying to configure Hilda's first smart phone and managed to delete her settings, so now she doesn't want to touch her mother's phones. Besides, it was always either Liam or Stefan who dealt with the technical things in the family. *I guess I have to learn how to do those things now*, Alicia thinks to herself.

'So we are obviously all going, yes? I know we said we'd spend the evening here, but this is such an opportunity ...' Hilda says, looking at Uffe.

Alicia looks at her mother. 'When is it?'

'What?' Hilda is staring at her daughter. Even Uffe is looking at Alicia. He's standing by the kitchen island, with one of Hilda's cinnamon buns in his hand.

'Don't eat that now,' Hilda snaps at Uffe and he puts the bun down on the kitchen counter. 'It's nearly dinner time!' Hilda gives her husband an angry stare, then turns back to Alicia.

'Midsummer's Eve is this Friday, silly,' she almost shouts. You know, Eriksson's Midsummer parties are the talk of Mariehamn, of Åland! Anyone who's anyone will be there.'

'Sorry, I was miles away. Of course we must go.' Alicia says and takes hold of the piece of paper again. 'Did you open the attachment? I bet there's an invite there with more information.'

'Oh,' Hilda says and turns on her heels. Moments later she's back with another piece of paper. Alicia wonders why she didn't just forward the email to her, but doesn't say anything. It's a stylish invite in black and white with images of dancing couples, champagne glasses and balloons bordering a text, 'Come and celebrate the magic of Midsummer with Family Eriksson'.

The party starts with lunch at 1pm and goes on past midnight, or whenever people want to go home. What a long bash, Alicia thinks and wonders how she can get out of it. When she looks up and sees that her mother's eyes are sparkling, she realizes there's no chance. She will have to go. A faint tingling on her skin tells her she is excited at the prospect of seeing Patrick again too.

'I've never been to the Eriksson's villa,' Hilda says, her voice breathless. 'Of course, like everyone else, I've driven past hundreds of times. They have those heavy iron gates now, so you can't see into the drive or the vast shoreline they own anymore, but ...' she stops abruptly, and exclaims, 'Oh, what will we wear! We'll have to pick something out of my stock and everyone in Mariehamn will have seen it already!' Hilda is staring at her daughter, her eyes wide and with one of her hands splayed over her chest in a dramatic pose. Not this again, Alicia thinks, but then she remembers she hasn't got anything suitable either. As if she's read her mind, her mother comes over and puts her arm over Alicia's shoulders. 'Don't worry, I have just the dress for you.'

On the day of the party, the skies are clear and the sun beams down as Alicia makes her way from the sauna cottage to the main house. Uffe has offered to drive Hilda's freshly washed and polished BMW. Two of his farm hands have given the brand-new soft-top a thorough going over. For over two hours they washed and scrubbed every inch of the exterior and then polished the chassis and the cream leather interior. The car looks brand-new.

So that people won't have to drink and drive, the Eriksson's have invited guests to park their cars overnight on their estate. Hilda is taking full advantage of the offer, and has ordered a taxi to take them home promptly at midnight. This, Alicia thinks, will give her mother another opportunity to make contact with the Eriksson's when they fetch the car the next day. She will be able to see the 'summer place' again. *Don't be so mean and churlish*, Alicia tells herself as she watches the streets of Mariehamn whizz past, full of revellers. The weather has brought everyone out to celebrate Midsummer on the islands.

They drive with the roof up to save Hilda's hair-do. Alicia's sense of being a teenager isn't helped by the fact that she is sitting on the back seat, almost doubled over in the small space, obviously not meant to be used by a fully grown person. Like a child being taken to an adult party, she'd rather be anywhere else right now. She wonders if she might be able to smuggle herself out before the twelve hours of merrymaking are over. She can't imagine she will have any fun among the Åland glitterati, most of whom will be the same age as her mother and Uffe. She brushes away thoughts of Patrick.

Still, it will be interesting to see the 'summer place', as the invitation calls (with false modesty) what Alicia knows is a vast estate at the southern tip of the peninsula. She's met Mia's parents in passing before, but she has never really spoken to them, nor has she ever been invited to their home. Alicia knows that not only is Mia's father a millionaire, but her mother is a famous author. That said, she is not a fan of her books, even though her works are celebrated all over Scandinavia and beyond and have been translated into several languages. To Alicia, Beatrice Eriksson's novels are too full of misery and death. She smiles when she recalls Liam's remark after reading one of her books—'I'm surprised she didn't commit suicide while writing this story.' At the time Alicia was angry with Liam's flippant dismissal of one of the most important books that had come out of Finland in years. The story, which centers on the famine under the Russian rule in the 18th century, won prizes all over Europe. But she had to admit, after reading *Frozen Hunger* she didn't wish to know any of the writer's other books, however much she would have liked to support an author from Åland.

Then there's Patrick. Alicia tries to brush away her stupid infatuation with the man. She knows she's being foolish, and that her feelings probably aren't reciprocated. Patrick is just being flirty; he's that kind of a man.

And what about the other day when they were having lunch? Didn't you share a moment then?

She tells herself to stop fantasizing about a married man and tries to concentrate on her mother's incessant chatter. She's talking about all the good Mr Eriksson has done on Åland, about the funds he's plowing into tourism and the charities he supports.

Alicia tunes out again and looks at the beautiful scenery. They're crossing a long, narrow bridge where the sea opens up on both sides of the road. The sun's rays glitter on the surface of the water and Alicia leans her head against the headrest. It's good to be home.

Soon they join a line of expensive cars, all just as well buffed and polished as Hilda's.

'We're nearly there!' Hilda says, with her voice trembling. 'How do I look?' she asks and pulls down the sun visor to check on her hair and teeth.

'You look fine,' Alicia says when her mother turns around.

They get out of the car and Hilda whispers to Alicia, 'You are stunning. That green color really suits you, and the chiffon fabric flatters your figure. I'm glad I managed to convince you to wear the high-heeled wedges with that dress.'

TWENTY

'Networking, that's what you need to do,' Mia says and gives Patrick a look. He knows she is disappointed that he's not come up to scratch.

'Tonight's your chance,' she tells him as they're getting ready in the converted boathouse on the morning of the party. 'Daddy invited the editor from *Expressen* just for you.'

Expressen is the other large evening paper in Sweden. Patrick has been put on notice of redundancy, something he hasn't shared with his wife. His boss at the paper told him everyone got the same notice, but he knows that's not true. He hasn't had a scoop in years. He doesn't care as much about his career as Mia does. He's fed up with the way *Journalen* sensationalizes the news. There are no standards in journalism anymore. But that doesn't matter to Mia and her parents. Her father, who has his fingers in many pies in Sweden too, just needs her daughter's husband to conform to the upper-class image he had of

Patrick when Mia married him. Little did Mr Eriksson know that he was just an ordinary *Norrbotten* Swede, who got lucky with a job in a major Stockholm newspaper. Even after ten years with Mia (and especially now, Patrick thinks) it's important that he has a good independent income.

He's married into a family with standing, with a prize-winning author to boot. Something he's often reminded about.

'All you need to do is to impress him with your ...' Mia looks Patrick up and down. 'Well, try at least to sound intelligent.'

Patrick doesn't say anything. He can't think of an equally suitable slur.

'Where are the girls?' he asks instead.

'In the house.'

Patrick thinks of his daughters in Kurt and Beatrice Eriksson's large house, scrubbed clean, watching a cartoon on TV, or playing on their iPads in one of the upper bedrooms. Mia got them ready hours before the party to give herself plenty of time to preen.

Everything needs to be perfect, that's how Pappa likes it.

Patrick has also been required to get ready in good time and is now standing dressed in his best linen suit in front of the floor-length windows of their converted boathouse, looking at one of the Viking Line ferries on its way toward Sweden. Patrick grabs the binoculars out of habit and surveys the ship through them.

'Are you even listening to me?' Mia says, removing the lenses from Patrick's hand. Her voice is gentle, too gentle, and Patrick looks at his wife. She's slim, but with a shapely body. Her legs, which are long anyway, are further elongated by the white outfit she's wearing.

'Isn't that boiler suit going to get dirty?' Patrick says.

Mia takes a deep breath and exhales slowly, throwing the binoculars on their vast *Hästens* bed, which takes up most of the bedroom. Her face is angular, all straight lines. With her hands on her hips. 'Jump suit, not a boiler suit. I'm not a fucking plumber!'

'All the same, red wine on that thing ...'

Now Mia has a knowing smile on her lips. 'Don't change the subject, darling.' She comes close to Patrick and presses her body against his. The top of the suit is open, almost down to her naval, and he pulls the side of the neckline away from her chest and peers inside. He sees one pink nipple on her pert little breast.

'No bra, eh? Who are you out to impress today?'

Mia lifts her dark brown eyes at him. Her smile has disappeared. 'Don't be nasty.'

'I'm not,' Patrick says, releasing his grip on her suit and taking a couple of steps toward the bed to retrieve the binoculars. Turning around and seeing his wife's shapely rear framed by the calm teal sea beyond the large window, he says, 'I can show you how nice I can be.' He reaches out to place his palm on one of Mia's buttocks, but she moves away just before he can make contact.

'Don't.' The expression on her face is icy cold.

Patrick sighs and continues to peer at the large red ferry. He sees people on the deck, gazing toward the coastline. There's a couple kissing, the woman's dress flapping in the wind. Patrick feels almost jealous of the man next to the smiling woman. He's forgotten how to be happy, he thinks, and resolves to try to appease Mia. Perhaps there's still hope? But when he puts down the binoculars and turns around to say something to her, he finds himself alone in the room.

Alicia sees Patrick almost as soon as she, Hilda and Uffe come around the corner and get the full vista of the magnificent house. Along with all the other well-dressed people, they've abandoned their car keys to a young guy with thick dark hair who directs them down a well-tended path toward a vast, modern building.

Valet parking in Åland, Alicia thinks. She's never even been offered it in London!

Patrick is dressed in a light-colored linen suit, with a T-shirt underneath. Somehow, he looks even more bronzed than he did a few days ago. He has a wide smile on his lips as he greets guests at the top of stairs leading to a wooden deck, which has been stained dark gray to blend into the rock surrounding the house. The place itself is covered in glass. A pair of tall windows facing the sea form the center of the house, with two long wings on either side, and sloping roofs half shading the glass. The house seems to be floating in the sea, which today is calm, blue-green in color. A slight wind is making patterns like fish scales on the surface of the water, and the sun is high up, the sky blindingly blue with just a few fluffy clouds breaking up the perfect impression.

Patrick is wearing aviator-style sunglasses, but Alicia can see from his smile that he has spotted them. He whispers something to a man standing next to him and steps down the stairs to greet them personally. He makes a few apologies as he walks toward Alicia, Uffe and Hilda, and a few eyebrows are raised at the attention they are getting. When he leans down to kiss Hilda's cheek, her mother's face lights up in awe. She moves her shoulders slightly lower down her back and lifts her head toward Patrick.

'How lovely of you to invite us!' she says and Patrick smiles. 'Not at all, it's a privilege to have you here.' As he says this, he glances at Alicia, who is standing behind Hilda and Uffe. Hilda introduces her husband to Patrick and the two men shake hands. And then he is standing opposite Alicia.

'Nice dress,' he says quietly against her ear as he bends down to kiss Alicia's cheek. His hand touches her back and she can feel his fingers through the thin fabric. The garment Hilda chose for her skims her body with three layers of fabric. The hem touches her calves but has slits up to her thighs, so that her legs are momentarily revealed when she walks. Alicia tries not to blush and is glad of the large pair of sunglasses she popped into her handbag at the last minute. She's sure her eyes will betray her emotions, so she keeps her shades on, even when Patrick removes his and gazes at her quietly. Just before the moment becomes embarrassing, Patrick says, 'Come and have a drink!'

As he leads the three of them toward a bar, Hilda and Uffe see someone they know and are pulled into a conversation.

'Just you and me, then,' Patrick laughs.

TWENTY-ONE

P atrick takes Alicia to a small bar set up in the main living rooms inside the house. Most people are staying outside, taking advantage of the brilliant summer weather, and the vast room is empty. Alicia gasps when she steps inside after Patrick. The decor is stunning; pared down with a gray color scheme, with just the occasional pop of color—a red scatter cushion here, or a bright yellow throw there. The floor is slate, and the walls, in which there are two massive fireplaces, are constructed out of gray stone. Patrick asks her if she would like champagne, and Alicia nods. A popping sound brings her attention back to Patrick, who is pouring the Moet into two long flutes.

'Is this where you stay when you're in Åland?' she asks when he hands her a glass. 'Yep,' he replies.

Alicia wishes she could put her sunglasses back on. She can feel his eyes on her, but she fears looking at him in case she betrays the speed of her heartbeat. Every time he comes near her, she wants him to move away, yet come closer at the same time. She can feel the heat of his body too well through the damned dress, which makes her feel naked.

'That really suits you,' Patrick says.

It's too revealing, I knew it.

Alicia lifts her eyes briefly. He isn't smiling anymore, but his lips are slightly parted.

'Shouldn't you be looking after your guests?' she says quickly.

'They're not my guests. Besides, I'm looking after you.'

Alicia sips the drink, glad to have the glass to hide behind, and to have something solid between her and Patrick. She looks up, trying to admire the high-ceilinged space, when she sees a figure leaning on a banister that runs between two oak staircases on either side of the room.

Mia.

'Hello Mia!' Alicia says and lifts her glass toward her old schoolfriend.

Well, not so much a friend.

Mia gives Alicia a quick glance and begins to make her way down one of the staircases. She's wearing an all-white jumpsuit made out of some silky fabric, Alicia notices. A belt made out of the same fabric is tied around her small waist. On her feet, Mia has high-heeled gold sandals, and she wears matching hooped earrings. Her dark curls are tied up in an up-do, with a few strands falling over her shoulders. She has barely any make-up on, just a dab of red color on her full lips. Her body is perfect for the outfit, as is her make-up. When she reaches them, she gives Alicia two air kisses and turns to her husband, 'A glass of that bubbly would be lovely, darling.'

Patrick looks back at the bar and realizes there are no champagne flutes left.

'Umm,' he says and looks at Mia.

She crosses her arms and lifts one eyebrow. 'Well, go and get some then! I'm sure Magda has some in the kitchen.'

'Men,' she smiles at Alicia when Patrick has disappeared through an opening in one of the stone walls.

'Amazing place!' Alicia blurts out. She desperately wants to take another sip out of her glass, but doesn't think it would be polite when her hostess is without a drink.

Mia smiles, but her eyes remain cold and almost hostile. She waves an arm into the room. 'Oh, this is where Mamma and Pappa stay. We're over by the cove. In a converted boathouse. It's tiny compared to this.'

'Right.'

Alicia is relieved to see Patrick re-enter the rooms with a small dark-haired woman wearing an old-fashioned white lace pinny over a dark-colored dress.

These people have servants?

The woman is carrying a silver tray filled with champagne flutes. She puts it down and looks up at Patrick. 'Here, let me, Magda,' he says, dismissing the woman with a friendly smile.

'At last!' Mia says, taking a full glass from Patrick. She gives Alicia another of her unfeeling smiles and then turns to wave at somebody in the garden through the open door.

'Excuse me,' she says to Alicia and turns to Patrick, adding, 'It's the Wikströms!' She floats out of the room, expecting Patrick to follow her.

On his way past, he whispers into Alicia's ear, 'See you later.' His lips almost brush her skin, and for a while Alicia stands still, trying to calm her breathing. She gulps down the rest of her champagne and decides to empty the bottle into her glass.

They can afford it, she thinks.

TWENTY-TWO

As the day wears on and turns into a glorious evening, Alicia's fears are confirmed—none of her friends are at the party. There must be at least a hundred people milling around the vast grounds of the house, but most of the guests are Kurt and Beatrice's friends, it seems. Hilda and Uffe also seem to know absolutely everyone. Her mother introduces Alicia to so many people that she cannot retain any of the names however much she tries. Hilda laughs and chats with everyone, and Uffe appears be in his element too, drinking beer and then red wine and schnapps when the food starts to flow. There's fish roe and sour cream served on tiny blinis, marinated herring with beetroot and pickled cucumbers, lobster tails on rye toast, new potatoes and delicious reindeer steak.

Occasionally Alicia spots Magda peering out from the main house, controlling the younger waiters and waitresses in similar old-fashioned outfits, as they weave in and out of the groups of people, filling glasses and offering food. Small frozen tumblers of different flavored vodka are passed around and men and women throw them down their throats.

Alicia steers clear of any strong drinks, but accepts the seemingly free-flowing champagne when it's offered. She's keeping herself away from Patrick, and clings onto her mother as if she is a child at an adult's party. She cannot trust herself around Patrick sober, let alone tipsy. Besides, she's always been a lightweight. It was Liam who could match Uffe's vodka-drinking, and sometimes Alicia wonders if that is the only thing Uffe admires about her husband. *Her husband.* Was she still strictly married to Liam? Or were they now separated?

Only occasionally does she glimpse Patrick, often in conversation with a group of men. Once she lifts her head and he is looking right at her. She is sure she blushes but hopes Patrick is too far from her to see it.

At around eight o'clock, when the sun approaches the horizon, Mr Eriksson stands up on a stool and gives a speech.

'Dear friends and islanders,' he begins in a low, quiet tone. The guests hush suddenly and all strain to hear their host's words.

'My family and I are delighted that you have been able to come and celebrate Midsummer with us in our small cabin.' Here Kurt Eriksson pauses and looks around the guests, most of whom burst into laughter.

'Small cabin indeed,' Hilda whispers loudly in Alicia's ear. She turns around and returns her mother's smile. But there's something about Kurt Eriksson that Alicia doesn't like. He is a tall man, with a slight paunch. In spite of this, he looks fit and handsome in his white linen trousers and striped blue-pink shirt. Alicia sees his Rolex glint in the sun and spots the almost compulsory footwear for wealthy islanders—Docker shoes. Mr Eriksson's hair is gray-blond and his eyes are pale, as if both have been bleached by a life spent in the sun. He's wearing a pair of expensive-looking sunglasses on top of his head. On the whole, he looks as if he's just stepped off an exclusive sailing yacht, which Alicia guesses he probably has. Alicia remembers her mother saying something about Kurt Eriksson speaking Russian and convincing some oligarch or other to come to the islands for a holiday. Many more followed in his wake, making the islands a prime holiday destination for Russians.

'He's a good man,' Hilda told Alicia.

Alicia is suddenly aware that Mr Eriksson's eyes are on her and she widens the smile on her face. The host nods toward their group, where Alicia stands with her mother and Uffe, a little apart from the other guests.

Turning his head away, Kurt Eriksson scans the lawn where the people are arranged below him. He invites all the guests to come down to the lower level of the garden, where a fully decorated Midsummer pole lies on its side. The Erikssson children, with the help of staff, have attached flowers and paper lanterns to the pole and now it's the job of two men to lift it up. One of them is the young guy who parked Uffe's car. Everyone cheers the lifting of the pole, raising their glasses to sing, 'Hurrah, hurrah', and then Mr Eriksson leads the crowd in the little frog song. When she was a child and living in Åland, it seemed completely natural to sing about frogs at Midsummer, but now it strikes Alicia as very strange. But funny. She smiles as old and young leap up to sing,

'Små grodorna är lustiga att se,
små grodorna är lustiga att se
Ej örön, ej örön,
Ej svansar have de.'

Most people also do the actions, waving their hands around their ears to show a lack of them, and on their backside to show the lack of a tail. Alicia laughs and catches Patrick's eye. He dances with his daughters until the end of the song, when Mia leads the two girls away. Alicia looks toward Uffe and Hilda, who are laughing with a group of their friends—or acquaintances—Alicia has never seen them before. When she looks back to where Patrick had been standing, he has disappeared.

TWENTY-THREE

All through the party, Patrick watches Alicia's slight frame appear from behind a group of people, or around the corner of the house, her pale eyes looking at him from a distance. If only Mia, in her ridiculous white boiler suit, wouldn't keep pulling him further away from her to meet this and that person. He doesn't understand why she still cares.

After the ridiculously overdecorated Midsummer pole is lifted up by the East European boys, and the frog song and dance is over, Mia decides it's time for the girls to go to bed. At first, both Sara and Frederica protest, but their mother is firm. Patrick sees that the girls are over-excited but tired, and he promises to go and kiss them goodnight when the party is over.

'Even if I'm asleep, will you do it, Pappa?' says Frederica, her eight-year-old eyes grave and her blond curls messy after the party.

Patrick kneels down in front of his two daughters and looks from one to the other. 'I promise.' He gives them both a kiss and adds, 'You have to promise to be good for your mother.' The two little girls both nod gravely, and as Mia takes their hands, she gazes at him and gives him an almost kind smile.

Patrick watches his wife and daughters walk toward their cabin. He suspects Mia will not read the girls a story, or tuck them in. She'll leave all that to the Finnish au pair she has employed for the summer. She's a nice girl and both Sara and Frederica like her. He knows that if he had offered to do the bedtime routine, it would have caused a further row. Deciding to make his escape from the party, he slips down toward the water, where he knows there's a little cove among the rocks that is not visible to anyone. When the girls were little and learning to swim, his father-in-law shipped in a truck full of sand to make a little beach. He also paid a fully trained lifeguard from one of his sports charities to come and give the girls lessons.

Patrick remembers how his own father taught him to swim the summer he turned five, well before anyone else in his neighborhood in Luleå. He and his parents lived in a two-bedroomed flat in a working-class part of the city. They both worked full-time for the city council, and he attended nursery school from the age of one. He was lucky that his granny had a small summer place in Kalix on the coast. It was a little hut with just two small rooms, a tiny kitchen, and an outside toilet, built by his grandfather. But it was close to a beach and that's where Patrick's dad taught him to float for the first time. It was a far cry from a private beach and a qualified private tutor.

Of course, neither girl used the cove beach anymore. The novelty wore off a summer or two ago, and now they liked to dive into the sea from the sauna at the tip of the peninsula, which formed part of the Eriksson family summer place. Or 'cabin'. As if! More like an estate, and the biggest one in Åland, of course.

What a ridiculous man my father-in-law is!

With his hands in his pockets, Patrick makes his way across the lawn, then down some steps and finally to a narrow path on a small triangle of land between two large boulders, where the sea laps onto the imported sand. Patrick kicks off his shoes and pulls his socks off. The cool sand feels good as it spreads through his toes. Toward the end of the day, the clouds had gathered and the sun is now hidden behind them, leaving pink streaks visible between the white, fluffy shapes. Suddenly Patrick gets an urge to jump into the sea. He takes off his jacket and pulls his shirt over his head without bothering to undo more than the first few buttons. He unzips his linen trousers and pulls them off with his boxers.

Running into the water, he ignores the cold. He feels like a boy again when the water reaches his calves, then thighs. There's a bit of shallow water, and then the ground drops dramatically where the artificial beach ends. Patrick dives in and the shock of the chilly water nearly makes him turn back again. It's early summer, and the few days of bright sunshine and temperatures above 20°C haven't yet managed to warm the seawater. Patrick perseveres and swims, taking long, regular strokes in a front crawl like his late father taught him.

TWENTY-FOUR

W hen the traditional games and singing around the pole have finished Alicia walks away. Even though she was quite young when she and her mother moved to Åland, she still thinks the Midsummer celebrations on the islands are wrong somehow. Her Finnish roots make her want to be by the shore, watching a bonfire being lit, as she must have done as a baby, when her mother and father were together. She didn't know her father at all; all she has is a photograph Hilda gave her when she got married. It's a picture of a man with a serious face in army uniform. Hilda said it had been taken when her father, Klaus, was doing his military service. He was just eighteen.

A year older than Stefan.

Growing up in Åland, Alicia would imagine her father living in the house by the sea in Helsinki in which she was born. She wonders now why Hilda never took her to see her father before it was too late. Hilda never wanted to talk about Klaus; the little Alicia knows has all been

126

extracted with difficulty. When she was seven years old, Hilda took her to *Svarta Katten* café after school and told her gently that Klaus had died. Nothing more was said about Alicia's father. As far as she knew, Hilda didn't even go to the funeral in Finland.

The light is fading a little now, helped by the shroud of gray clouds. She walks toward the shoreline, down a path to a small cove with a tiny sandy beach. As she gets closer, she spots someone in the water. The person turns around and Alicia sees who it is. Surely it can't be ...?

TWENTY-FIVE

Patrick is swimming back toward the beach. He doesn't spot the woman standing by one of the boulders until he has nearly reached the shallow water by the shore. He stands up and smiles at Alicia. The water comes just above his hips.

'Come in, it's wonderful!' he shouts.

He can't see her face properly, but he thinks she's considering it. Then he can see she's shaking her head. She forms a funnel with her hands and replies, 'Do you have a towel?'

He shakes his head and continues walking toward the shore, aware that he is naked. He wants her to see him, even though he knows the cold water will have diminished his manhood somewhat. As he gets closer, he is holding her gaze, and to his delight he sees she is not shy, but looking at him. He goes to the gym at least three times a week, plays football regularly and knows he's in good shape. Suddenly Alicia, in her thin dress that the slight sea breeze has plastered to her body, revealing a slim but shapely figure, bends down and picks up his shirt.

He walks toward her and she hands him the shirt.

'To preserve your modesty.'

'Thank you,' he says but instead of placing it over his hips, he takes the linen shirt and uses it to dry first his face, then his chest and finally between his legs. All the while Alicia is looking out to sea, but he knows she is trying to keep her gaze away from his body, because just now, when he lowered the shirt from his face, her eyes shifted quickly away from him.

Patrick rushes to pull on his pants, not bothering with underwear, because he can feel a movement in his groin. Looking down, he sees he's just in time, and tucks himself in.

'You missed out,' he says, sitting down next to her on the rock. He means the swim, but knows she will get the double entendre.

And he is rewarded with a smile.

He sees she's taken off her sandals and is burrowing her toes in the sand.

'Did I now?' she says, and her smile reaches her eyes and widens.

Patrick is so close to her that their thighs are touching. He wants to put his arm around her, but is afraid she will bolt.

'How did you find this place?'

'Has the beach always been here?' Alicia and Patrick speak at the same time and both laugh.

'My father-in-law made this for the girls.'

'Ah,' Alicia says. 'Lucky girls.'

'Yeah, not that they appreciated it. Not then, not now. I'm the only one who comes swimming here nowadays. It's my secret place.'

Alicia turns her head and looks at him, 'What are you escaping from?'

For a moment Patrick considers Alicia, noticing the thin lines around her mouth and how her eyes have a sadness etched into them even though she is smiling. He wants to touch the curve of her jaw, pull her face close to his and kiss her.

'Isn't it obvious? All this,' he says instead.

Patrick throws his arm out, pointing toward the house behind the large boulders. They hear faint party noises; someone has put on music. All of it seems far away to him. He feels as if he's sitting on a desert island and the only person who matters is this vulnerable, beautiful woman next to him. 'Besides, you're one to talk about escape. I believe you're on the run as we speak.'

Her large eyes stare at him, and the grief in them fills him with sudden, strong desire. Her lips are slightly parted. An invitation. He needs to kiss those lips now. He bends closer and presses his mouth to hers. He's hungry for her. He puts his left hand onto her neck to pull her close, and his other hand finds the small of her back.

Alicia pulls herself away. She's breathless. She stands and smooths down her dress to disguise how strongly she feels.

'You shouldn't have done that,' she says and picks up her shoes from the sand. She doesn't dare look at Patrick.

She loved the taste of his lips on hers; the desire she can feel emanating from his body.

And hers.

Patrick is quiet and Alicia moves her eyes toward him. He's still sitting on the boulder, leaning on his hands, which are placed either side of his body. Alicia can see his muscles flex. His eyes are a darker shade of blue now, and she has to turn her head away to avoid sinking into them.

'I can't wear these!' she laughs, stealing another sideways glance at Patrick. She's banging her wedges against each other, but the wet sand is sticking to the inside and soles.

Alicia sits down next to him again, facing the small beach, where the water laps gently against the sand. The only sounds are from the party beyond the boulders, further up the bank behind them.

'Wear mine,' he says, pushing his shoes toward her feet.

'No thanks,' Alicia says and they both giggle uncontrollably.

I must be very drunk. I don't have any sense of guilt about kissing another man.

'I love champagne, must have just had too many glasses of the stuff,' Alicia says, between bouts of laughter.

'I'll remember that,' Patrick says, then he is suddenly serious. He touches Alicia's cheek. 'I hope this wasn't just too much drink?'

Alicia looks into his brilliant blue eyes. She sees there are specs of brown in the aquamarine and that his eyelashes are unnaturally long and dark for a man.

For a man with blue eyes.

She says nothing but allows Patrick to put his lips on hers, and once more they kiss. This time, Patrick is gentle; he doesn't use his tongue as he did before, but gently presses himself against Alicia. She pulls away again.

'I like you,' Patrick says breathlessly.

Alicia touches his lip, and another cut on the side of his chin.

'You haven't learned to shave yet?' she says and smiles.

But Patrick is serious. He doesn't reply but silently takes hold of her hand and kisses the inside of her palm. Alicia's insides riot. Her head spins in a rush of desire. She glances down at Patrick's linen trousers which clearly reveal his arousal.

A sudden bout of loud laughter makes them both turn their heads toward the party, which they can't see from below the bank, but which is very close. Anyone— Mia, Kurt Eriksson, Alicia's mother, or Uffe—could at any moment walk down and see them sitting like this.

They are both married and Patrick has two little daughters.

Alicia pulls her hand away and gets up. She decides to rinse her feet in the water. When she walks back, Patrick tries to take hold of her hands. But now, shaken awake by the sounds of the party, she turns her head away, acutely aware of the proximity of Patrick's real life. His wife and children are in the boathouse, which she could see lit up in the distance as she walked to wash her feet in the sea. And her parents too—or mother and Uffe—are there, talking to their friends, being pleasant and civilized, unaware of what's going on between Alicia and Patrick. While they have been acting like any good guests of the richest man on the islands, Alicia has been kissing the son-in-law of the benefactor. And what was Patrick doing? How could he behave like that, so close to his wife and children? The children he was leading in a traditional Midsummer dance only moments ago? Or was this what he did all the time? To punish his rich father-in-law?

'You OK?' Patrick now says. His face is serious, his eyes searching, trying to lock onto Alicia's. But she won't look at him, can't look at his face. She must get away and pretend this never happened.

'I have to go,' she says, getting up, and putting her sandals onto her still sandy feet, praying that no one will spot her wet canvas shoes under her flimsy dress. It's all the fault of the dress; she knew it was too sexy, like an invitation to Patrick. Perhaps he'd taken it as a sign that she wanted him.

Oh my God, what have I done?

'Alicia,' Patrick says, but she's not listening.

Alicia bolts off the beach and onto the path. She's slipping in her damp shoes. Only once when she's on the other side of the large boulders does she dare to look back. But Patrick hasn't followed her. She can just spot the top of his blond head framed by the beach and the sea beyond it. For a moment she stops and sees that he's lit a cigarette. She can spot the red burning light of the tip as he sucks on the filter.

TWENTY-SIX

Alicia wakes up to a ping on her phone. She gets up quickly, still used to being on call in case Stefan is in trouble somehow. Her head hurts from the quick movement and as she reaches toward the illuminated screen of her phone, she remembers. She'll never again be called to fetch him from a party after a night bus has failed to arrive, or a friend has let him down.

The screen shows a message.

'You OK? You disappeared and I couldn't find you anywhere. P'

Alicia stares at the words. There's a persistent hammering on her temples. How much did she have to drink last night? She scans the room and spots a packet of painkillers in the corner. Birds are happily twittering outside and the sun, which barely dipped below the horizon last night, is blasting into the room through the large sea-facing window. Alicia swallows two pills with a glass of water and opens the door to the beautiful early morning scene. The sea is calm. A family of mallards is swimming in a long line in the distance, and the reeds covering the shore are gently swaying in the light sea breeze.

You could almost feel content here.

Alicia goes inside and fetches a throw to cover herself; the morning is sunny, but there is a chill in the air. She sits down on the porch, which Uffe, on her mother's instructions, has extended into a deck the same size as the main room in the sauna cottage, where Alicia sleeps on a double sofa bed. She glances at the phone again and finds herself smiling at Patrick's message. She thinks back to last night; the way it took them seconds to attach themselves to each other. How exciting, yet so wrong, it had felt to touch another man's lips. How taut Patrick's body had been when he emerged from the sea. How easily he had lifted up her chin and kissed her. She should not reply to his message. But in spite of herself she taps the phone and writes, 'Good morning. I'm fine. You?'

'Flying. When can I see you again?'

Alicia's heart begins to beat harder. She wants to write, 'We can't do this.' or 'This is wrong, you know that.' Instead she types, 'Monday at the office?'

There's no reply to this message. Alicia waits for a few minutes, then decides to go for a morning swim. That will sort the headache, which is bouncing behind her temples. Inside the cottage, she exchanges the blanket for a towel and walks swiftly toward the jetty a few meters along the shore. She leaves her phone behind on purpose. She wants to play it cool. She'd already made one mistake by replying to him far too soon.

What am I thinking?

This is all wrong. He is married with not just one child but two. And to an old friend of hers. Well, not a friend exactly, but at least an old school mate. And she is still not even separated from Liam. Alicia resolves to reply 'No' to the next message, whatever Patrick asks.

At the jetty, Alicia glances quickly around, but there's no one to be seen. It's just half past eight on Midsummer Day and everyone is still in bed. Alicia pulls the T-shirt she wears as a nightie over her head and lowers herself into the water. The cold hits the skin of her calves and thighs and is a shock, but Alicia walks quickly through the shallow water, almost running into the deeper sea. She doesn't want anyone along the shore to see her naked. She wants to feel the caress of the water on her body. Soon, she's taking long strokes, in a perfect front crawl.

Pleasantly tired from her swim, Alicia slowly approaches the sauna cottage, trying to resist the urge to run to her phone to check if Patrick has replied. All through her time in the cold sea, she has not stopped thinking about him, or about what happened last night. She feels guilty but she cannot stop thinking about him, so she shoos away thoughts of Mia and the two little girls. It was Patrick who initiated the kissing; if anyone should be feeling bad it's him, and he obviously doesn't. *Flying*, he had written. Flying because of her, Alicia?

When she gets closer to the cottage, Alicia is surprised to see her mother sitting on one of the chairs on the decking.

'Nice swim?' her mother shouts.

Alicia nods and waves a greeting. From the distance Alicia can't see her phone. She's sure she left it on the table outside. What if Hilda saw Patrick's reply? What if he'd replied with something sexy? Alicia pulls her towel a little tighter around her naked body and bends to kiss her mother on the chin.

'I'm wet, sorry,' she says as a droplet falls on Hilda's crisp white linen shirt.

'That's OK.' Hilda takes a hankie out of her shirt sleeve and blows her nose. Now Alicia sees she has red-rimmed eyes.

'You've been crying?'

Hilda nods. 'It's Uffe.'

Alicia sighs. 'What is he supposed to have done now?' Her words come out harsher than she anticipated, and Hilda lowers her head and puts the hankie to her eyes. 'You always take his side,' she says.

'Look, I've got to get some clothes on. Have you seen my phone?' Alicia says, putting her hand on Hilda's shoulder, trying to sound nonchalant about the phone and caring about her mother at the same time. Hilda doesn't look at her, but nods at the window sill.

The screen is black. Alicia snatches the mobile and runs inside. There it is, a message from Patrick. It doesn't look as if it has been opened, but Hilda could have seen it displayed on the screen.

'I can barely wait. Meet me outside von Knorring on Monday at 12 o'clock?'

·   ·   ·

Ten minutes or so later, she's sitting opposite Hilda, her hands holding hers.

'Tell me what happened.'

This is not the first time her mother and stepfather have rowed, but as they've got older, the arguments have become worse and more frequent.

But her mother seems to have changed her mind.

'It's nothing,' she says, affecting a bright tone. She looks at Alicia and takes her hands away.

'Where were you yesterday?'

Alicia is caught short with this sudden change of subject.

'What do you mean?'

'You disappeared during the party.'

Hilda's eyes are sharp, and Alicia very nearly crumbles under her gaze, ready to reveal everything to her mother. But surely Hilda can't have seen Patrick and her together? They were away from the party for only an hour, if that. It was very quick and very passionate, she thinks, and she cannot help a smile forming on her lips.

'What are you not telling me?' Alicia's mother demands.

'Nothing, I was just thinking of the drive home.'

They had taken a taxi home. The driver had been an older man with a huge moustache, which Hilda, after copious glasses of champagne, had found hilarious. Uffe knew the man and it was left to him to try to hold up conversation while Hilda made faces in the back seat. Alicia thought that her mother had behaved really quite badly, but at the time she had also found it funny.

'Is Uffe upset about the taxi driver last night?'

'What?' Hilda says. 'No, it's just money, boring, boring money!'

TWENTY-SEVEN

A licia forces herself to sit down and have a coffee after Hilda returns to the main house. She's shocked by what her mother has told her. She had no idea her parents had money troubles. Seeing how little Hilda was making at the shop had been a surprise, but she thought Uffe's farm was very profitable—enough to cover Hilda's losses. She had never discussed money with her stepfather; her mother wouldn't entertain it. All issues relating to the support she had as a student had been done through her mother.

Alicia recalls a time at a Midsummer dinner when she had thanked Uffe for everything he had done for both her and her mother. Hilda had risen from the table and come back several minutes later puffy eyed. Later that evening she had argued with Alicia in front of Stefan, who had been just seven at the time. Rows with Hilda were never understated affairs, and Alicia had learned to avoid them, but on that occasion, fueled by too many schnapps and wine during dinner, she had confronted her while helping with the dishes. She had put her arm around Hilda's shoulders and asked what was the matter. Her mother's reaction was explosive; she began shouting how Alicia had never appreciated the efforts she'd made to support her through university, nor since, and did she have any idea how much food cost? Or how many hours she spent scrubbing the house and the sauna cottage to make it ready for Alicia and her family? Or how much time she devoted to looking after Stefan, and cooking breakfast, dinner and supper for them? Alicia was and had always been an obnoxious, ungrateful girl.

That time, Alicia had moved away from her mother, and put her arms over Stefan's narrow shoulders. She was about to turn away, knowing that nothing she could say could make her stop, when, without even a glance at Stefan, Hilda threw a plate at her daughter and left the room. Luckily, her aim was poor and the dish ended up on the kitchen floor between Alicia, Stefan and the sink.

Alicia's heart had been beating hard, but she forced herself to remain calm. She heard her mother stomp up the stairs and slam her bedroom door. Turning to Stefan, who had wrapped his arms around Alicia's waist, burying his head into her lap as he had done as a small child, said, 'Don't worry, *Mormor* is just a bit upset. She will be fine tomorrow.'

The look in the boy's blue eyes nearly broke Alicia's heart. 'It's OK,' she said and hugged him hard.

Alicia sent Stefan to watch cartoons on the TV in the lounge, where she could keep an eye on him, swept up the remains of the broken plate, and finished clearing the table and doing the dishes. As usual, Uffe had gone to his office well before the argument to listen to the late news on the radio, and Hilda's outburst had eluded him. After half an hour, when she hoped her mother had calmed down, Alicia climbed the stairs to her mother's bedroom, determined not to start another argument, but to restore peace for Stefan's sake if no one else's. She knocked on the door.

'Yes?' had come a faint reply.

Alicia opened the door slightly. Seeing her mother lying on the bed on her own, with her face red and swollen from tears but without fury in her eyes, she stepped inside the room. Her mother had remodeled the house Uffe had been born in, adding an attic and extending the master bedroom with a wooden balcony and an en-suite bathroom on the middle floor. Alicia had been inside this room only once before, when Hilda had proudly presented the new interior. The walls of the room were dark, and there was a large wooden bed in the middle. The overhead lamp was off, but Hilda had her bedside light on, which cast a somber glow into the room and over her dramatic facial features.

When Alicia walked slowly toward the bed and looked down at her mother, Hilda brought an arm out from under the blankets and said, in a miserable, small voice, 'Sit down here, Alicia.'

'I'm sorry,' Alicia had said and took her mother's hand. She felt fourteen, or perhaps fifteen years old. Her mother's scent reminded her of the many nights they would stay up late together, watching a romantic film on TV while Uffe was in his office, doing the paperwork for the farm.

'Don't be,' Hilda said and gave a faint smile.

Alicia bent down and hugged her mother.

'Goodnight,' she said and left the room.

After this incident, Alicia was careful not to raise any subject that implied Uffe was supporting her and Hilda. The summer after the outburst, Stefan begged to be left behind in London to stay with a friend for the summer. He was just eight. In the end, Alicia managed to convince him to come, but she'd been careful not to upset her mother since. Talking about money now would, she was certain, cause a similar reaction.

TWENTY-EIGHT

During the first three days back at work, Liam doesn't see Ewa and he is relieved. He is supposed to be on holiday, so there's no contact between them, as planned. But on the Friday afternoon, as he enters the hospital in St John's Wood where he has a private clinic, she's there. Wearing her blue nurse's uniform, and with bright red lips, she looks up at him and smiles.

'Didn't think we'd see you today, Mr O'Connell,' she says with a smile full of meaning.

Liam keeps his face steady. 'Change of plan. I believe you have some patients for me?'

Ewa grabs a clipboard and follows him into the consulting room. Liam puts his briefcase down, but remains standing behind his large desk. He faces Ewa, who closes the door behind her and, with her back straight, showing off her large breasts, straightens her mouth, and with serious, widened eyes asks, 'What happened?'

Liam looks down at his desk.

'Nothing,' he says and stretches his hand out, to indicate he wants Ewa to hand him the files. 'Who do I have today? Any new patients?' he says, sitting down, not looking at her.

Snapping into her professional role, Ewa briefs Liam on who he will see. The day is already filled with patients, even at this short notice. As Liam listens to Ewa rattle off the names and their medical history, he wonders how he can ever be away, even on a short holiday, without people suffering because of his absence. He makes notes, with his head bent. He's suddenly aware that Ewa has stopped speaking. He lifts his head and sees her standing in front of him, with the clipboard pressed against her ample chest, gazing at him with an expression he can't read.

'Are you going to tell me what's going on?'

Ewa's eyes are startlingly dark against her artificially colored blond hair. She always wears bright red lipstick to match her long nails, something Liam used to find irresistible, but now, he thinks, she looks like a painted doll to him. *How can you fall out of love—or lust—so quickly? In a heartbeat?*

'Nothing. I just decided to cut my holiday short. And for good reason, it seems.' Liam lowers his gaze to his papers again, but Ewa isn't shifting.

'I'm not talking about why you are back,' she says, and walks around the desk to stand next to him. He can feel her arm slide along his shoulders and he feels her breast brush the side of his jaw. Her scent of musk and cigarettes is strong and for a moment Liam thinks of her soft belly, of the curve of her back when he makes her climax.

Then, his thoughts go to Alicia, his wife, and her eyes, full of sorrow, but also full of love for him.

I hope she still loves me.

I have to be strong.

Liam gets up. His movement forces Ewa to drop her arm.

'Not here, not now,' he says and looks at her.

The woman's eyes are even darker, if that's possible. Great big inky pools, ready to brim over. He feels bad for her, but he never promised her anything. They were always clear on that. No divorce, no declarations of love, just fun. Liam reaches over and takes Ewa's hand. 'Look, we can't carry on. I ... and Alicia, we need to ...' he looks to Ewa for help but the woman is just staring at him with those eyes. She blinks and Liam is afraid a tear will fall from her lashes, but luckily she keeps her composure.

The door to his office opens suddenly and another surgeon, his younger colleague, pops his bald head in. He sees Liam and Ewa standing next to each other, holding hands. 'Sorry, didn't mean to interrupt,' he says and disappears.

Liam drops Ewa's hand and curses under his breath.

Ewa lifts her chin up, then turns on her heels and walks through the door.

Liam sits down again and has only a minute or two to recover before there is another soft knock on the door. Sighing, he says, 'Come in.'

TWENTY-NINE

Patrick looks tall and tanned leaning on the bonnet of his car by a small parking lot opposite *von Knorring*, an old steamer that has been turned into a bar and a restaurant in the East Harbor. His car is just behind a new seafood restaurant on the old concrete jetty. Alicia had spent the morning in the newspaper office, sorting out her next story, about the newly released employment figures on the islands. She could not concentrate on the words, or the figures, and had failed to make any sensible connections that would have provided an interesting thread to the story. Her deadline isn't until the end of the week, so she allows herself to be excited about meeting Patrick. She's wearing a red Marimekko cotton dress that comes just above her knees and a pair of Swedish Hasbeens clogs.

When she was getting dressed at the sauna cottage that morning, she noticed that her daily swim in the sea had made her legs and arms firmer and her skin bronzed. The dress fell attractively over her firm bum, and she had decided to wear her best underwear, bought at an expensive boutique before ... she shook her head to stop her thoughts going to Stefan. Instead she found the matching shoes and made sure she had her phone on. There were no other messages from Patrick and Alicia had only replied to the last one with a thumbs-up emoji.

The Island life suits me, she smiled, looking at herself in the full-length mirror Uffe had installed in the cottage at her mother's behest.

In the car on the way into town, Hilda remarked, 'I like that dress on you.'

Alicia tried to ignore the question in Hilda's voice, and just smiled at her mother.

Alone in the sauna cottage, Alicia had made up her mind to meet Patrick today, nothing more. She wanted to find out why he had kissed her, and whether their connection was real, and not just the result of too much alcohol and the Midsummer spirit. Alicia remembered how as a girl, she and her friends would place wildflowers underneath their pillows on Midsummer Eve. According to old Nordic folktales, if you did this, you would dream of your future lover on that magical night.

What nonsense!

But when Patrick talked about his daughter's near-death, it felt as if he'd been describing the torment she feels over Stefan. Of course, he can't know exactly how it is, because his daughter survived, but ... Alicia feels as if Patrick is the only person who can understand her. She knows seeing him is wrong, but what if they became just friends?

. . .

Alicia can see Patrick watching her as she walks along the road running parallel to the harbor. There are a few people milling around, lowering their sails or setting up to leave the jetty. The outside tables in the *Club Marin* café are all taken up by sailors and tourists, enjoying their drinks and talking loudly. There are a few parked cars beside the walkway. The Finns and Russians dock their sailing boats on this side of the Mariehamn peninsula, and the harbor is full. Hoping she doesn't bump into anyone she knows, Alicia quickens her step. She is a few minutes late—on purpose. But now that she is here, she can't wait to see him.

There is a slight wind, which makes the rigging of the sailing boats rattle against the masts. Alicia brushes a few strands of hair away from her face and tries not to run toward the man who is waiting for her. As she gets closer, something about how he moves from one foot to another and fidgets with the leather strap of his bag, indicates that he too is eager to touch her. She can hear the blood pulse in her head, and for a moment feels faint.

She stops two paces from where he is standing. She can smell his scent.

He looks sideways, checking for other people, but no one seems to notice them. The seafood restaurant is full, as is *von Knorring*. Even the old harbor hut, which is now a bicycle hire place, has a line outside. High season in Mariehamn.

'Come here,' Patrick says but he does the opposite, closing the small distance between them and taking Alicia into his arms. He plants his lips on hers and she relaxes into his kiss.

'God, I've missed you,' Patrick says when at last they manage to release each other.

Alicia can't speak. She nods, looking into Patrick's blue eyes, committing them to memory. She now realizes that she could never just be friends with him. This feels right, this is where she wants to be, with this man who understands her pain. She is at peace yet anxious at the same time, certain and doubting, happy and afraid. But not guilty anymore. How can you feel remorse when you have found someone so precious; someone you can find a safe harbor with?

'I have a boat; we can take it out and find a place for a picnic?'

Patrick pulls something out of his shoulder bag and reveals the neck of a bottle of red wine.

'Sounds good,' Alicia says through the hammering of her heart. She is trying to calm her breathing, and to fight the urge to touch Patrick again. But she knows it's dangerous; anyone in the busy harbor could see them. Besides, she knows she mustn't appear needy. But Patrick also seems paralysed; he's just standing in front of her now, smiling.

'It's down there, shall we go? I have an extra wind breaker and a pair of trousers for you onboard if you get cold out on the water.'

'You've thought of everything,' Alicia says. Still she isn't moving.

'I'm delighted to see you,' Patrick says. His expression is soft, but Alicia can see desire in his eyes. She feels color rise to her face.

'Me too.'

Patrick makes a move as if to kiss her again, but Alicia takes a step back and puts a hand up. 'I don't think we should ...'

Patrick's smile disappears for a moment and Alicia wants to take him into her arms. She shouldn't have reminded him of their hopeless situation. Because that's what it surely is, impossible?

And wrong.

But suddenly his lips smile and he guides Alicia toward the wooden boardwalk, which she passed on her way from the newspaper office. 'It's the fourth jetty along from here,' he says.

As they walk toward the rows of boats, Patrick leans on Alicia and whispers in her ear, 'Just wait until we get onboard.'

Desire rises up in Alicia as if an army of ants had begun crawling down her spine. She turns and lifts her eyes to him. 'You have to catch me first,' she says and starts skipping down the wooden walkway. She knows full well he can't follow her at the same pace without it looking as though they are a couple and playing some kind of lovers' game. Alicia doesn't know what excuse he has given Mia for this outing, but she doesn't care. If this afternoon is all they have together, she is going to enjoy every minute of it.

THIRTY

As they pass the first jetty, jutting out of the broad walk, they see a couple wearing matching white sailing jackets having coffee onboard a sailing boat. Alicia nods to them and smiles, and they nod back, unsmiling. 'Finns, why do they always have to be so serious!' She remembers Liam exclaim on more than one occasions. She brushes away any thoughts of her uncaring, cheating husband, and glanccs at Patrick, who is keeping his head down.

Did he know them?

The islands are small and everybody knows everyone else. What's more, the Erikssons are like celebrities in Åland, but she hopes Patrick isn't as well-known as his wife and father-in-law. Alicia, at least, didn't know him by sight before. And judging by the way she was talking about Patrick before the interview, her mother hadn't been aware of his connection to Mia Eriksson either. Otherwise she would have mentioned it, Alicia is sure. He's from Sweden, after all, and has never lived on the islands. There are no schoolfriends who could pop up from anywhere. As Alicia watches him walk along the second jetty, she wonders why Patrick doesn't seem to be concerned about being seen? It was a risk to kiss by the beach during the Midsummer party, and now, meeting up in the middle of town, where anyone driving past could recognize them, is careless, if not foolhardy. Is he doing this to hurt someone? Mia? His father-in-law?

Oh God, what am I getting myself into?

Patrick's boat is moored about halfway down one of the jetties. To Alicia, *'Mirabella'*, as it says on the hull, looks like a medium-sized sailing boat. She imagines it was expensive, but then she knows nothing about boats. Having lived most of her life on the islands, she feels slightly embarrassed about her ignorance, so makes no comment about the vessel.

She watches Patrick lean down and step onboard, hoping her body, which is aching to touch him, doesn't betray her desire. When he turns to help her with his hand, the touch of his fingers sends another jolt through her. His hand is warm, and she holds onto it even when she's standing safely on the wooden decking.

Finally, Patrick lets go. 'You can get changed in there.' With a slight movement of his head, he indicates a hole between two seats. The boat has a large steering wheel in the middle of the stern.

'Sure,' Alicia says. 'Where are we going?'

Patrick smiles, 'Not too far, but far enough.'

Alicia is certain she has blushed under Patrick's gaze. Standing so close to him in a confined space is torture.

She inhales his particular scent of pine needles and leather.

'The galley is below, and there's also a loo.' Patrick hands her a pile of clothes and picks up a life jacket from a cabinet. Alicia steps through an opening, which takes her below to a cabin with a seating area arranged along the bulkhead. It's clean and tidy without any visible signs of family. As she turns around to perch herself on the leather seat, she sees through another opening a double bunk made up with white sheets. Her heart quickens at the sight of the bed. Although there are no visible signs of anyone ever having been onboard, she wonders if this is where Patrick sleeps with Mia. Her heart is racing.

Calm down, you knew what you were doing when you kissed him on Midsummer's Eve. And when you agreed to meet him again. This is what you want.

Alicia realizes the boat is new; there is a faint scent of furniture polish and the leather on the white seats is hardly worn. No children have been playing here, or eating at the teak table, which has a perfect shine. The woodwork in the hull above the seating and the cabinets is gleaming.

How much does a boat like this cost?

Suddenly Alicia hears the roar of the engine and she can feel the deck below her move. There is a rocking motion and she quickly puts on the sailing jacket Patrick has given her. Ignoring the trousers, which look too large anyway, she adds the life jacket, then climbs the few steps out of the cabin and up into the daylight.

'Sit down,' Patrick says, nodding at the seat on the side of the steering wheel. Not looking at her but concentrating on maneuvering the boat out of the harbor, he points toward a coolbox behind Alicia. 'There's wine and beer in there. I'll have a *Karjala*.'

Holding onto the side of the boat, Alicia sees there's champagne and a rather good Sauvignon Blanc, plus several bottles of beer in the bottom. She smiles. She's certain the champagne is meant for her. He said he'd remember how much she loves the stuff. Alicia opens up two bottles of beer, hands one to Patrick and takes a sip out of the other as she sits back down. She finds a pair of sunglasses in her bag and watches as they pass the *von Knorring* restaurant boat moored at the end of the old concrete jetty, and then on toward the open sea.

'This is nice,' Alicia says, raising her voice above the roar of the engine.

Patrick reaches his hand across the space between them and squeezes her knee. 'I've been thinking of nothing else but you for the last three days.'

'I meant the boat,' Alicia replies with a smile.

Patrick presses her leg once more and also grins, 'Cheeky.' He removes his hand and slows the engine down as they approach the Sjoland canal.

'I didn't know we were coming this way,' Alicia says. 'I think I might need to go down below.'

Patrick looks over to her. 'What do you mean?'

'What if my mum or Uffe, or someone from the farm sees me in your boat?'

Patrick's smile fades. He replies to Alicia in a dry tone, 'Just keep your glasses on, I'm sure you'll be fine.'

They pass the canal in silence, following the three other boats that had been in the line for the swing bridge to open. Alicia wonders why he is annoyed at her. She was trying to protect them both, surely? If their affair—*if that's what this is going to be, an affair?*—came to light, Patrick would be the one to lose the most, wouldn't he? Marriage to the richest family in the islands must have its benefits, surely? So why would he not care if Alicia was seen in his boat. Is she here just to make Mia jealous?

Alicia looks at Patrick's profile. His straw blond hair has been mussed up by the swirling sea breeze and his lips are in a straight line. Paler laughter lines are visible along the side of his mouth. The white polo shirt under a navy sailing jacket brings out his bronzed skin. His chin is clean-shaven, but she can see a few pale hairs pushing through. No cuts today, she notices. She wants to run her fingers along that chin, feeling the rough bristles against her palm.

'That's where I am,' Alicia says when they are on the open sea. Patrick has put the sail up and the boat rocks gently from side to side as they are moved along by the strengthening wind. She points at her sauna cottage and the jetty, from where she takes her morning (and some-times) afternoon swims. The jetty, with Uffe's rowing boat tied to it, looks tiny from this distance. The green wooden building is barely visible between the reeds in front and the thicket of pine trees behind the building. Uffe and Hilda's white house, standing high beyond the potato fields, is more visible from this far. In the distance, Alicia can see a red tractor working on one of Uffe's fields. She wonders if her stepfather is driving the vehicle. She's sure no one would recognize them at this distance, but she wonders what he w*ould he say if he knew what she was doing?*

But what does Uffe know? He has no idea what Alicia's life is really like. He's never been a father. He's never lost a son.

'Good, I can drop you off there later,' Patrick says as if it was the most normal thing in the world. Once again Alicia wonders what he's thinking. Wouldn't it look odd to Uffe and Hilda if they saw her being dropped off by Patrick? In a flash sailing boat like this? She looks at him, but he is concentrating on the water and steering. Suddenly he runs along the deck and indicates for Alicia to duck. With great skill he moves the sail to the other side and they change course.

THIRTY-ONE

The little island Patrick chooses for their picnic is uninhabited and looks barely bigger than one of Uffe's potato fields. Patrick drives his boat to a small cove, and after turning off the motor, expertly floats the vessel toward the gently sloping rockface. Before the hull hits anything, he jumps onto land with a rope in his hand. He puts his foot out to soften the blow as the vessel makes contact with the rock, and then moves the boat sideways. There is no mooring as such, but a single ring attached to a pole where Patrick hooks the rope and secures the boat. Alicia is impressed. She's been on the water with friends and Uffe, of course (her mother is afraid of water and doesn't even swim in the sea), but she knows that to maneuver an expensive boat on your own when there are no jetties, is not easy. It requires experience.

'How did you know about this place?' Alicia asks, as she gazes at the cool box that Patrick has brought out.

'It belongs to a friend,' Patrick says.

He places a blanket on the rocks and hands Alicia two glass flutes; he begins opening the bottle of champagne. The pop makes them both laugh, and they down the first two glasses, full of froth, in a few mouthfuls. Patrick refills the flutes and settles himself down beside Alicia. As he stretches out, supporting himself with his elbows, Alicia sees the short sleeves of his polo shirt strain over his muscles.

How many times has he done this? Taken a girl to an island that belongs to a friend?

'Lie down beside me,' Patrick says, reaching out to Alicia with his hand. She can't resist him.

Patrick brushes hair away from her face and looks deeply into her eyes.

'Is this OK?'

Alicia melts, 'It's lovely. You've thought of everything.'

Patrick nods, but he's not listening.

'Can I kiss you?'

Alicia bows her head, already mesmerized by his strong arms, blue eyes and his soft voice. And those velvety strong lips. She wants to melt into them, into him and never leave.

When they come up for air, Patrick says, in a hoarse voice, 'Let's get back onto the boat?'

Alicia smiles into his eyes. Ever since she saw the white sheets of the small cabin below, the image of Patrick's body lying there, naked, has been haunting her. She wants to examine every detail of his strong chest, arms, thighs and legs. She wants to run her fingers along his tummy, to follow the line of hairs on his chest to the place between his legs. The desire in her is making her feel faint.

Patrick practically carries Alicia back over the rocks to the boat. Pulling his jacket and white shirt off, he places one hand on Alicia's neck and uses the other to take off her jacket. He then reaches under her dress and along her thigh to her knickers, which he deftly pulls off. As they tumble onto the bed, Patrick turns Alicia around, saying, hoarsely, 'You'll hit your head.'

He enters her almost as soon as their bodies hit the sheets. Feeling his hardness inside, she gasps and arches her back. He moves in and out, then stops for a moment to remove her dress and pull down her bra. He gazes at her breasts. It feels as if his eyes are caressing her skin. Taking one nipple in his hand, he pushes hard into her. She finds his mouth and they kiss, but then he pulls away to suck on her nipples, one by one. Unable to hold on any longer, she comes. Her pulsating grip makes him groan and he also climaxes.

Afterwards, as they lie between the sheets, Alicia examines the ceiling of the little alcove containing the bed. They are lying with their heads toward the galley, underneath the bow. Alicia smiles as she remembers how Patrick had turned her over and around when they fell onto the bed earlier. She'd felt like a rag doll in his grip.

She cannot remember sex like this. She hadn't thought about anything but Patrick, and how to satisfy and please him. She places her hand on Patrick's flat, hard tummy, and then on his thigh.

'Again?' She can hear a smile in his voice, even though she can't see his face from where she is lying in the crook of his arm. She's fully sated, and although she knows this sense of overwhelming warmth and mellowness will eventually disappear, she is determined to enjoy it to the full. She lifts herself onto her left elbow and glances down at Patrick's erection. 'Do you have time?' she says.

'Now I need something to eat!' Patrick throws his jeans on, leaving his boxers on the floor of the cabin, where he threw them earlier. Alicia hears him clattering on the upper deck and soon he's back with his rucksack. From the bed, she watches him set out red wine, bread, ham and cheese in the galley. Suddenly, she is also ravenous. She slips on her dress and sits down opposite Patrick at the teak table. He pours the wine into two glasses taken from a cabinet over the small sink in the corner.

'We could live on this boat, couldn't we?' Alicia says between bites of her open sandwich.

Patrick looks at her in alarm. His mouth is full of food and he puts a hand over his lips, still gazing at her. His blue eyes seem more piercing somehow.

Alicia is embarrassed. 'I didn't mean ...'

Patrick takes a gulp of wine and looks down at his food.

'Look,' he begins, lifting his eyes again. 'I'm not sure you understand my situation?' He has a serious expression on his face.

Alicia is staring at him.

This is it. He's going to say, 'This was fun', next. And you have no knickers or bra on under your dress because you thought he would want to have sex again after eating.

Patrick bites his lower lip.

Alicia panics. She can't hear this. She gets up and, picking up her pants and bra from the floor, rushes into the tiny toilet in the corner of the cabin.

'Alicia,' Patrick says, but Alicia isn't looking at him. She's trying to get into the small space, but the door won't open.

'Let me,' Patrick says behind her. She can feel his hot breath on her neck, but she ignores it and waits for him to unlock the door. It seems you have to pull it toward you and then turn the handle.

'Thank you,' Alicia mumbles into her hands, which are holding her underwear. Inside, she sits on the toilet seat and puts her head in her hands.

Mustn't cry, mustn't cry.

She takes a deep breath and exhales slowly. What does Connie, her grief counsellor say? 'You can always breathe; it's natural. When you feel overwhelmed, just stop and concentrate on your breathing. Think of nothing else, just air going in and out, in and out.'

After she's calmed down a little, Alicia has a quick pee, washes her hands and face, and puts her underwear on. She struggles in the small space, but finally manages to pull her dress over her bra and knickers and step out of the bathroom.

'You OK?' Patrick says. He's bent over, not able to fully stand in the cabin.

Alicia smiles at him, holding the sides of her mouth up even though all she wants to do is flee the boat and swim to the nearest shore. She knows she needs to keep calm, appear cool, and let Patrick take her home.

'Could you take me all the way back to Mariehamn?' she says, trying to appear calm and collected. She doesn't add, 'As soon as possible,' but Patrick seems to get the message and fusses with ropes and pulleys to make the boat ready, while she clears the galley and puts the food and wine back in the rucksack. When she hears the engine start, she realizes that he intends to take them back with horsepower. Much less romantic than sailing.

This was a big mistake.

THIRTY-TWO

Hilda is in the back room, unpacking two boxes of summer wear that have just arrived from her supplier in Italy. When the door chime sounds, she shouts, 'Just one moment, I'll be with you shortly.'

When she enters the shop, she's surprised to see a man. Men very rarely—if ever—visit her shop unless it's to buy something from her small line of jewellery and handbags as a present for their wife or girlfriend. She can count with the fingers of one hand the number of male customers she's had during the five years she's owned the shop. The man looks foreign, Russian, and immediately she takes a couple steps back. He's wearing a light beige bomber jacket with a pair of cotton trousers and an expensive pair of loafers without socks. There's a single gold stud in one ear and a small, black tattoo on his hand, between his thumb and forefinger. He also wears two rings on his fingers, both heavy, shiny gold. He's a large man, and he fills Hilda's little shop with his bulk.

The man crosses the room and comes to stand close to Hilda. He is so tall, and his chest so broad, that he obscures her view of the street. The man bends down and puts his lips close to Hilda's ear. 'We have a mutual friend,' he says.

Cold shivers run down her spine. She reaches out her hand to support herself on one of the rails of special offer tops in the middle of the shop.

The man is now looking around him. 'Where are your most expensive dresses?'

'Why?' Hilda whispers.

'Our mutual friend needs a small gift for his lady friend.' He continues, his cold eyes on Hilda, 'Because you have been a naughty girl, haven't you?' The man gives a brief grin, but soon this becomes a mock sad face.

'I am going to have a very good month, so I can catch up ...' Hilda stammers.

The man looks around the shop, 'You busy?'

There was no one there. No customers, not even tire-kicking Swedes, who pull the clothes off the rails to hold them up against themselves, glancing briefly in one of the long mirrors on either side of the shop. They never buy, or put the garments back in the right place again.

'It's a slow day today. The week after Midsummer always is, because people are out in the archipelago with their families. But they'll soon get bored of each other and come into town. People argue when they are on holiday and then they need to buy something to make themselves feel better,' Hilda realizes she is talking uncontrollably, but she can't stop herself. 'Tomorrow will be very busy and ...'

He places one fat finger across his lips, interrupting

her. 'Shh.' The man bends down so that his face is very close to Hilda's again. He smells of alcohol and cigarettes and very strong aftershave. 'No talking, just doing. We need money next week.'

Hilda nods. 'You will have it, I promise.'

'I said no talking,' the man whispers, and he straightens up. He glances around the shop and his eyes fix on three dresses displayed close to the till.

'But now, a small gift to keep our friend calm, yes?' The man says.

Hilda nods and moves toward the items the man is looking at.

'You like this dress?' she asks, picking out a silver lamé thing she had foolishly bought in three sizes at a Stockholm fashion fair last fall. With a price tag of 495 Euros, it hadn't had any takers in Mariehamn. The one person, a very pretty blond girl from the islands, who liked the dress, lifted it off the rail and exclaimed, 'That's more than my monthly rent!' Hilda's margin on the dress is now just 25 Euros. She should really charge more like 600 Euros for it.

'What size?' she turns around and asks the man.

He looks blankly at her.

'Is she 36, 38 or 40?'

When the Russian doesn't reply, Hilda adds, 'What size is the lady?'

'I take all,' the man says and Hilda gasps.

The Russian grins and says, 'You put them in silk paper, make look nice.'

For a moment, Hilda hesitates. It occurs to her that the cost of the three garments comes to over a thousand

Euros and that she should be able to deduct that from what she owes the Russians, but she keeps quiet. Her heart is beating so hard she can hardly hear herself think. With shaking hands, she packs the dresses one by one into her special pink tissue paper and then into one large plastic bag. She should, according to the law, charge the man for the bag, but again she says nothing, just hands the package to him.

'Tell him I will have the money next week.' Hilda says with a dry mouth.

'He know,' the man says, and takes the bag. Again he gives one of his brief grins, and says, 'Nice doing business with you.' Then he walks into the street.

Hilda leans against the counter. She wants to cry, but she lifts herself up and brushes her brand-new Birger et Mikkelsen skirt with her hands to calm herself. She will be fine. She always manages and she will manage this situation too.

Uffe walks along the edge of one of his fields. The earlies are nearly in flower and look healthy. His eyes follow the line of the dark green plants and then stop at his house. The white structure looks magnificent with its new paint and dark copper roof, which gleams in the late afternoon sunshine. He's proud of this house, the home where he was born and which his father built with his friends and relatives from the village. Would his parents, long gone now, approve of all the modernizing Hilda had instigated during the past two decades? Her standards are high, with every detail—a door handle, the color on the walls, kitchen appliances and bathroom fittings—having to be just so. Nothing but perfection will do for Hilda.

Uffe has lost count of the times they've argued about the works. When Hilda greets him at the door with a look like a storm warning, her arms crossed over her chest, he finds it best to say nothing. She will soon tell him how he is at fault. Usually he hasn't seen some minor mistake that the builders made while Hilda was at the shop. He's got tired of pointing out that he could not afford the time away from the farm, especially from supervising his laborers, most of whom spoke no Swedish. But to Hilda, his time in the fields didn't count as any kind of useful excuse, even though the land provided all the money Hilda spent on the house. And everything else.

But this is the limit.

Uffe nods to one of the Romanians standing smoking a cigarette outside the red cottage and then turns away from the house, deciding to take another tour around the fields. He shakes his head. How can Hilda be so stupid as to get into debt? Credit cards were one thing, she'd been there before. Uffe can't remember how many times he has bailed out Hilda from that particular trap. But this; this is different. No amount of money will ever get Hilda out of this bind. To accept a loan from a man like that?

He curses under his breath. He knows this is his fault. He should never have got involved with the man, but he thought Hilda had more sense than to accept money from him. Besides, when and where did that happen? Uffe was too upset to find out the details. He had stormed out of the house when Hilda, tears in her eyes, finished the tale of her latest financial catastrophe.

At first, he had stood in front of her, mouth open, not able to utter a word. She must have seen in his eyes how bad it was. Of course, she had only told him because she had no choice. He is—as always—the last resort. She said that she was three payments late and that there had been threats. She assured him that the article in the *Journalen* by Patrick Hilden would bring in customers from Stockholm, and she could then start the payments again, but frankly, Uffe doubts it. Even though he knows nothing about fashion, something Hilda has repeatedly told him, he knows enough to understand that no woman would come from the capital of Sweden to buy clothes in a tiny shop on the Åland islands. As usual, Hilda is being naive—some might say stupid.

'You are incredible,' was all Uffe said. He couldn't trust himself not to shout at her, which he would never do. It isn't right. His father had never in his life raised his voice to his mother and had taught Uffe to respect women in the same way.

But Hilda is testing his patience to the limit. When he left Hilda standing alone, he heard her shout after him, but he'd ignored her. He knew she wouldn't run after him and make a show of herself in front of the farm workers, but all the same, he turned on his heels as quickly as he could, put his rubber boots on and walked rapidly along the edge of the closest field to the house. He had now walked two rounds, but he's still not calm. He needs more time to think, so he decides to do another round. He knows the two young lads will be watching him from the red cottage, wondering what's up, but he doesn't care.

· · ·

Hilda is fuming. The one time she reaches out to her husband, who promised to love and honor her, Uffe flees and doesn't say anything. Hilda needs a glass of white wine. It's only 5pm, but she has to have something to calm her nerves. It's an emergency after all. On second thoughts, when she opens the fridge, she decides on something stronger and goes in search of Uffe's drinks cabinet in the 'best' room to pour herself a whisky. The strong liquid warms her throat, and she takes half a glass more. She needs to drive later, so she better not have a third, she thinks, after gulping down the second.

With the alcohol inside her, she can breathe more easily. The nervous anger is slowly dissipating, and she considers her options. If Uffe will not help her, she will need to negotiate with the Russians. But how to get to the main man? The thugs he sends to collect the money don't even speak Swedish properly, so how can she make them understand that she needs more time?

THIRTY-THREE

Alicia is getting ready to leave the newspaper office when Patrick appears next to her cubicle. He has his hand on the bright blue divider, where Alicia has pinned useful information such as the Intranet codes and the staff telephone lists that the personnel woman gave her. There is also a picture of Stefan taken in their garden in Crouch End in London, with him smiling into the camera.

'You off?' Patrick asks.

Alicia is aware of Frida, the only other person left in the office listening in on their conversation. Most people, including the editor, have gone hours ago. Alicia wanted to stay to map out a piece on Russian influence on the islands, but is hitting a brick wall each time she comes close to any useful information. Of course, she knows that there are strict rules on ownership of land and assets by non-Åland residents on the islands, but she also knows that there are ways both wealthy Swedes and Finns get around those rules. Why couldn't Russians do the same?

'Yeah, my mum's giving me a lift home,' Alicia says, not looking at him.

'I emailed her the PDF of the article just now.'

'Thanks, I'll tell her.'

There is a silence. Alicia, having placed her laptop into her backpack, picks up her cotton jumper, tucks her chair under the desk and tries to smile at Patrick. What does he want? Surely the fact that she hasn't answered any of the texts since that disastrous boat trip would be enough to make him understand she doesn't want anything more to do with him.

She feels like she's been played.

Before the boat trip, she thought they meant something to each other, but the way he reacted to her remark about living on his boat—as if she wanted to stay there— showed that all he wanted was a quick summer fling. She's been feeling stupid ever since, especially because Patrick said nothing about it during the journey home. She pretended to be OK, but she didn't let him kiss her when he dropped her off in Mariehamn. All of his previous bravado had been just that, showing off. It was all a game, she decided. A rich man's game to get her into bed. She's done playing games with him.

'Any plans for the weekend?' Patrick says, his blue eyes squarely on Alicia. Suddenly she has an image of his naked body lying on the white sheets of the bunk in the cabin. She can recall the fair hairs on his chest and the thin line reaching down between his legs. Flashes of their love-making—or sex—invade her brain.

She must stay strong.

'Spending it with my family,' Alicia says pointedly,

trying to steady her breathing and hoping the words come out without any show of emotion in them. She is aware that Frida is now listening to their conversation.

Patrick turns around and gives a nod to Frida, who smiles briefly then looks at her screen. Gazing back at Alicia with those flirty eyes of his, Patrick says, 'Mia is taking the girls shopping in Stockholm. I thought I might talk to you about the article we're working on?'

Alicia is fighting a smile forming on her lips, but failing.

'But if you can't meet up, I'll walk you out and tell you my theory?' Patrick says. He moves to touch her elbow, but she is quicker and pulls her arm away.

She nods and says, 'OK'. She can hardly say no to a suggestion like that in front of Frida, and he knows it.

'See you Monday,' Alicia says to the intern as she begins to walk toward the door. She can feel Patrick's body behind her, too close. As soon as they're in the stair-well and the door has closed, he takes hold of Alicia's arm and turns her around to face him. 'You're driving me crazy. I need to see you!'

'Not here,' Alicia hisses and glances up the staircase. The space is open to all the offices in the building and Birgit—or anyone—could at any moment step out and see them. When her eyes return to Patrick, she can see his face is full of emotion. His grip on her arm is strong.

'You're hurting me,' Alicia says in a low voice.

Patrick lets go, dropping his arm to the side of his body. Alicia sees now that he is unshaven, and that his clothes are crumpled.

'What happened to you?'

'I need to see you.'

Alicia sighs. 'OK, I'll tell my mother I need to work late.'

A smile forms on Patrick's lips.

'Just for a talk,' Alicia says pointedly and Patrick nods.

'And we go our separate ways. Where shall we meet?'

'I know a place,' Patrick says and begins to tap on his phone.

Alicia goes back inside the newspaper office and tells Frida she's forgotten something. She doesn't want the girl to think that she left with Patrick. She taps a message on her phone, and makes a show of looking for something in her desk drawers. When her mother replies to say she is in the car waiting for her, Alicia assures Hilda that she will make her own way to Sjoland later. She picks up her bags again and goes out via the ladies. She gives herself a wash, just in case, using the shower placed for just that purpose next to the loo. She isn't sure what Patrick is going to say to her, but she thinks it will be good to get things out in the open. Perhaps he isn't playing games after all?

Who am I kidding?

She will be strong and not jump into bed with him. She thinks about the message she's received from Liam where he says he's sorry and that he's finished with Ewa. She hasn't replied. She is so confused. Why has Liam suddenly changed his mind? He has been pleading with her to talk to him, but she is still too angry to do that. Besides, she now feels guilty for sleeping with Patrick, although when she did, she thought her marriage was over.

What a mess.

Trying to think about something else, she remembers her promise to look over her mother's new plans for the garden in Sjoland. Secretly, she is glad she doesn't have to spend another Friday night listening to Uffe and her mother squabbling. Hilda is never satisfied with what Uffe does in the house, or the yard. He hasn't watered the flower beds, or the hanging baskets enough, or he's given them too much water. Or the gravel paths that crisscross the yard between the barns and the main house are, in Hilda's view, neglected and full of weeds. Each time Uffe sits down on the small bench he's placed under the oak tree, Hilda will find him something that needs fixing immediately. Uffe doesn't often complain, but occasionally he will mutter something under his breath, and a small quarrel will ignite between the couple.

Their harmless altercations, which she and Liam once thought endearing, are now beginning to get on Alicia's nerves. Besides, she suspects there's more to it than she's previously imagined. She is afraid they have serious problems with money, and that what her mother told her on Midsummer Day is not an exaggeration. Her stepfather looked more and more morose when he talked to Alicia about the future of the farm, and having seen the accounts in Hilda's shop, Alicia can only conclude that Uffe is pouring cash into the venture to keep her mother happy. She wonders if she should be brave and talk to her mother about it. It isn't right that Hilda is putting the future of the farm in danger.

Looking at herself in the bathroom mirror, Alicia sighs. Who is she to lecture anyone about morality? She's been with a man, a father of two little daughters. And she is breaking her own marriage vows. Not that they matter anymore. Liam broke them first, and now he is full of remorse.

He's too late.

Alicia looks at her phone and sees that Liam sent another message last night. He asks when they can talk (again) but she doesn't intend to reply. Why should she talk to him? Alicia glances at her watch. It's just past 5pm on a Friday night, or 7pm in the UK. *Whatever he says, she bets her husband is in that Polish nurse's arms right now.*

She takes her red lipstick out of her purse and applies a liberal amount to her lips. She tidies her eye make-up and wishes she'd taken mascara and eyeshadow with her to work. Still, she doesn't look bad. The daily swimming and sunbathing have given her skin a healthy glow. Her Swedish Hasbeens clogs make her legs look shapely and she is pleased with the general effect she sees in the mirror. She will not go to bed with Patrick, or not again, but at least she looks presentable. Perhaps she should lighten up a little? It is summer, the sky is clear and the sun is still high in the sky, it's warm, she's back home in Åland, doing a job she loves, and it's Friday night.

THIRTY-FOUR

As Alicia walks onto the street, she gets a message from Patrick.

'We can talk in peace here.'

The address attached is on the western side of town, a bit too far for Alicia to walk so she decides to take a cab. She picks one up from a rank on Norra Esplanaden and steps inside a large Mercedes car. Luckily the driver doesn't say a word during the ten-minute ride.

She cannot help but smile when she sees the new blocks of apartments right by the sea. This area used to be a fishing harbor and she remembers coming here with Stefan to look at the boats and buy fish for supper. Now all that remains are a few red and white huts and a stone jetty to one side of the new development, with a new wooden wharf further along the shore full of expensive-looking yachts. It's still sunny, but the wind has got up and she can see the boats bobbing up and down and the surf rising on the sea.

The block of apartments has around ten floors,

making it unusually high-rise for Åland. The façade is covered in balconies, with some facing the sea, the sun glinting off the smoked glass; many have smart wicker furniture. The buildings must be brand-new, she thinks, for there are some building materials under a tarpaulin to the side. She finds the correct block—the nearest one to the sea—and when she enters the number Patrick gave her on the intercom, she hears his voice. He tells her to step inside the elevator but not to touch any of the buttons, and then buzzes her in. When the doors close, the lift begins to move, as if of its own accord. Alicia follows the light that indicates the different floors and when she's at number ten, the doors open straight into a vast penthouse apartment with floor-length windows affording a full vista of the open sea. Involuntarily, Alicia gasps at the view. She is speechless when she steps onto the light parquet flooring.

'Please come in,' Patrick says and she takes a step further inside, dropping her bags on one of two low-slung sofas that face each other. The apartment is furnished tastefully and very understatedly in pale gray and white. A white rug echoes the white of the kitchen units and there's a long table with leather-backed chairs arranged at one end of the huge room. A vast painting of a seascape in grays and blues covers one wall while a balcony, enclosed by sliding glass doors, wraps around one corner of the flat. She recognizes the style from the Eriksson's summer place. Is this Mia and Patrick's apartment? Surely he wouldn't invite her to their home—or one of their homes?

'Come and have a look at the view,' Patrick says,

stretching his hand toward Alicia, beckoning her. He opens the sliding balcony doors and indicates for Alicia to step in.

There are no other buildings or blocks of apartments between them and the sea. The ones in view to the right are well below them. Alicia thinks this building must be on a higher elevation, somehow. Or it has an extra floor, not visible from below. She looks at the old red fishing cottages, which seem minute from this far up, like pieces of Lego. Further on, at sea, a yacht is making its way toward the shipping lane, with its sails taut against the wind, the hull creating a V-shaped wash behind it. Alicia is amazed how fast it's moving. To the right there's the new jetty, where the few boats gently rock in the water, and further on the ferry port. One white ship, and a smaller red ferry are moored at the harbor, and uncon- sciously she checks her watch. It's half past five. One of the two large ferries from Finland and Sweden that dock in Mariehamn twice a day is due in soon. They sail right past this balcony, Alicia thinks. She looks around and sees a basket full of girly toys in the corner of the space. A chill runs through her body and she shivers. She turns around to look at Patrick.

'Is this where you live?' she asks.

Without smiling, Patrick nods.

Alicia, who has been leaning on the balcony railing, moves away from the edge. She doesn't want to touch anything here.

This is Patrick and Mia's family home.

'It was lovely for you to show me where you live, but I'm afraid I have to go now,' Alicia says, stepping out of the balcony. She goes to pick up her bag, but Patrick is beside her, grabbing her arm.

'Don't go, please.'

Alicia is seething. 'You are something, aren't you? Do you have any morals at all? Or is this what the rich boys in Åland do? Take other women to their marital home? How dare you!'

But when Patrick pulls her into his arms and kisses her, Alicia can't resist him. They tumble onto the sofa and continue kissing. It isn't until Patrick puts his hand inside her skirt that she suddenly comes to her senses.

'No,' Alicia manages to say, and as abruptly as they started to make love, they both stop. Panting, Patrick gets up and goes to the open-plan kitchen. Alicia grabs the side of the sofa, gets herself up and, smoothing down her skirt, sits down. She watches Patrick, whose shoulders are moving up and down. His head is bent, as he leans onto the immaculately tidy kitchen counter.

'I'm making coffee, do you want some?' he asks after a short while. He sounds out of breath.

When he doesn't get an answer, he turns around and goes over to where Alicia is sitting. She is fighting tears; how did she get herself into this mess? Faced with Patrick's family situation, she can't continue with the affair. She just can't take a father away from his two little girls.

Patrick is now kneeling down in front of Alicia. He gives her a tissue and puts his hands on Alicia's knees, then seeing her expression removes them. 'Please don't cry,' he says, letting his hands rest between his legs.

'I can't do this,' Alicia sobs. 'You are married. With children.'

Patrick looks at her, his blue eyes sad. He gets up with a sigh and comes and sits next to her on the sofa. 'I don't know what to say. You know we're not happy. Mia ...'

'Stop!' Alicia shouts. 'I don't want to hear any excuses!'

'OK, let's not talk about her. But I have to tell you I've never felt like this before. You ... you make me crazy. I can't stop thinking about you. I need you.'

Alicia realizes these are the words she wanted to hear after they made love on his boat. Why didn't he tell her this before? Why had he let her believe this was just a summer fling? All the way back on the boat, Patrick must have noticed how quiet and upset she was. If he really cared, surely he would have said something then?

She turns her head and lifts her eyes up to Patrick. With the sun suddenly pouring in through the windows, she sees there are dark circles around his eyes. He's wearing his customary white shirt and jeans, and looks tanned, but dishevelled. His blue eyes are as piercing as ever, and his lips, drawn in a straight line, give way to lines around his mouth. Alicia has an overwhelming desire to kiss those lips. She places a hand on Patrick's cheek. 'I need you too.'

Seconds after she's uttered the words, Patrick's mouth is on hers. He lifts her up to sit astride him and presses his body against hers, so she can feel his erection through the jeans. She pulls herself away, but Patrick is holding tightly to her. And it feels good, so very good.

Why should she be responsible for his family?

But an image of Liam and Stefan, when their son was about the same age as Patrick's girls, eleven, comes to her mind. They are messing about in the water by the sauna cottage. Alicia remembers that Uffe had cleared the reeds from the jetty, so that Alicia could see them from the veranda. She had some kind of deadline to meet for the FT, and had her laptop on the small table in front of her. But she wanted to join her boys in the water and couldn't concentrate.

Alicia puts her hands on Patrick's shoulders and firmly pushes herself away from him.

'I can't do this—not here,' she says, panting.

She clambers off Patrick and stands up, smoothing down her skirt again, and buttons up her blouse. Before he has time to react, she grabs her shoes and bag and goes to the elevator. Luckily, it's still on the top floor, and Alicia, now panicking, wanting to get away from this place, steps inside.

THIRTY-FIVE

Alicia walks for what seems like ages to reach a taxi rank. Her feet are aching, and her bag suddenly seems much heavier than it was this morning. Tears are running down her face, but she doesn't know what she's crying about: Stefan, or her futile desire to have another child, or the now certain break-up of her own marriage, or the disastrous affair she's embarked on with Patrick.

She feels so stupid. How did she think that sleeping with someone else, someone who is also married, would make her grief for Stefan, her desire for a baby, or Liam's affair, any better? But she has decided now. No more Patrick, no more sneaking around the islands to meet up. No more telling lies to people like Hilda or Uffe, no more feeling guilty about breaking up a family. She feels awful about what they have already done, but she has to trust Patrick not to breathe a word to Mia and to start repairing his marriage.

Just as she sees a taxi waiting at the rank on *Norra Esplanaden*, her phone pings. Automatically, she reaches for the mobile in her handbag, but when she sees who it's from she hesitates. But there's a sentence on her screen that she cannot ignore.

Mia and I are separating. She's leaving me.

Half an hour later, Patrick and Alicia are sitting at the kitchen table, facing each other.

'Thank you for coming back,' Patrick says. His hands are resting on the table, his fingers laced together. Alicia remembers how those long, thin fingers were all over her body moments earlier. He lifts his eyes to Alicia's.

'This is what I wanted to talk to you about.'

Alicia nods. After she read the text, she replied to say how sorry she was. Patrick telephoned her and offered to pick her up from wherever she was. Alicia agreed. She decided she would not go to bed with him, if this was a trick, but she didn't believe it was. He sounded sad, and sincere, on the phone, and thinking back, the news explained a lot of his earlier behavior. The bitterness toward his in-laws at the Midsummer party; his apparent lack of concern about being seen with Alicia; the hesitation on the boat when she made a stupid joke about living on the boat.

Alicia hadn't been in Patrick's car before, but it was no surprise to her that he drove a brand-new black Mercedes soft top with cream leather upholstery.

How is he going to survive without Mia's—or, rather, her father's—money?

'Nobody knows about this. So, I'd appreciate it if you didn't ...'

'Of course not!' Alicia exclaims. She touches Patrick's hands, squeezing his knuckles.

'We want to spend the summer with the girls as normal. Mia is going to move here, her father has a job for her in Mariehamn.'

Alicia watches Patrick's face as he speaks. His eyes are as blue as ever, but there are lines around them and a strain around the corners of his mouth. She now realizes the hurt, pained expression that she sees on him has attracted her. It mirrors her own, she's certain of it.

Patrick's eyes fall down to his hands. He opens his palms and squeezes Alicia's fingers between his own.

'I am considering what to do. I'd like to be close to the girls, so ... perhaps go freelance.'

Again, Alicia wonders what he will do for money. Surely a freelance journalist was just as poorly paid here as in the UK? She guesses he didn't have to worry about maintenance payments.

'We're still working out the details but I'll have this flat, car and the boat. Mia never goes onboard anyway and she spends most of her time in the summer place. Plus they've got other blocks of apartments to choose from closer to the center, where I'm certain Her Ladyship would rather be.'

The bitterness of Patrick's last sentence takes Alicia by surprise. As he utters the word 'Ladyship' his face contorts and shows the anger he obviously feels.

Was she unfaithful? Does he still love her?

'I don't want to pry, but what happened?' Alicia asks

carefully. She squeezes Patrick's hand in a show of encouragement and support.

Patrick sighs and removes his hand from Alicia's. He straightens his back and without looking at her says, 'I'm a disappointment, apparently.'

She hears that hostility in the tone of his voice again.

Alicia waits. She tries to control her own feelings. She realizes that he slept with her to punish Mia; it was an act of revenge. She wants to ask whether Mia has slept with someone, and whether he still loves her. But to ask these kinds of questions would show how much she, Alicia, was investing—had already invested—in the relationship. It's clear to her now, clearer than it has been for all of the short time they've known each other, that for him this is about something else. It's about his own marriage, and it is certainly not about Alicia. She could be anybody. Yet Alicia tries to suppress the jealousy and anger that begins to bubble inside her. Besides, isn't she also taking her own frustrations with Liam out in this relationship?

Her reticence is soon rewarded.

Patrick leans back in his chair and rubs his chin with his hand. He is gazing over Alicia's shoulder through the tall windows overlooking the sea.

'She met someone last year. A successful businessman like her father. Not a useless liberal journalist like her husband. They all knew about it long before I did.'

'When did you find out?' Alicia asks, trying to control her voice.

Patrick looks at her again, but doesn't say anything.

And then Alicia knows.

Anger and jealousy again rise inside Alicia and she forces herself to breathe normally. She feels used. She gets up, but Patrick takes hold of her wrist.

'Please, I can explain. You don't understand.'

'No need, it's all clear. You got bad news and decided to take revenge with the first available woman. I'm glad I could be helpful.' She can hear the emotion in her voice and is ashamed. Her voice is trembling, she's sure of it. She has to get out. She moves toward the elevator again, the second time that evening.

'You've got it all wrong!' Patrick says. When Alicia doesn't reply, he continues, 'At least let me drive you home.'

Alicia lets out a dry laugh, 'Please don't feel obliged!'

But when she sees the expression on Patrick's face she once again changes her mind. He looks so drawn, so miserable, that she feels sorry for him. They have both used each other. Why did she allow herself to be kissed on Midsummer Eve? And why did she go willingly with him on a picnic to the archipelago? Wasn't it as much an act of revenge for her as she now knows it was for Patrick?

They ride down the lift in silence, and do not speak during the fifteen-minute drive to Sjoland. As they cross the bridge, Alicia is about to ask Patrick to drop her off a few meters from the sauna cottage so that they won't be seen from Hilda and Uffe's house, but then decides against it. Patrick doesn't care who knows about them, and neither does she. Not now. Besides, this affair isn't going to carry on, so it really doesn't matter. Alicia can always say that Patrick was among the people she'd spent the evening with if her mother or Uffe sees her get out of Patrick's fancy car. She will think of something.

She turns her head to look at Patrick's profile as he drives on the empty road. It's not dark even though it's gone 9pm, and she can see glimpses of the sea on the left-hand side of the road as it dips close to the shore. They are nearly at her sauna cottage.

'Turn left down the track there,' she points to a small turning.

As she gets out of the car, she bends down at the open door and asks, 'Does Mia know about me?'

Patrick looks at her and says, 'You really don't think much of me, do you?'

'Thank you for the ride,' Alicia says and closes the door.

As she walks along the lane toward the sea and the sauna cottage, she can hear the engine of Patrick's car as he reverses up the small bank to the road. She is relieved to see that there are no lights on in the cottage. At least her mother isn't sitting there waiting for her. She gets the key from its hiding place under the flower pot on the decking and unlocks the door. It isn't until she's inside the cottage, lying on her sofa bed, that she relaxes and stretches out. What an evening!

Uffe is still up, sitting in his office, gazing at the sea, when he sees an unfamiliar car turn into the sauna cottage. His guts churn when he sees it's a black Mercedes. Surely Dudnikov wouldn't put the frighteners on his step-daughter too? Moments later, he can see the light in the cottage come on, and the car pull out and head back on the road to Mariehamn. He spots a blond man in the driving seat of the open-top car and feels such relief when he sees it is the Eriksson's son-in-law that he almost laughs out loud.

THIRTY-SIX

The water is cold, but Alicia likes it just so. She dives in, letting the chilling water run over her face, arms and legs. The freezing sea clears her mind and forces her to move her body faster, emptying her head of any other thoughts but the sensation of her heart pumping quicker, making the blood course through her veins. Soon, she feels as one with the water and begins to enjoy her own speed, her own agility. Alicia takes long strokes, and slowly the chill diminishes and disappears. Now the sea around her seems warmly embracing. This is the part she most enjoys; when her body acclimatizes and she feels strong and confident in her own ability in the water. She wonders if she could swim all the way to Finland. Stopping at the many islands on the way, she is sure she could do it. She tries to remember if anyone has attempted such a race, like swimming across the English Channel. Perhaps she could be the first, she thinks, when she finds herself near the shipping lane about a kilometer from the shore. Wonder what Patrick would think if I swam to Finland, she smiles.

Don't think about him!

Alicia turns back and sees the reeds along the shoreline swaying in the wind, either side of the jetty, where Uffe has cut them right down. She's swam farther than she's ever done before but decides to carry on. She has tons of energy left in her body; she could swim until she reaches a small inlet on the other side of the open water. She could rest there until she has to turn back.

These early morning swims are her favorite hour of the day on the islands. When Stefan was small, this was the only time during the family holidays when she could please herself, stop being mum and just be Alicia.

When Stefan was older, she would slip out of the house, safe in the knowledge that either Liam (if he was there—he often came over for just a day or two during the summer, while Alicia and Stefan spent weeks on the islands) or her mother would occupy Stefan while she was in the sea. She'd walk slowly down to the shore, listening to the birds and slip into the cold water.

As she remembers, the calmness of the morning is suddenly broken by a loud motorboat, and a triangle of wash around and behind it cuts the scenery in half. She sees there's a Russian flag at the stern. Alicia stops and treads water. She realizes she may be in danger if she goes out any further. The boat looks far too close to her and has no intention of changing course.

Suddenly alarmed, Alicia turns around and dives as deep as she can. Holding her breath, she concentrates on moving her legs and arms in a breaststroke just as her swimming teacher on the islands taught her all those years ago. 'It's all about the rhythm,' she had said. 'Keep the strokes strong and use your hands as paddles. Kick hard to propel your body, keeping the arms long. Don't rush and you'll go faster.'

She hears the deep hum of the engines roar above her.

When Alicia surfaces, she turns around and watches the boat make its speedy way toward the Sjoland canal. She can see a lone man at the helm. Didn't he spot her in the water?

She takes a deep breath before making her way back toward the shore.

Back on the wooden jetty, panting, she sits down and wraps a towel around her shoulders. Listening to the sounds of the sea birds all around her, Alicia closes her eyes and lets the sun warm her face. There is now a thin layer of cloud shading the sun, but the rays are still warming on her skin. She realizes she hasn't thought about Stefan for the past few minutes, while concentrating on getting back to the shore. She has also not let Patrick and his problems into her mind.

It's over, she's convinced of it. She is ashamed that she let herself be seduced by someone like that, but she was vulnerable, so she must forgive herself.

Whatever he says, Liam is probably at this very moment back in the arms of his nurse, so why shouldn't she try out another man? But Alicia cannot help but feel dirty and used; more than anything she feels stupid for thinking a man like Patrick would find her attractive and desirable. Images of their love-making—or sex—onboard the boat flash in front of her eyes. It did *seem* as if he was into her, but Alicia's emotions may have been blinded by her own desire. Alicia lifts her legs up and wraps her hands and the towel around her knees. She decides to ignore Patrick from now on. She has enough worries with Hilda and Uffe. How is she going to be able to broach the subject of money with her mother without a huge argument? Perhaps she should talk to Uffe instead?

THIRTY-SEVEN

'I hear you're sleeping with my husband,' Mia stands with her arms crossed outside the newspaper office.

It's a Monday morning, past ten o'clock, and Alicia is running late because her mother has overslept. Reeking of alcohol, Hilda had allowed Alicia to drive. It wasn't Alicia's day in the newspaper office, but her mother should already have been in the shop, especially now that she'd given notice to her assistant to 'save money'. Getting her mother together and on the road was a novelty. As Alicia parked the car and said goodbye to her outside the little boutique, she resolved to talk to Uffe as soon as possible.

That morning when she saw Hilda's red-rimmed eyes she knew she needed to ask her what was going on, but she was preoccupied by a message she'd received from Harri earlier that morning. The body of a boy had been found in the waters around Sjoland, near the sauna cottage, and he needed Alicia to cover the story. She wondered if she should inform him that she had never reported on crime, but Harri was the editor, and she wanted to make a good impression, so she typed *'I'm on my way,'* got dressed quickly and ran to the main house to see if Hilda had yet left for work.

Now Alicia, her head already full of concerns for her mother and the story she is required to cover but doesn't know how to write, regards Mia. She's wearing a huge pair of dark sunglasses, red lipstick and a sleek trouser suit. Not exactly summer wear for the islands; more like an office outfit one would wear in Stockholm or London.

'I'm sorry, I'm running late,' Alicia says and she tries to walk around Mia to reach the door to the newspaper office.

Mia steps in front of her again and leans in to speak, close to Alicia's ear, 'I always knew you were a little tart. At school you'd go around with that blond head of yours held high, like a primadonna, as if you were somebody. Which you weren't. And then after you moved to London, you blanked me every time I saw you in town.'

Alicia sees how angry the woman is but she has no time for her now. Besides, she couldn't give a monkeys about Patrick and his little domestic argument. She is well out of it.

'Look, I don't know what's going on, but I need to get to work.'

'Are you, or are you not, sleeping with my husband?' Mia asks. 'I demand an answer.'

Who's being a primadonna now?

Alicia tries to keep calm. Mia has her arms crossed and appears taller than Alicia, and she wonders briefly how come she doesn't remember her being so lanky at school, but then she notices the sky-high heels.

'No,' Alicia replies, trying to look Mia in the eyes through her dark lenses. She knows this is a half-lie, but at the same time, she has no intention of sleeping with Patrick again.

Her reply seems to take Mia aback and she doesn't stop Alicia as she walks around her and into the *Ålandsbladet* building.

'You're a liar,' she hears Mia shriek behind her back, but Alicia quickly runs up the stairs. She hopes the woman will not follow her. A scene with the jealous daughter of the owner in front of the editor is all she needs.

When Alicia enters the open-plan office, the first person she sees through the glass of the editor's office in the far corner is Patrick. He's standing opposite Harri's desk, with the leather satchel slung across his jacket. He's nodding to something Harri is saying. Neither he nor the editor have spotted Alicia yet.

What the hell is he doing here—again?

Alicia steadies herself and walks confidently past Frida and another junior reporter, who are both watching her. She nods to them and opens the door into Harri's glass cubicle.

Patrick doesn't look surprised to see her. He glances at her without smiling and she nearly asks him, '*Do you know your wife is downstairs accosting reporters on their way to work?*' but her thoughts are interrupted when Harri says, 'Oh, good, you're here. Patrick has offered to take you to the crime scene on his boat.'

Alicia meet's Patrick's eyes. His hair is ruffled, which makes him look even more handsome than usual. She notices he has shaved this morning.

When Alicia doesn't say anything, Harri asks, 'Did you read the police report I sent you?' 'Yes,' Alicia replies. She had quickly scanned it while waiting for Hilda to get ready.

'Off you go then,' Harri says. He's gazing at both her and Patrick in turn, and Alicia is sure he's noticed the tension between them. When neither moves, Harri adds, 'Everything OK?'

'Yes,' both Patrick and Alicia say in turn.

'Get a move on then!'

THIRTY-EIGHT

'You OK?' Patrick asks and touches Alicia's elbow.

They are out of the office and walking down the stairs. His touch through the thin fabric of her cotton blouse runs through her body.

How am I to resist this man?

'Sure, but I ran into Mia outside the office,' she says, trying to pour cold water over both his tenderness and her own weakness.

Patrick stops and stares at her, 'What, where?'

'Outside, just now.'

Patrick runs his hand over his face and Alicia notices that he's cut himself shaving again. There is a small nick at the side of his face, and a stream of blood has run down his chin where he has rubbed it.

'You're bleeding...' Alicia says, taking a tissue out of her handbag and, after a moment's hesitation, handing it to Patrick rather than wiping his chin herself. She touches the side of her own face to indicate where the mark is.

'Ah, thanks,' Patrick says and rubs the tissue against his face.

'You OK?' Alicia asks.

'Yeah,' Patrick says. He crunches the napkin in his palm and gazes at Alicia. She sees he too has red-rimmed eyes much like her mother. Has everyone else on the islands been binge-drinking overnight, Alicia wonders.

'I didn't go home last night—I mean home to the Eriksson's summer place,' Patrick says. His voice is quiet.

'Right,' Alicia says and carries on walking down the stairs, but Patrick stops her, taking hold of her arm again.

'What happened with Mia?'

Alicia is suddenly weary, fed up with being these wealthy people's piggy in the middle.

'Nothing,' she replies and frees herself from Patrick's grip. 'You coming?' she says over her shoulder and hears Patrick following her down the stairs. When they reach street level, she's relieved to see Mia is no longer there.

'The boat is docked in the East Harbor,' Patrick says and he chin nods toward the sea.

'I know,' Alicia replies.

Patrick gives Alicia a quick glance. 'Of course you do,' Patrick says and grins.

Patrick and Alicia hardly say a word to each to other on the way to the harbor. When they get to the moorings, Patrick offers Alicia his hand, but she lowers herself onto the boat without as much as a glance at him. When she's onboard she avoids looking at the ladder leading to the cabin below. She is trying hard not to think about the day they spent in the bunk, wrapped around each other.

Harri has given them a grid reference for the place where the body has been found. At the *Sjoland* canal they see a police boat. Patrick nods to the three shapes onboard the other vessel. As they leave the canal, and speed up toward the open sea, Patrick says to Alicia, 'We can't go as fast, but I know the way.'

Alicia nods. She digs out a hairband from her handbag and ties her hair back to avoid the wind blowing it into her face.

Moments later, they dock on the side of a small rocky island, right next to the police boat. The three police officers are gathering equipment on top of a small hill. Alicia sees one of them walk toward the edge of the island, holding some police tape. His head dips down as he climbs down the bank.

A policewoman turns around as they step off the yacht. 'It's Alicia, isn't it?'

'Hi,' Alicia replies and adds, 'I didn't know you'd moved back to Åland, Ebba?'

'Likewise.'

Alicia walks the few paces along a rocky island and regards the policewoman. She's wearing a midnight-blue police overall and white rubber gloves. She's changed since their schooldays and looks more assured, a little more filled out, although she is still lanky and a head taller than Alicia. Her dark hair is cut short and she isn't wearing any makeup at all, which makes her look freshly scrubbed. When, years ago, she bumped into Ebba in the corridors of Uppsala university and heard that she too was studying there (criminology, while Alicia was studying English), she thought they might become closer friends, but somehow it didn't happen. She heard later that Ebba was working with the Stockholm Police.

Alicia is brought back to the present by Ebba's voice. She's issuing commands to the other policeman. There are two men standing next to her old schoolfriend, one an older man, wearing shorts and carrying a case, and another one, a younger male police officer in an all-blue overall like Ebba's.

'Simon, you help Gustav with the body and take the pictures. I'll deal with the press.'

'Where's the body?' Patrick asks Ebba. He is standing next to Alicia, and she is trying to ignore the effect the closeness of his body has on her. They are facing Ebba, who has her eyes on Alicia and Patrick, regarding them gravely.

'How did you know about this?' Ebba asks.

Patrick smiles, 'Oh, come on, Ebba, we get live police reports.'

'You two know each other?' Alicia asks, glancing at Patrick and then at Ebba.

'Everyone knows everyone else here, surely you know that?' Ebba says drily, and adds, 'But you've made a wasted visit. I can't let you near before we've made our investigations. And definitely no pictures,' she says as she sees Patrick dig his mobile out of his pocket.

'Just for my own reference?' Patrick replies, holding firmly onto his phone.

'You don't want me to confiscate that, do you?' Ebba says and smiles.

'OK,' Patrick replies with a sigh, 'Be like that.' He puts the phone back into his pocket.

As they stand there, the third policeman re-emerges from behind a rock and waves them over.

Without a word, Ebba begins to move toward the sea's edge, followed by an older man carrying the heavy case. Patrick and Alicia look at each other, then start walking behind the two policemen. As they approach the sea, the young policeman points to a shape in the water.

He is lying face down, his limp body tangled in the reeds. His thin, fully clothed shape moves with the gentle waves of the sea wash. Alicia stares down at the torso and sees in her eyes Stefan, or how his lanky figure would have looked in the morgue. She regrets she didn't insist on seeing him; her mind's image of how he looked is far worse. There's blue and white police tape strung across two thin, twisted pine trees sprouting from the rocky ground as if by a miracle. The tape is for show only, Alicia thinks. Who would come to a little outpost like this?

Ebba glances behind her to where Patrick and Alicia are standing, but she doesn't say anything. She moves carefully down the side of the rock that leads down to the water. With one foot on a stone close to the boy's head and another resting on the main rock face, Ebba squats down to take a closer look. Alicia's stomach turns as she sees the swollen state of the corpse. The body is puffed up underneath a dark-colored parka and long shorts. The half-upturned face of the boy looks pasty, bloated and blotchy. Ebba steadies herself on the rock and leans in to take a close look.

Alicia moves closer, stepping over the police tape.

'Stay there!' Ebba shouts, but Alicia replies, 'I think I know him.'

Ebba stares at her and then nods in agreement.

Alicia puts her other hand to her mouth and nose to stop herself from smelling anything as she takes the few steps down the slippery rock. She squats down beside Ebba, who reaches out to steady her. Alicia looks at his legs and sees the plaster cast on his bare left foot. It too is discolored with a greenish yellow hue, but there are still a few scribbles left visible. His friends must have written stuff on the cast.

'He is—was—just a kid,' Alicia says.

THIRTY-NINE

Alicia thinks about her stepfather. How shocked Uffe would be to see the boy in that state. He is a good man, Alicia knows that. He looks after his staff well, too well in her mother's opinion.

'He keeps asking them to come into the house and then I have to feed them!' she's often said to Alicia. When she was growing up there were two farm laborers who came back each summer to work for Uffe. They were both born and bred in the Åland islands, and Uffe had known them since childhood. But when Eastern Europe opened up to the West and cheaper foreign labor became available, Uffe began employing first Estonian boys, then Polish and now Romanian. It has never occurred to Alicia to ask Uffe where he found the temporary labor; she assumed the boys themselves turned up on the doorstep of her stepfather's farmhouse in Sjoland.

'Oh my God,' she hears Patrick say behind her. He's standing on the rock above Alicia. The sun is shining directly into Alicia's eyes so she can't see his expression fully. Taking her hand away from her mouth, she holds onto the rock and straightens herself up. Patrick reaches his hand out to help her up the bank. This time she takes it and he pulls her up.

Alicia looks around the little island where the police and Patrick have moored their motorboats; how has the boy ended up here, on this small rocky outcrop? There are clumps of grass in the middle and around the edges, but mostly it's just a flat, stony surface with patches of moss.

Alicia is shivering even though it's a very warm day, with little wind and silent except for the seabirds and the occasional sound of a motorboat somewhere in the distance. They are just ten minutes or so away from her swimming place in Sjoland. She hears the sound of an engine, but it soon fades and gives way to the twittering or squawking of the birds. There isn't much habitation in the surrounding islands. One jetty juts out from a shore-line, about 500 meters away, and Alicia can make out an old boathouse, and then a large wood-clad villa further up the hill. The water looks shallow between the larger island and the one they are standing on. Alicia wonders if the little outpost is owned by the people with the jetty. In her mind's eye, she can see children swimming from the larger island to the smaller one, laughing and drying themselves in the sun when they reach the other shore.

Her own childhood.

What a deserted, beautiful place it would be if it wasn't for the dead body of a young man floating between the reeds just a few meters away.

The older man with the heavy case edges down

toward the body, while Ebba, helped up by the young policeman, comes to stand next to Patrick and Alicia.

'So who is he?' Ebba asks.

'His name is Daniel. He works—worked—for my stepfather.'

Patrick makes a sound. Since the exchange with Ebba about his phone, Patrick has been unusually quiet. Alicia now looks at him. His face is very pale.

'You OK?' Alicia asks. Ebba is regarding them both.

'Yeah, I keep thinking I should take notes, but I don't seem to be able to think straight.'

'Shock,' Alicia says.

Patrick nods.

'You didn't cover anything like this in Stockholm?' she asks him.

Patrick shakes his head. 'No, I was more political and financial crimes.'

Ebba coughs, ending Patrick and Alicia's conversation abruptly. Her face is grave.

'Tell me everything you know about him,' Ebba says, and chin nods back to the other end of the island.

'I haven't really met him, just seen him from afar. He works as a casual laborer for Uffe, and stays in one of the cottages, that's all I know. The plaster cast is from an accident he had with the tractor last week.' Alicia shivers. She pulls her arms around herself. 'I mean, I *think* it's him ...' Suddenly Alicia is afraid she's mistaken.

'OK. I don't want any of this in your paper,' Ebba says.

Patrick nods, again not uttering a word, but Alicia

replies, 'Surely we can say that a body has been found here?'

Ebba sighs. 'OK, but no details about his ID until we know more about what's happened and can contact his next of kin.'

'How do you think it happened?' Alicia asks.

Ebba looks at Alicia, but doesn't answer the question.

'Wait here, I may need to ask you more questions,' she says instead and moves toward the police tape to talk to the older man.

Alicia and Patrick are kept on the island for another half an hour, while the police move back and forth between the body and their boat. Eventually, the young policeman fetches a gray plastic body bag. A few minutes later, the three policemen carry the dead body into their boat.

'You can go now,' Ebba says with her head bent over her notebook, not looking at Alicia or Patrick.

They travel back to Mariehamn in silence. Patrick doesn't put the sail up, and the noise of the engine provides Alicia with an excuse not to talk to him.

'What an infuriating woman,' Patrick says as they pull up to the jetty in the East Harbor.

'Yeah, I remember she was a bit of an odd-ball at school,' Alicia replies.

Patrick is standing in the boat, facing her with his hair mussed up by the wind.

'Sorry, I forgot she was a friend of yours,' he says, gazing at Alicia from under his eyebrows.

Alicia climbs onto the jetty, not waiting for Patrick's help. She's holding onto the strap of her canvas handbag, which she'd slung across her body as she got out of the boat.

'You were very quiet out there,' she says, looking closely at Patrick's face. She's standing above him, watching him getting ready to leave the boat.

'Not used to seeing dead bodies, I guess,' he says, lowering the fenders, locking the doors to the cabin and putting away their life-jackets. As he steps out onto the jetty, he leans down and makes sure the fenders are in place to protect his precious boat.

'Right,' Alicia says.

'I'm off then.' Patrick says. But he only stands opposite Alicia, looking down at her.

'Oh, you're not going to write the article?' Alicia says, surprised. She's still not sure what his role at the newspaper is, nor what is expected of her.

'This isn't exactly a story for the finance section,' Alicia says, 'so I assumed ...'

'I told you, I don't work for *Ålandsbladet*.'

'So why were you here today?'

'To give you a lift, of course,' Patrick says, a smile playing on his lips.

Alicia feels stupid. She looks down at her shoes and nods, 'Well, I should thank you then.'

They stand on the jetty facing each other. Alicia isn't looking at him, she can't, because she knows what will happen if she does. Instead, she glances down the jetty and into the restaurant at the far end of the harbor. A few tourists are walking on the path that runs along the wooden jetties, and a cyclist passes them.

Patrick takes her hand, 'Look, can we start again?'

Alicia lifts her head and sees the sincerity in his face. He's standing so close to her now that their bodies are nearly touching. Her breath is caught in her chest and for a moment she can't speak. But then she remembers the anger in Mia's face a few hours before, and the pain in Patrick's when he spoke about their break-up.

Those two aren't finished with each other.

'Look,' Alicia begins. She briefly squeezes Patrick's hand, then lets go and steps backward to put some space between them. 'You need to sort things out with Mia. Perhaps in a few months' time, when ...'

Patrick's face shows no emotion when he says, 'OK, I understand.' There's a pause, then he adds, 'I guess I'll see you around?'

Alicia stands still for a moment and then walks away. At the end of the jetty, she turns around and sees Patrick still looking at her. She nods and makes her way quickly toward the newspaper office.

Harri is so excited about having a scoop with the body of the Romanian boy that he convinces Alicia to write the story up in spite of the promises she made to Ebba.

'I'll clear it with her, don't worry about that. We know the Police Chief, and he'll be fine about it.'

Reluctantly, Alicia writes a brief report about the discovery of the body, leaving out the connection to Uffe, which she hadn't mentioned to the editor. She just quotes 'unnamed sources' saying that the boy was from Romania and had been working as a farm laborer on the islands.

Moments later, she sees it's been uploaded to the

paper's online version. As she re-reads her own words, the article strikes her as too simple, as if she's forgotten something. Bloody Patrick, he keeps getting into her thoughts, clouding them. She needs to be a good journalist and to learn new skills to keep the job at *Ålandsbladet*. For now at least. She doesn't know if she's going to stay indefinitely, but at least for now. The money she earns comes in handy.

But she had no idea when she was offered the job by Birgit that it involved working with all the breaking news. When she'd returned from seeing the body Harri had said, 'Everyone turns their hand to anything here.'

He swept his hand across the newsroom, where just two people were sitting, Frida and a younger boy, just as they were when she'd met Patrick there earlier. 'Those two are both interns, they are not ready to tackle an article like this.'

The pieces she wrote for the *Financial Times* were rarely needed quickly. She often had a few days to write a report on a company, or a feature explaining the impact of a possible interest rate rise, or the effects of the fall in the UK pound after the Brexit vote. Only when she worked on the 2008 financial crisis, did she remember having to turn in stories fast. But she's a trained reporter and she knows she can handle anything. Better than Patrick, it seems. Bloody man! Alicia decides enough is enough. She will control her emotions from now on.

FORTY

That evening after the discovery of the boy's body, Alicia convinces her mother that she is too tired for a nightcap after dinner. She wants to collect her thoughts about Patrick, about the boy, and think about Stefan in peace. Seeing the dead Romanian has brought back her own fabricated images of Stefan's body after the accident. She curses Liam, who kept her away from her son. *Think of the positives.* She forces herself to remember how Stefan loved the islands, how he made friends here. Suddenly, she realizes she doesn't know any of the youngsters he used to 'hang out' with as he put it. She resolves to find out from Hilda who they were - surely she would have heard from a friend of a friend who Stefan befriended?

Alicia tries to empty her mind, and uses the techniques her psychologist, Connie, had taught her.

'Notice everything around you, look at the trees, take in the color of the sky, the fluffy clouds. Breathe in and out.'

Alicia sits on the wooden decking outside the sauna cottage and watches the birds dip in and out of the water, picking up insects off the surface, trying to think only about the beautiful nature around her. But her mind wanders and she thinks about the young Romanian man instead. Both Uffe and Hilda were shocked to hear of Daniel's death. Uffe wanted a glass of whisky straight away but then didn't have wine with dinner, whereas Hilda drank several glasses. At the end of the meal her mother was slurring her words and giggling. She acted so inappropriately that Alicia exchanged several glances with Uffe during the meal. Alicia didn't say anything about her drinking, but resolved to talk to Uffe, again, about it, as well as the money worries. The alcohol, the rows and the losses the shop was making must be linked, surely? As soon as the police found out what had happened to the boy, they could move on with their lives.

Again, Alicia forces herself to think about her surroundings. It is a still evening, with the sun hovering over the horizon, and she sits on the decking, trying not to think about anything, and just concentrating on her breathing. She thinks how amazing it is that the sun will only dip down a couple of hours before midnight and emerge again around 4am, leaving a dusk that never gets truly dark. It's now 9pm, and there is no sign of darkness. This is what she has missed in London. The quiet peace where you can really gather your thoughts.

This is her favorite time of the year on the islands. The end of the day, when the wildlife around her is busy calling each other, or feeding their young, is magical. Watching the calm sea in front of her, she spots a pair of birds emerge from the reed bed and dive elegantly, hardly breaking the glinting surface. Alicia holds her breath as she waits for the bird to emerge. She thinks they are Artic loons, which have an amazing ability to stay under water for several minutes, and her suspicion is confirmed when she sees the first bird emerge a couple of meters away from where it entered the water. Alicia wants to clap but is afraid of alarming the wildlife around her.

A noise of a motorboat cuts through the landscape. A wooden rowing boat with an outboard motor attached to the back is heading across the shipping lane toward the island opposite, a young man holding onto the tiller. When the boat disappears around a point, peace is once again restored. Alicia closes her eyes and concentrates on the natural sounds around her: the soft rustling in the trees and the lower sound of the reeds swaying in the breeze. The birds are twittering warnings to each other.

Suddenly a noise she doesn't recognize makes Alicia open her eyes.

'Your mum said I'd find you here.'

Ebba stands with her feet wide apart, her hands in the pockets of her trousers. She isn't in uniform anymore, but she still looks as if she is on duty, with the same water-proof coat she was wearing earlier, now over a plain white shirt bearing the logo of Finnish police force—a gray sword and the head of the Lion of Finland against a blue background. On her feet she wears sensible black, flat shoes, which Alicia suspects are police issue too.

'So what happened to your promise not to write about the body?' Ebba has her eyes on Alicia.

'Sorry, Harri said that you'd be OK with it. Apparently, he knows the Chief of Police.'

'Yeah, the same man who chewed my head off when he saw what you'd written.'

'Sorry,' Alicia says. 'I'm still new at the paper. I couldn't refuse it.' Alicia tries to smile at Ebba. 'Please sit down?'

Ebba plonks herself on a chair next to Alicia.

'Apology accepted. Besides, I knew that would happen, but I thought it'd be Mr Eriksson's son-in-law who would write about it, not you.'

'Me too,' Alicia says, trying to avoid looking at Ebba, and instead studying her hands.

Ebba regards Alicia silently for a moment before speaking. 'We've definitely identified the boy.'

'Oh,' Alicia says, 'that was quick.'

'I've also just spoken with your mum and dad.'

'You mean my mum and Uffe?' Alicia remarks.

Ebba raises an eyebrow and scratches her hair. 'Sorry, yes, your step-dad.'

'That's OK. It's just that I don't, never have, called Uffe "Dad".'

Ebba exhales. 'Let's cut the crap. We didn't know each other that well at school, nor at uni, so I can be excused for not knowing the ins and outs of your family relationships.'

'Sure,' Alicia says. She's surprised at Ebba's tone, but recognizes her direct manner. She was just the same at school and university.

'But what's the issue, what more can I tell you? I came

to see the body because of my job and happened to know who it was. That's all,' Alicia says.

'Why didn't you tell me about you and Patrick?' Ebba says, looking straight at Alicia.

'I didn't think it was relevant.' Alicia is hoping Ebba is referring to the fact that she knows Patrick.

'See, that's where I disagree.' Again Ebba lifts her eyebrows. 'It seems a bit of a coincidence that a boy you and your boyfriend both know turns up dead ...'

'Colleague,' Alicia says. 'Look, I've just started at *Alandsbladet* and Patrick, who didn't know Daniel, offered to take me to the island on his boat. That's all.'

Ebba looks at Alicia, raising an eyebrow, 'I bet he offered,' she mumbles and before Alicia has time to reply, continues, 'So you're living here now? You're not registered as living here. We have your home address as ...' Ebba refers to the screen on her phone, 'Crouch End, London?'

Alicia looks down at her hands, 'Yeah. Sorry, I'm not sure what I am going to do.'

Ebba makes a note on her phone and looks at Alicia again. Don't forget you have three months, after which you have to register your move from one EU country to another. The rules still apply until Brexit.'

Alicia sighs, 'OK. Give me a break, will you!' She grins, trying to remind Ebba that even though they weren't the best of friends before, they're not exactly strangers now.

But Ebba isn't having any of it. 'I don't make the rules,' she says, not returning Alicia's smile. 'Going back to my investigation, can you tell me how exactly you and Patrick came to the scene?'

'I told you—we were covering a story. Harri called me into his office this morning and Patrick was there. He offered to give me a lift. Apparently *Ålandsbladet* isn't wealthy enough to own a boat of its own.'

'But I thought you were a financial journalist, not a breaking news reporter,' Ebba says and crosses her arms.

Alicia groans. 'Yes, that was a bit of a surprise to me too. It seems there are no such distinctions here.'

'Right,' Ebba says, and continues. 'Your step-dad filled me in on the unfortunate incident with the tractor, and their working relationship.' Ebba's glance settles on Alicia once more. 'It's a shame you didn't let me know about the connection before. Any reason why you didn't?'

Alicia bites the inside of her lip. She hadn't mentioned this to Ebba because she wasn't sure whether the farmworkers' work status was above board. She is well aware that Uffe takes on summer staff without worrying too much about permits and taxes. She is almost certain Daniel and his Romanian friends were paid cash in hand, no questions asked.

'I didn't want Uffe, or my mother, to get involved in something that had nothing to do with them. Besides, I wasn't even sure it was him.'

'Hmm,' Ebba says, still keeping her eyes on Alicia. Alicia is beginning to feel uncomfortable, as if her old schoolfriend is accusing *her* of something. Instead of saying this to Ebba, however, Alicia keeps quiet.

'Anything else you'd like to tell me? Any other small

details about the boy you have kept to yourself, in case it would get someone else in trouble?'

'No, of course not.'

'Nothing to do with your son, Stefan?'

Alicia stares at Ebba. Suddenly she feels very cold. She can't speak.

Ebba continues, 'We have reason to believe the two youngsters knew each other.'

FORTY-ONE

Alicia can't sleep that night. Images of Stefan involved in some crime on the islands, speeding fast on a motorcycle, or his body being replaced by that of the Romanian boy creep into her dreams and she wakes with a start.

Finally, when she has tossed and turned in bed for what seems like hours, and when she sees the light streaming into the room through the small window and making an oblong pattern on the pine log wall, she gets up. She looks at her phone and sees it's a few minutes past 6am. The birds are already singing outside, noisily making preparations for the day ahead.

Alicia gets out of bed and fills the coffee machine Hilda has brought to the sauna cottage. They already had a small fridge for beer, and Alicia has brought some butter, rye bread and cheese for breakfast. She needs to be more independent of her mother and Uffe.

From now on, she plans to take the bus into town

rather than rely on Hilda's lifts to the newspaper office. Her mother's time-keeping is terrible, and her drinking, which Alicia knows she must mention, worries her sick. She plans to leave a note at the house later, or discuss it with Uffe, who's usually awake early. As well as the drinking, Alicia is seriously worried about their money troubles. She needs to speak to Hilda, but has no idea how she will broach the subject. And she can't do anything until the matter with poor Daniel has been settled.

With a hot, steaming cup of black coffee, and a woollen throw around her shoulders, Alicia goes to sit on the terrace and watches the sun, which is already high over the horizon. It looks like being another bright and hot day, with just some hazy clouds scattered over a deep-blue sky. She can see a row of sailing boats moving slowly around. They are gathered in the shipping lane, waiting for the swing bridge to open so that they can make their way through the Sjoland canal and into Mariehamn's East Harbor. These are early risers, she thinks.

Later, the town will be full of tourists and the restaurants and cafés buzzing. She hopes Hilda's shop will be filled with customers too.

Alicia pulls her knees up and turns her thoughts to what Ebba said about the Romanian boy, Daniel. Alicia feels ashamed that she never even met him. He had just turned eighteen, so he was exactly the same age as Stefan. And Daniel knew Alicia's son.

'Two friends, both dead now,' Ebba said in that serious, level voice of hers. Her intelligent eyes were on Alicia, as if waiting to hear how she could explain it. But, of course, she wasn't able to do that. How could the policewoman imagine she would have an explanation when she didn't even know the two boys were close?

They'd sat in silence for what seemed like hours, on the same terrace where Alicia is now, watching the birds duck in and out of the reeds. 'Look, I'm not sure what you are saying. How do you know that Daniel knew my Stefan?' she asked Ebba.

'There are messages on his phone. And photos of the two of them—and a girl.'

'Who?'

'We don't know yet.' Ebba sighed and stood up. 'Come and see me on Monday at the station. I should have more information by then.'

Alicia nodded.

'Have a good weekend,' Ebba said and disappeared around the corner of the cottage.

Now, sipping her coffee, Alicia resolves to find out who that girl is. Surely there must be something on Stefan's phone or laptop. She needs to ask Liam to look through any images. Alicia picks up her phone and sees the latest messages Liam has sent her, all gone unanswered. She types in a few words, rereads what she has written, and then deletes the word 'sorry'. She realizes she's not sorry for having kept her distance from him. Liam is still her husband, that is true, but as far as she is concerned they are separated.

When, two hours later, Alicia makes her way up to the

house, her mother is standing by the kitchen window above the sink, looking over the fields and the sea beyond. She's clutching a cup of coffee.

'Hi,' Alicia says.

Her mother turns around and Alicia goes and hugs her. Hilda's eyes are red again, and she looks so miserable that Alicia has to ask, 'What's the matter?'

Her mother turns back to the window. Alicia sees Uffe walking along the side of one of the fields, and they follow his slow progress to the end of the path until he disappears into the narrow strip of pine trees separating the rest of Uffe's farm from the house.

'Oh, the boy's accident has upset us both,' Hilda says.

'It's terrible,' Alicia agrees. She decided during her morning swim that she will not mention what Ebba told her about Stefan, Daniel, and the unknown girl. Not until she has a chance to find out from the policewoman who the girl is.

'Do you want breakfast?' Hilda asks. Alicia realizes that her mother is still in her dressing gown.

'No.' Alicia tells her mother that she plans to take a bus into town. She sees relief in Hilda's eyes.

'Aren't you going in today?' Alicia asks.

Hilda glances at her daughter. She can see her expression change to a wary one. 'Oh, the summer girl is there today.'

Her mother smiles and turns around, giving her daughter the message that the matter is closed.

Hilda offers Alicia Uffe's old bike, but Alicia decides against the rusty old thing. She plans to buy one in the shops in the fall, when the tourist season is over and prices plummet for things like that.

If she's still on the islands then.

FORTY-TWO

The first person Alicia sees when she enters the newspaper office is Patrick.

Why is he constantly hanging around here?

'There's a meeting with Harri at 9am sharp. You and I are covering the murder case,' he says to Alicia.

She stares at Patrick. She glances at her watch and sees it's nearly 9 o'clock already.

'Murder?'

'Come on,' he says and touches the small of Alicia's back, pushing her toward the glass cubicle where Harri is already sitting, talking to Birgit. The personnel woman is standing with her back to the general office and there is another man sitting down, with only his blond hair visible. When she opens the door, forced by Patrick behind her, Alicia immediately recognizes him. Kurt Eriksson—the majority owner of the newspaper and the most famous man on the islands.

'Where's that girl?' Harri says as soon as Alicia and Patrick enter his fish-bowl of an office.

'Called in sick,' Birgit says. The woman is holding a stack of papers. Did she ever go anywhere without them, Alicia wonders.

'If that's all,' she now says, looking at Harri. The editor nods and Birgit leaves the room, closing the door behind her.

Alicia feels Kurt Eriksson's gaze on her. He coughs. It's just a small sound, barely audible, but it stops Harri in his tracks.

'Ah, and Kurt, please meet Alicia, our newest recruit. From London,' he adds and lifts his chest a little.

If only they knew, Alicia thinks and looks at the famous millionaire, who stands up and extends his hand to her.

'Hello again. We met at Midsummer,' Alicia says and takes his hand.

'Yes, of course,' Kurt Eriksson says and moves his eyes toward Patrick, who is now standing next to Alicia. His face hardens from the polite smile directed toward Alicia just a second before.

'I believe you know my son-in-law?' he says, bringing his face back to Alicia with a false smile on his lips again. Alicia notices his pale eyes have the same, cold, expression in them. His tan has an orange hue, and his artificially blond hair has been professionally styled to look naturally ruffled. Close up, he looks far too young, his skin a little tight and thin across his face. He is wearing a pink striped shirt, tucked into dark navy chinos, revealing a slightly extended but firm stomach, and gives off a scent of expensive aftershave. No tax-free junk from the Viking

Line ferries for this guy, Alicia thinks, and she pulls her hand away.

'I hear you've worked for the *Financial Times*?' he says and gives Alicia a smarmy smile.

'Yes,' she replies, and wonders whether to add that she was a freelance reporter, but decides against it.

There is a silence and Alicia wishes more than anything that she could turn on her heels and leave the room.

'Right, I want you two to go and talk with the police, come back and write a thousand words,' Harri says, ignoring the polite chit chat Kurt Eriksson has started.

'I'm not ...' Alicia says, but Harri puts his right hand up, palm facing Alicia.

'If you want to go full-time for the next few weeks, we've just OK'd it with the shareholder.' Harri nods at Kurt Eriksson, whose smile widens but still doesn't reach his eyes.

'What the hell?' Alicia spits at Patrick when they are outside the newspaper office, walking toward the police headquarters a few blocks away along the East Harbor. The wind has got up and the rattle of the sails and rigging in the wind is so loud it's almost deafening. They walk right past the spot where Patrick's boat is moored, where he first invited Alicia onboard.

'What have I done?' Patrick says, stopping in the middle of the path. He is wearing another white shirt (*how many does he own?*), black ripped jeans and his suede jacket.

'What are you even doing here?' Alicia faces Patrick,

her hands on her hips. 'You don't work for the paper, and you don't want to be involved in this story.'

Patrick touches Alicia's arm, and in spite of herself, the contact sends a jolt deep inside her. She shrugs Patrick's hand away. 'I'm waiting. What is going on?'

Patrick runs his fingers through his hair and Alicia can't help but find the gesture endearing. The breeze catches the blond strands and a few fall back onto his face. Alicia is glad she put her own hair up in a ponytail this morning.

'Look there aren't many suspicious deaths in Åland, so this is big. Plus you aren't experienced in this kind of thing.'

'And you are? When we saw the body you told me you'd never covered crime. I'm a big girl, I can do this!' Alicia almost shouts the words.

Patrick lifts his eyebrows. 'Yeah sure, but we don't have anybody who has written about something like this. So it makes sense if we put our two heads together.' He regards Alicia for a moment and then stretches his arms out in front of her. 'Honestly, that's all it is. Harri just wanted me to help you out.'

'I told you, I don't need any help,' Alicia says, but she is close to being convinced. She turns on her heels and continues walking along the path by the jetty to the police station.

Patrick hurries to catch her up and takes her arm. 'I knew you'd come around.' He grins like a little boy and Alicia shrugs her shoulders, detaching herself from him.

'Don't get any ideas,' she says, but she cannot help a smile forming.

FORTY-THREE

They walk along Strandvägen in silence, passing the Hotel Arkipelag and the library. Images of visiting the place with Stefan flood Alicia's brain. She glances over at Patrick and wonders if she should tell him what Ebba said about Stefan knowing Daniel, but decides against it. She will try to speak to Ebba on her own. They cross the main thoroughfare of the town. In the distance, the sun, now high in the sky, is reflected on the surface of the sea. The light bouncing off the shifting water is blinding and Alicia has to shade her eyes. She's forgotten to bring her sunglasses.

The police station is an old 1950s building, clad in dull gray cement. They have to wait for Ebba. Patrick and Alicia sit on green plastic chairs.

'I need to speak to her privately first,' Alicia, when the door eventually opens and Ebba gestures for them to enter.

Patrick has already stood up.

Alicia turns and looks at him, 'Please?'

For a moment Alicia thinks that Patrick will insist on coming with her, but then he relents and sits back down.

'Before you ask,' says Alicia, 'I have no idea why he's here. Something about crimes against persons being rare on the islands.'

Ebba doesn't say anything. She folds her long legs behind a light pine desk and points Alicia toward one of two chairs set against the table.

'As far as I'm concerned I'm speaking to *Ålandsbladet* when I'm speaking with you.'

Alicia nods in agreement.

Ebba leans across the table and adds, 'But I have to tell you something off the record first.'

She is looking at a screen in front of her and turns it around toward Alicia.

'Or, rather, I have to ask you some questions.'

'OK,' Alicia says. She's got her phone in her hand, with the notes app opened, just in case she needs to jot down some details.

'Do you know this young woman?'

Alicia gasps. The hair color and length are different, and her cheeks are a little less plump but the face is unmistakable. 'Yes,' she replies.

'Thought so.'

'What has Frida got to do with anything?' Alicia asks.

'How do you know Frida Anttila?' Ebba asks.

'She works as an intern at *Ålandsbladet*.'

'And before that?'

Alicia shakes her head, 'I met her for the first time the day after I started at the paper.'

'That's strange,' Ebba says, staring at Alicia, as if trying to determine whether she is speaking the truth.

'What is this? What has Frida got to do with anything.'

'I'm asking myself the same question,' Ebba says. She turns the screen back toward herself and taps it.

There is a silence during which Alicia stares at Ebba, trying to understand what the policewoman is getting at. Eventually she cannot stand it any longer. 'What is it?'

When Ebba still doesn't reply, Alicia gets it. 'She knew Stefan ... and Daniel! She's the girl in your picture?'

Ebba nods and turns toward Alicia, calmly eyeing her. 'That's why I can't quite understand how you didn't know her,' she says.

Alicia sighs. She too, is amazed how she didn't get to know the young people Stefan hung out with during their holidays. Looking back, there was always the conflict between her and Liam getting in the way. He didn't want to spend time on the islands, while Alicia was always desperately trying to make him love her home.

What a waste of time; I wish I'd never tried.

'I don't know, but I just never met his friends here. He didn't have many, you know. We were always here when everyone else was away in their summer places, so Mariehamn was just full of tourists ...'

Ebba puts up her hand as if to stop Alicia speaking.

She leans over the desk again. 'I need to tell you something. But none of this can go into the paper. Or to be known by anyone else. Is that clear?'

Alicia nods.

'We have reason to believe that Frida and the deceased had a very close connection to your son. Several images from security cameras around the city indicate that they spent some time together in central Mariehamn last summer. Plus we have witness statements from a home where Frida's mother, Sirpa Anttila, is being cared for that say they visited her together on several occasions.

'I didn't know,' Alicia says and gets up. She wants to go and talk to Frida. She'll get her home address from Birgit and pay her a visit.

'Sit down, there's more,' Ebba says. Her expression is serious. 'We believe she is pregnant.'

Alicia sits down. Her head is spinning. 'Sorry, what did you say?'

Ebba shrugs her shoulders. 'I'm just telling you so that you know about her condition before you speak with Ms Anttila.' She gets up and adds, 'Of course, we need to speak with Frida ourselves first, but at the moment we cannot get hold of her. So if you do find her, can you ask her to contact us as soon as possible.'

Patrick watches as Alicia storms out of the police detective's room.

'What's going on,' he says and runs after Alicia, onto the street, but she waves him away and starts walking fast toward the bus station. He is confused. If Alicia has got a scoop out of the police she would head toward the newspaper offices and not in the opposite direction, surely?

When Patrick returns to the grim police headquarters, the constable at the desk tells him Ebba has also left. Cursing under his breath and not knowing what to do next, he walks down Hamngatan, where he has left his car in the multistory next to the Hotel Arkipelag. His thoughts turn to Mia and the divorce.

What is he going to do? He knows his career at *Journalen* is over. He's never going to win any prestigious prizes for his writing however much he wants to. What he needs to ensure now is that he is still going to be involved in the upbringing of his two girls.

Kurt Eriksson, his father-in-law, is a rich and powerful man. Patrick knows he has never liked his Swedish son-in-law. Perhaps in the early days when he saw how happy his daughter was. But lately, after Mia's affair, everyone can see the marriage is anything but blissful. Patrick feels the man's disappointment in his fledging career as a journalist. But what would he have him do? Work 12-hour days and let his children be looked after by a paid help?

In Stockholm, Mia is always busy with the Eriksson's estate business. It's mostly Patrick who fetches the children from school and takes them to their ballet and riding lessons. It's becoming easier, now they are older and sometimes take themselves on the bus and *tunnelbana*, but Patrick is overprotective, of his eldest in particular. He will never forget that night when he thought they were going to lose little Sara, and the memory of her limp body in his arms as he carried her to the car in the dead of night. Or how she looked lying on the emergency ward bed with her eyes closed and her damp hair spread either side of her pale head, as if she was a little sleeping princess.

And he's known about Mia's affair for ages. He knows their relationship hasn't been good for years. They haven't had sex for twelve months. The images of Alicia's slim, strong body writhing beneath his own come into his mind. Alicia's got under his skin, he knows, but he's not sure she feels the same. She seems to think that he and Mia aren't over and he doesn't know how to convince her otherwise.

The confirmation that the marriage was at an end came the morning of the Midsummer party. It was long overdue. Patrick had surprised himself at how calm he'd been. He told Mia that he would want to share custody of the girls, and she had nodded. Not in agreement, he knew, but in acknowledgement of his demand.

'I am going to move to Mariehamn. With the girls,' she replied, regarding him with cold eyes. He tried to recall the last time she had looked lovingly at him, but he couldn't remember.

Patrick said nothing. He just nodded. Afterwards, he was proud of himself, because he didn't want an argument, and he didn't want Mia to back him into a corner. She was a brilliant negotiator, a skill learned at her father's knee. And he needed time to think about his own options. What was there for him in Stockholm, really?

Patrick changes his mind and returns to the multi-story. He decides to go back to the newspaper offices. Perhaps Alicia has returned by now.

FORTY-FOUR

Frida cannot get out of bed. She knows she needs to go and see her mum, but her limbs are so heavy. She's been crying so hard since she saw the news on the online version of the newspaper the previous day that her eyes are swollen and her head hurts. Perhaps she's coming down with something. She lights another cigarette, although she knows she should stop, and drags herself over to the French doors and the small patio in front of her flat. Or, to be more precise, her mother's flat.

She still misses her mother's presence in the three-roomed apartment. The place is so quiet without the low humming of her mum as she cooked by the stove in the kitchen, or her laughter in the evenings when she watched old Finnish comedies on TV. Although Frida knows her mother will never come out of the home, she still hopes that a miracle may happen and her mum will return to normal.

What if I don't go today, will she even notice?

Frida takes a long drag from her cigarette. She's sitting wrapped up in her duvet on a kitchen chair, blowing the smoke out through the open door. That's when she sees her.

Quickly, Frida puts out the cigarette in a flower pot she uses for that purpose and shuts the door. As she closes the curtains, she sees Alicia walking toward her with a determined gait. *Fuck, fuck, fuck.* Frida swears and goes back to bed.

The knocking starts almost as soon as she's back in her bedroom.

'Frida, I know you're there. I just want to talk!' The woman shouts through the door.

Shit, she'll alert the neighbors. An old hag who lives next door would love nothing more than to complain about Frida to the council.

'Coming,' she shouts back. Still wrapped up in the blanket, Frida goes to the door and lets Alicia in.

'Thank you,' the woman says politely.

Frida eyes her up, 'Sit down there,' she says indicating a beaten up green velour sofa. 'Let me get some clothes on.'

Alicia surveys the room where Frida lives. It's not exactly dirty, all the surfaces in the kitchen by the living room are clean and there's only a faint smell of smoke. All the furniture is old, though, and the sofa where she's sitting has a frayed head and armrests. There is an expensive-looking oriental rug in the middle of the room, but that also looks worn-out. The walls are lined with dark wooden bookcases, filled with old hardback volumes and the occasional china figurine. This isn't a young woman's home, Alicia thinks, as Frida reappears wearing a loose dress. Looking at her, Alicia can clearly see there is a bump.

Frida sits down opposite her in an armchair belonging to the same suite as the sofa.

'What do you want?'

'You didn't come to work today and no one has been able to get hold of you.'

'So? I called in sick. Besides, you're not my employer.' Frida has crossed her arms over her chest, making the bump even more pronounced. Her face looks blotched and the purple color of her dress clashes with the blue of her hair, making her look as though she is in fancy dress. A clown.

'How far gone are you?' Alicia asks.

That takes Frida aback. She heaves her back straight, and her eyes stare at Alicia. They are very bloodshot.

She's been crying.

For a moment she is afraid that the girl will get up and hit her.

'What's it to you?' Frida says after a while. Still, there is anger, or defiance in her voice.

'Is it Daniel's?'

'No!' she says. Frida is now staring at Alicia.

'Whose then …?

Suddenly Alicia knows.

'Surely not Stefan?'

Now the girl breaks down. She lowers her head and

begins to sob into her hands. Alicia immediately gets up and goes to hug her.

'There, there,' she says and rocks the bulk of the girl back and forth. Finally, her crying subsides.

'Why didn't you tell me? You knew I was Stefan's mother, didn't you?' Alicia asks as Frida wipes her face and blows her nose loudly into some kitchen paper. It was the only thing Alicia could put her hands on when the crying started.

Frida nods, 'But Daniel was going to help me. And I have this apartment, and the job at *Ålandsbladet*.' She blows her nose again and Alicia fetches more paper.

'Why?'

Frida looks up at Alicia. Her eyes, with swollen lids, are large. Alicia sees that she is truly devastated.

'Do you know what happened with Daniel?' Alicia asks gently.

Now Frida's eyes widen, 'No, do you?'

Alicia shakes her head. 'He drowned but there are suspicious circumstances.'

'Yeah, that's what it said online.'

Alicia says, 'I know, I wrote the article.'

Frida smiles for the first time since Alicia stepped inside her apartment. 'Sorry, I'm being dense.'

Alicia squeezes Frida's shoulders. 'No, you're not.'

They are silent for a moment. Alicia wants to ask all sorts of questions about when Frida is due, how she had met Stefan, did he know about the baby, but she tries to hold fire. She doesn't want to scare Frida away. She looks at the girls' bulging tummy and suddenly feels such joy. In there is a precious thing, a part of her beloved Stefan. A part of her. And a part of Liam. Suddenly Frida starts speaking.

'We first met at the summer confirmation camp when we were both really young. But it didn't start properly until last summer. He was so nice, Stefan, you know?'

Alicia looks at her eyes and nods. She feels tears prick behind her eyes but she controls them and waits.

Frida continues, 'When we met again, last year, that was it. We fell in love. My mother had just been taken into hospital and Stefan was so good about it, taking me to see her on his moped.' Frida is playing with the frayed piece of tissue in her hands, and now lifts her eyes to Alicia. 'Or Uffe's.'

Alicia nods. 'Go on.'

'We spent the whole summer together and in the fall I was accepted onto a language course in Brighton. We met there every weekend until ...'

Alicia thinks back to the fall frantically. And then she remembers, Stefan said he had a friend in Brighton, but she doesn't remember that he went there *every* weekend.

'Sometimes I'd come up to London. Stayed in hostels,' Frida says as if she's read Alicia's mind.

'When did you find out?' Alicia asks carefully after Frida has been quiet, in her own thoughts, for a few minutes. She knows this grief well, it takes over and then you are gone to the world. Poor girl, she's now lost two of her close friends.

'November, I'm nearly eight months now.'

Alicia is shocked and sees the packet of cigarettes by the French doors. 'You shouldn't be smoking.'

Frida lowers her head. 'I know. I've cut down to two or three a day.'

Just as well she doesn't look like she's having a baby, Alicia thinks. She's heard of expecting mums being humiliated in public places if they as much as look at a cigarette, or an alcoholic drink.

'It's really dangerous for the baby,' Alicia says, trying to sound gentle. She takes hold of Frida's hand.

The girl nods and says, 'Daniel told me that all the time.' Tears start running down Frida's face again and Alicia puts her arms around the girl and says, 'I'm here now. I'll take care of you.'

On her way back to the bus stop, Alicia gets a message on her phone.

It's from Ebba, *'Did you get hold of Frida?'*

'No,' Alicia taps in reply. The last thing that girl needs is brusque questioning by Ebba. No. The longer she can stay at home and calm herself down, the better. For Frida —and the baby.

The baby! Alicia stops walking. She's going to be a grandmother! And she's not even forty herself! As this realization hits her, the whole of her heart fills with love toward Frida and the child she is carrying.

Will the baby look like Stefan?

Alicia begins walking again, dreaming about a little boy or girl with Stefan's blond curls and hazel eyes. Of course, Frida is also blond, at least when she hasn't dyed her hair the colors of the rainbow. Alicia smiles to herself. She finds Frida's odd style endearing now. She hasn't felt this happy for months. Not since she lost Stefan. What a wonderful gift this is! She imagines herself being at the birth, supporting Frida through the last stages of her pregnancy, and holding the newborn in her arms.

Another ping from her phone brings Alicia back to the here and now. As she digs out her mobile again, she resolves to stop fantasizing and slow down. Frida might not want her to interfere; she must be careful not to over-power her. She needs this baby more than she has ever needed anything, so she must make sure she will not lose it before the little thing is even born. Frida seems a very independent young woman, and Alicia understands that. She has to respect her wishes above all else. First there is the issue of Daniel's death. She needs to shield Frida from its horrible consequences.

When Alicia's eyes reach the phone, she sees the message is from Liam.

'I can't find anything on Stefan's laptop but I know he knew someone called Frida at the summer camp. I can tell you more if we talk. Please call me?'

It occurs to her that Liam is also going to be a grand-parent. Should she tell him now? No, she needs to wait until she has had more time with Frida and has talked through all her options. She deletes his message. She has no desire to talk to Liam.

Alicia knows Frida is seeing a doctor regularly at the health clinic. That is how Ebba found out she was expect-ing. She is surprised that the police have access to such information, and that Ebba was allowed to tell her, but knowing the islands, she is aware that rules are often ignored. She remembers when she had conjunctivitis as a child, and her mother went to get some drops from the chemist. The woman who served her already knew Alicia was off school with an eye infection. Her class teacher had told the other kids to keep away from her as it was very infectious.

'This island mentality is something else,' she remembers her mother muttering as she applied the lotion to Alicia's eyes. At the time, Alicia didn't understand why Hilda was so upset, but as she got older, she understood how suffocating it could be when everyone knew everyone else's business. It was the reason she eventually left to go to university and never returned.

Until now.

FORTY-FIVE

Patrick sits in the deserted offices of *Ålandsbladet*. He knows that Harri is struggling to make money from the newspaper and that the advertising takings are down, making it necessary to slim down the operation, but it seems there is never anyone around.

It's true that it's the height of summer, and most people are on holiday, but it seems Harri is relying on just Alicia and a couple of interns to produce the paper at the moment. He looks at the editor in his glass cubicle. He's written most of the articles for the latest edition himself, with the ads and announcements coming from two members of staff working alongside the personnel woman on the second floor.

Patrick glances at his watch. It's nearly 2pm. If Alicia doesn't show up, he'll have to produce a piece on the Romanian boy's death on his own and he has absolutely nothing to go on. Yesterday Harri asked him to help Alicia out, but there was no mention of a fee. It is unbelievable how they use him. The only reason he comes to the offices in summer is to make himself useful. This year, there's also Alicia.

Alicia.

He was hoping he could take her out to lunch again, even take her to the flat, but there's no sign of her. Where could she be?

He doesn't want to go back to their summer cottage. Now that negotiations on the divorce settlement have started, the atmosphere at the Eriksson's villa is even more stifling. Even spending time with his daughters is fraught with the possibility of being told how useless he is. Only last week, when he was there for a night, his mother-in-law had stomped into the kitchen to get a glass of water and found him giving the girls ice creams. 'Those will spoil their appetite for dinner,' she had said, not even glancing at Patrick, before floating back to the vast living room.

Magda had been in the kitchen too, preparing dinner, and Patrick had made a conspiratorial face to her behind his mother-in-law's back. They all laughed, including the girls, but Patrick had had enough of his in-laws. When he was rid of them, he would give Sara and Frederica as many ice creams as they wanted. So what if they have too many sweet things every now and then? Patrick spent his days helping out at the newspaper to avoid being constantly humiliated. But being near Alicia was also a bonus. He is surprised how quickly he's become infatuated by her. Just the thought of her face near to his makes him smile. The Midsummer night was magical too. He couldn't remember the last time he'd wanted to kiss anyone so badly. He needs to convince her he is serious.

He sees Alicia enter the office before she spots him. He gets up from the desk where he has been waiting and walks toward her.

'What happened to you?' Patrick says. He's trying to keep his voice level, but judging by Alicia's face, his words have too much urgency in them.

Alicia shrugs, but she looks happy, which is strange. Patrick cannot help but smile in return.

'You've had good news?'

Alicia regards Patrick for a moment. She looks over to where the editor is sitting. Patrick knows he has his door open.

'It's complicated,' she says in a low voice.

'Try me,' Patrick replies, moving closer to her. He takes in her scent of flowers and sunshine. It's just the two of them in the vast office, but Patrick knows the editor can hear everything through the open door. 'Let's have a coffee,' he says, indicating with one hand the small kitchen to the side of the office.

Alicia nods.

Inside, Patrick and Alicia sit opposite one another. Alicia, taking a deep breath, begins to talk.

Alicia didn't think she would blurt everything out to Patrick, but she realizes she has a dilemma. The only thing she could write about Daniel would be an interview with Frida on what sort of person her friend Daniel had been. She decides to tell Patrick the truth.

'Wow,' Patrick says when she's finished. 'I thought she was just a bit fat,' he says as if to himself.

Alicia slaps him on the arm, but she can't help the smile that keeps spreading over her face since Frida told her the news.

'Who's the father?' Patrick asks. When he sees Alicia's expression, he opens his mouth, then closes it and nods, 'Of course, I get it now!'

Alicia can't say anything. Talking to Patrick about Frida and the baby has made it even more real to her. Plus she doesn't know if Frida will mind her sharing the news. Although, it will soon be visible to everyone.

She realizes she doesn't care about the paper, the story or anything except protecting the baby. She's close to tears, happy tears, and instead of saying anything more, she bites her lip.

'OK?' Patrick says, leaning back in the chair.

At that very moment, Harri steps into the kitchen.

'This is very cozy,' he says.

'Just talking about the case,' Patrick says and Alicia nods.

After the editor has left, Patrick and Alicia write their thousand words without mentioning anything about Daniel's personality. They decide to simply say that he had friends on the islands and worked on Uffe's farm. The decision to mention Uffe was difficult. In the end, Patrick convinced Alicia that they had to give Harri something.

FORTY-SIX

When Patrick and Alicia walk out into the late afternoon sunshine, they are tired but relieved. It had been hard to convince Harri that the article contained everything they knew about the death of that poor boy. She could tell the editor sensed there was something they weren't telling him.

When they're outside, Patrick takes Alicia's hand. 'Look I know you don't believe me, but Mia and I are over.'

For a moment she doesn't say anything, doesn't even look at him. But she doesn't remove her hand from his either. When, at last, she lifts her pale eyes up to him, he has to fight the urge to kiss her. Instead he says, 'Why don't you let me take you out to dinner? I know a fantastic place.'

She gazes at him and hesitates. 'I don't know. I'm not dressed for going out.'

Seeing his chance, he moves a little closer to her, making sure he doesn't lose eye contact. 'It's a place in the archipelago used by sailors, so no one dresses up to go there. They cook freshly caught fish and have their own smoker for *abborre*.'

He knows most islanders who live abroad miss the local delicacy of wood-smoked perch. The fish taste different here, sweeter than the European species, because it swims in the brackish waters of the Baltic.

Alicia bites her lower lip and again Patrick has to control himself not to bend down, take her into his arms and press his mouth onto hers. But he has to be patient. He sees she's tempted.

'I'll behave, I promise,' he says and grins.

And that does it.

'OK,' Alicia says.

Alicia is again sitting next to Patrick on his boat. This time she's wearing more suitable clothes, a pair of jeans and one of Patrick's jumpers over her T-shirt. When she saw the Henri Lloyd logo on the navy knit, she smiled, but pulled it over her head anyway. The garment smells of him, and wearing it makes Alicia feel excited and safe at the same time. They've passed Sjoland canal and Uffe's farm, and her sauna cottage. Patrick said it would take about 45 minutes to reach the small Getviken island where the restaurant is. He sends a text to the owner to make a reservation.

'As I thought, Bertil's got freshly caught *abborre* in the smoker,' Patrick told Alicia as he read the reply.

Alicia smiles at Patrick now. They are traveling fast, so there's no point in trying to talk. Instead Alicia enjoys the fresh sea breeze on her face and leans back to catch the rays of the sun.

The restaurant is as remote as Patrick had promised. Five or six tables are set in a small wooden building. The owner, Bertil, a gray-haired, shortish man with a round belly, greets Patrick and Alicia at the jetty with a wide smile. Alicia wonders if he knows Mia and whether everyone on the islands will know about Patrick and her after tonight, but she decides not to care, if Patrick doesn't. Which he doesn't seem to. Instead, he jokes and laughs with Bertil, whose lined, weather-beaten face reflects a life spent fishing in the waters around his island. He takes Alicia and Patrick around the back of the restaurant to the smoker, where the delicious smell of charred fish fills Alicia's nostrils. Suddenly she's famished.

Patrick places his hand protectively around Alicia's waist. 'Alicia here has come back home just because of this.'

Bertil laughs and Alicia explains that she's lived in London for the past eighteen years.

'Oh,' Bertil exclaims. 'Well, you won't get anything like this in England,' he says and adds, 'Now you two, aren't you thirsty after your long journey? Go inside and Miriam will give you something to drink. I'll bring these little fellows in when they're ready.'

Alicia cannot remember when she last enjoyed food so much. Before the *abborre*, which is served with new pota- toes covered in chopped dill, Bertil brings them *gravad siik*. The whitefish is marinated in salt, sugar and pepper to perfection and goes perfectly with the sweet rye bread and homemade butter, which Bertil proudly explains is his wife, Miriam's, specialty.

To Alicia's relief, the restaurant is almost full with tourists. There's a large group of men from Finland who've arrived in three sailing boats, which are docked at the small harbor, as well as two other couples. Everyone is served at the same time from a small selection of freshly cooked dishes made from locally sourced fish and meat. The Finns take schnapps and sing drinking songs, and Alicia, Patrick and the other couples occasionally join in.

They sit opposite each other in a corner of the fishing cottage. The table has a small candle in the middle, but the place is shrouded in half-light due to the low ceiling and tiny windows. All evening, Patrick's eyes are fixed on Alicia's. It's impossible not to be affected by the general happy mood of the place, or Patrick's attentions.

As they are served coffee, she wants to ask Patrick so many questions about himself, Mia, and the situation. But she doesn't want to break the mood of the evening. She refuses dessert, but when she hears it's homemade *Åland's Pannkaka,* she gives in and agrees to share a portion with Patrick.

After the meal, which Patrick insists on buying, they step into the pale light of the day's end. Patrick takes her hand and they gaze beyond the small jetty to the sea. Boats rock gently against their moorings and the scenery is even more breathtaking than at home in Sjoland. The sun is going down, suffusing the horizon in flaming orange, red and yellow. The light is reflected on the still water. There is no wind at all, and the sea beyond the cove has a surface like glass.

'Shall we have a swim?' Alicia asks Patrick. It's a spur of the moment suggestion. Really, she wants to talk to Patrick about his marriage, what will happen to his daughters, and about Frida and her pregnancy. But the evening, after such an incredible day with the news of the baby, has been so wonderful that she decides the conversation can wait. Perhaps Patrick will tell her about his future plans of his own accord, when he is ready.

She can see he's surprised by her suggestion, but says, 'Wait here. There's a place around the back that's private.' He walks down to the jetty and disappears inside his boat. A moment later he comes out carrying two large striped towels and a blanket.

Neither has brought swimming costumes.

When they get to the small rocky cove, Patrick spreads the blanket on a little grassy mound between two large rocks. He gives Alicia a grin and takes his shirt off. Following his example, Alicia pulls her jeans down and her T-shirt over her head. She doesn't dare to look at Patrick when she unhooks her bra and slips her knickers off. Instead she runs into the water and shrieks as the cold hits her calves and legs. She should be used to it by now, she thinks, as she lowers herself down and begins to take long strokes, her body relaxing into the cooler temperature of the sea. Suddenly, Patrick pops up from under the water and takes hold of her. They kiss, until breathless.

'We need to swim, it's too cold,' Alicia says.

'You think so?' Patrick says and grins. He's staring at

her nipples, which are half-covered by the water. 'I rather like the effect.'

Alicia laughs and splashes water over him. She turns toward the open sea and begins to make strong strokes. As usual, the sensation of the water on her body calms and excites her in equal measure. It's almost too pleasurable.

After the swim, they sit wrapped up in the towels, watching a seagull bullying a flock of smaller birds. The only sounds are the bird calls and some music from the restaurant on the other side of the island. Patrick leans over to kiss Alicia and she lets him. But when he begins to explore her naked body beneath the towel, she stops. 'What if someone sees us?'

'Hmm?' Patrick murmurs, not hearing what she said. He's caressing her left nipple while kissing her neck, his other hand moving downwards from her belly.

Alicia pushes him gently away. 'Let's get dressed and take the boat somewhere more secluded?'

FORTY-SEVEN

Liam drives along the road from Mariehamn to Sjoland, thankful that he doesn't have to stop to wait for the bridge to open. He sees from the dashboard that it's quarter to midnight, yet the horizon is still pale yellow. The nightless nights always take him by surprise. In London it would be pitch-black now—except for the streetlights of course. He's pleased how quickly he'd disembarked. He is sure they got stuck in long lines in the past, though to be honest, he doesn't really remember. Because he didn't plan this trip, he'd ended up paying over the odds for the flight to Stockholm, and for the car at Stockholm airport. He'd got to the ferry port in Kapellskär just as the previous ferry was leaving, so had a long wait for the last transport of the day. For some reason he felt he needed to get onto the islands that same night.

During his long four-hour wait he had time to think as well as sleep. Several times he wondered if he should send Alicia a message, but he resisted the temptation. He knew he had let her down with his earlier behavior, and leaving like he did, so he wasn't sure she would want to see him now. It was best to surprise her, he thought.

He wonders now, as he makes his way along the deserted road toward Hilda and Uffe's place, if—once again—he is being stupid, coming after his wife like this, but he thinks he needs to give it one more chance. He knows he's been a fool, having an affair behind Alicia's back. She is the one he wants. He needs her, especially now.

He's glad to see a light in the sauna cottage as he turns into the little lane. He thinks back to all those summers they spent here, where he never felt at ease, but could see how happy it made Alicia to be home. He could understand her delight in how Stefan took to the islands; almost as if he had been born there. Perhaps Liam was jealous of the close connection between his son and wife? He doesn't know. All he is certain of now is that he was stupid not to see how much Alicia will always mean to him, and how much the islands mean to Alicia. But he is here now. He will even try to enjoy the sauna, if that's what it takes to get Alicia back.

'Do you know that you just had sex with a soon-to-be grandmother?' Alicia says and laughs. She's in Patrick's arms and for the first time since she doesn't remember when she feels almost completely happy. They are in Alicia's sauna cottage, lying on her sofa bed, listening to the evening chorus of the birds outside. After leaving Getviken, Alicia surprised herself by suggesting they drive back to Sjoland. She's fed up with going around worrying what people think. She will tell Uffe and Hilda the truth if they see her with Patrick. She can't wait to tell them about Frida's pregnancy anyway. After the news about Stefan's baby, she's almost giddy with the possibilities for the future. And Patrick could be part of her life here.

Patrick squeezes Alicia closer and kisses the top of her head. Alicia is amazed how quickly they fell back into each other's arms, and how quickly she felt comfortable being naked with a new man. She lifts herself up on her elbows to look at him, to make sure he's real. With the movement, she reveals her breasts and Patrick gives them an approving glance.

Laughing, Alicia takes hold of his chin and says, 'What again?'

'Well, if you insist?'

As they start to kiss, they are interrupted by the sound of an engine outside. Wheels are crunching against the small lane Uffe prepared with hardcore.

FORTY-EIGHT

When Liam knocks on door, he is nervous. There's a blind covering the windows overlooking the decking, but he can make out movements inside. Next, he hears steps on the wooden floorboards of the sauna cottage.

'Who is it?' Alicia says through the door.

'It's me, Liam.'

There is a long silence, and then more commotion inside. Liam doesn't understand. It sounds as if Alicia is talking to someone, but the voices are low and Liam can't hear what is being said. It sounds as if they are speaking in Swedish.

Eventually, Alicia opens the door. The first thing Liam sees is the unmade sofa bed. To one side of it, stands a man, wearing a white shirt, rumpled and unbuttoned, with a pair of chinos, with bare feet. He thinks he recognizes him, but he can't process who he is. Liam turns to Alicia, who is also barefoot, wearing a long striped Marimekko T-shirt. The shirt, or dress, barely covers

Alicia's buttocks. Liam notes how bronzed and slender her legs are, and then how ruffled her long hair is. She looks blonder and her face has a healthy tan, like the rest of her body. Is that a blush on her cheeks?

And then it hits him. Suddenly he realizes what he is seeing. As if in slow motion, he notices the man is putting on his shoes, picking up a set of car keys and walking toward Alicia, who is still holding the door open to Liam. The man bends down to kiss her—his wife, for God's sake —on the lips (*lips!*).

'Are you sure you are OK?' the man asks Alicia.

She nods and touches his arm briefly. Intimately.

The man nods to Liam, with a serious face, brushing past Liam's jacket and disappearing out of the door. Bizarrely the first thought that comes to Liam is where this man's car could be, but he ignores his stupid old brain and tries to concentrate on understanding what his eyes are seeing in front of him.

Alicia, his wife, is looking at him. The room is messy, and filled with the sofa bed. The duvet is half on top of the sheets and half on the floor; one of the two pillows is also on the floor. There's a bottle of beer on the floor too, with a glass of wine on the narrow coffee table, which has been pushed to the side of the room. Liam tries to remember when he last saw a scene like this and suddenly realizes he is thinking about his son's bedroom when he'd had friends over. They too had been drinking beer and wine, and there was a similar mess. He remembers telling them off and asking where the alcohol had come from.

'You've turned into a teenager, now, have you?' he asks Alicia.

What a stupid thing to say.

He hears the sarcasm in his voice and tries to calm himself. His thoughts are filled with the image of the man and Alicia in that bed, drinking beer and wine.

'Are you coming in?' Alicia now says. She has her arms crossed over her body, no longer holding onto the door.

Liam realizes he hasn't moved from the threshold of the sauna cottage, so he steps inside the messy room.

Alicia removes some clothing from one of the wood-framed chairs. Liam remembers joking that they must be pre-war, because the woollen fabric was so threadbare. Now his jibe seems childish, or even visceral, a betrayal of his deep resentment against Alicia's close connection to these islands.

Betrayal, that's the word.

Alicia is sitting on the bed, facing Liam. She's dumbfounded by his sudden appearance. Acutely aware of the shortness of her night-shirt, she tugs at the hem, and then lifts her legs up and tucks them underneath herself. She thinks with horror about the scent of sex that must surely linger in the air of the small cottage and fidgets with her wedding band. She's only aware of this because she sees Liam glance at her finger. She stops and forces herself to speak.

'You should have let me know you were coming.'

'Clearly,' Liam replies in the crisp, cool, sarcastic tone she used to hate.

Alicia regards her husband with what she hopes is a

cool gaze. What right does he have to sit there and judge her? Obviously, it would have been better if he hadn't walked in on her and Patrick, but really, she has every right to find someone to comfort her, considering he has been sleeping with another woman for months.

'How's your little nurse?' Alicia asks. She is angry now and wants Liam to understand that she does not feel any shame. Why would she?

She can see her words take him aback. He presses his hair down at the back of his head and looks away from Alicia, toward the small window at the side of the cottage. Alicia sees he's wearing his light wool 'traveling' jacket over a crisp checked shirt, a pair of chinos and his old brown Dockers on his feet. He's not wearing any socks, and Alicia can see a few dark hairs peeking out between the tops of his shoes and trouser legs. He looks younger and slimmer, and she wonders briefly, out of old habit and before she can stop herself, if he's been feeding himself. He looks tired too, with untidy (for him) longish hair that lands on the collar of his jacket and half covers his ears. Alicia's anger subdues a little. How familiar Liam's athletic shape is, as he sits opposite her in the small sauna cottage, where they often slept.

'It's over,' Liam says, lifting his eyes to Alicia.

'That's alright then,' Alicia says. It's her turn to be sarcastic, but she regrets her words as soon as they've come out.

Liam is slumped in the chair. He's holding onto the old wooden arm rests. It's as if what he witnessed as he entered the sauna cottage is only just registering. His eyes are downcast and he looks crestfallen when he says, 'I don't suppose it matters now.'

Alicia then takes a snap decision.

'We're going to be grandparents.'

Liam straightens his back and stares at Alicia.

'What do you mean?'

'It's a miracle, I know. Frida, a girl from Åland, was Stefan's girlfriend and she is about to have his baby.'

Alicia tells Liam about the newspaper office and about Frida, Daniel, and how she found out. When Liam doesn't say anything, Alicia moves toward her husband and squats next to him, taking his hand. 'I know it's a lot to take in and believe me, I was equally shocked. Frida is a lovely girl, a bit different, but a really nice young woman at the bottom of it all. She is eight months gone, so there's not long to wait now. Just imagine, we will have a little Stefan in our lives!'

'You've got yourself a job here? Does that mean you are planning to stay? And leave me?'

Alicia gets up and goes back to the bed again.

'I'm not sure. It's a long story. I literally popped in to enquire about freelance work and they offered me a part-time job.' She is smiling, but seeing Liam's serious face, she adds, 'I didn't know what to do after you left. I didn't want to come back to London, so ... but that's not important now. We are going to become grandparents. If you wish to be involved, that is.'

Liam brushes his hand over his face. 'Are you sure this isn't some kind of ... hoax, or joke, or something?'

Alicia takes a deep breath.

'Never mind,' she says, trying to control her voice,

which has suddenly started trembling. 'You don't need to believe any of it.' Alicia is quiet for a moment while she fights the tears that are welling up inside. 'For me, it's the most wonderful thing that has happened to me since ...' Alicia swallows and manages to keep her composure. 'I will welcome this little miracle into the world and into my life, but I know for certain we can do it without you.'

With this Alicia gets up and goes over to the door. 'And now I think you should leave.'

Liam sits in his rental car, driving toward Mariehamn. He is numb and shocked by the man he found with Alicia. He just cannot process it in his mind. How could she have begun an affair with someone? And so soon? Liam knows he hasn't got any rights to Alicia, even if she still is his wife, but he is devastated that she has betrayed him.

He is tired and suddenly enormously hungry. As he approaches the junction that will take him into the city, he sees a van selling Finnish meat pastries and hot dogs. He drives over and orders a pie with a sausage. There are a few youngsters, swaying and clearly drunk, eating hot dogs out of greaseproof paper. They watch silently as Liam pays and takes his pie to eat inside the car.

He wonders if his son used to come to this fast-food joint when they were here on holiday, while he and Alicia were sleeping in their bed in the sauna cottage, unaware of his nightly escapes. Could it be true, Liam wonders? Could there really be a girl here who was impregnated by Stefan?

But when?

He knows that the last time Stefan was on the islands was in August last year. Whatever happened must have happened in the late fall. Is this girl (was it the same girl Stefan had fallen in love with when he was fifteen?) claiming that Stefan traveled over just before he was killed? Or did she come over to London? That is more likely, Liam thinks, but he shakes his head at the thought. How easy it is for someone to claim to a grieving mother that her son has miraculously made her pregnant? Surely it must be a cruel sting.

Liam decides that he will not travel back to London on the early morning ferry as planned, but will take a room in one of the hotels in town and find out the truth. He will need help. Perhaps Hilda will help him? She has always had a soft spot for Liam. But first he needs to get some sleep.

As soon as Liam has shut the door behind him, Alicia puts her head in her hands and takes a few deep breaths. She is so angry and also sad that she doesn't know whether to scream, laugh or cry. Instead she gets up and pummels the bed with one of the pillows from the floor. A ping on her phone stops her.

'*Are you OK?*'

The message is from Patrick. Alicia stares at the words displayed at the top of the screen. She asked Patrick to leave when she discovered it was Liam standing outside the sauna cottage. She now wishes she hadn't. And then she realizes that she wouldn't talk to him about how she is feeling even if he was there. What is she feeling? She is so confused that she doesn't know her own mind.

Patrick will not understand the connection she has with Liam. In spite of everything, their marriage has been a good one. Liam was a good father, he is kind, generous and intelligent. And even funny. Or, at least they used to laugh a lot together before. Before Stefan was taken away from them.

She knows the affair with the nurse is partly her fault. She drove him away, not letting him into her own grief. Or comfort him in his. All she could do was keep herself breathing through the first days, weeks and months after the accident. Connie always says during their sessions that breathing is natural, but Alicia never feels she can take the air flowing through her body for granted. It's getting easier now, but only since she's been here, at home on the islands.

What about Liam? Is he telling the truth about the nurse? Is it finished? And why was he so skeptical about Stefan's baby? Now her anger has abated, she hopes Liam's reaction to the news about Frida and her pregnancy was simply shock, and that with time he'll come around. He would be a wonderful grandfather, as he was a father, Alicia is sure of it. And turning up like he did tonight must mean that he wants their marriage to work.

Alicia puts her head in her hands and takes deep breaths. She goes over to the small sink and fills a glass with water. When she gets back to the bed, she sees her phone. She wants to give Liam one more chance. Alicia finds his number on her phone and types in a message. But when she's done, a message pings.

'I'm out of town during the day tomorrow, but I need to see you. Meet me 6pm at the jetty in East Harbor. Kisses, Patrick.'

Alicia looks at the message and shakes her head. How can he think that they will continue seeing each other while Liam, who is still her husband, is in town? She can't decide what to say, so she resolves to get some sleep and reply in the morning. She turns the lights off. In the semi-dark, listening to the wildfowl calling to each other, she wonders how her life has got so complicated. Then when she remembers the shape of Frida's round belly, she thinks about the baby, and how wonderful it will be to hold a small version of Stefan in her arms. She has been given a new chance at life and she is going to take it. If she has to carry on alone, without Liam, or Patrick, so be it.

FORTY-NINE

Svarta Katten used to be Stefan's favorite café in Mariehamn when he was little. He grew out of the place when he hit his teens, but Alicia is certain he still had a soft spot for the *Ålands pannkaka*, the oven-baked semolina pudding with jam that the little café was famous for. As she climbs the stone steps to what is really just a sand-rendered residential house, she remembers the last time they visited the place together. She smiles as she recalls that Stefan wanted coffee instead of Fanta with his pudding, and how this simple request made Alicia realize her boy was growing into a young man. Alicia takes a deep breath and selects an open cheese and salad sandwich from the glass cabinet.

Inside the café, she sees that Frida is already sitting at one of the sofas in the largest of the small rooms that make up *Svarta Katten*. The interior is a little like a grandmother's house, with several tiny parlors leading into one another, with mis-matching sofas, comfy chairs and tables scattered through the small spaces. Lace curtains hang from the wood-framed windows, increasing the sense of being in someone's home rather than a café.

Alicia had the idea to meet here last night. She knew Liam would know the place and she wanted him to remember how much Stefan loved the islands.

'How are you feeling?' Alicia says as she sits down opposite Frida. She pushes the sandwich toward the girl. 'In case you didn't have time for breakfast.'

She wants to kiss Frida on the cheek, but she's afraid she may be appearing too familiar, or oppressive. They don't know each other well, after all. The sandwich is enough of a risk, she thinks, but Frida accepts it without a word. Although they have the large belly, now visibly a baby bump, very much in common, they only met a few weeks ago.

Frida doesn't smile when she nods and says, 'Yeah, OK.' She does, however, add, 'Thanks,' as she takes the sandwich.

She's wearing a green dress with black capri-length leggings underneath. She has large yellow hoops in her ears and her signature Doc Martens on her feet. This time they are red. With her blue hair, she is not unlike a human kaleidoscope. Alicia smiles at Frida. It seems she is no longer trying to hide her pregnancy, which Alicia takes as a good sign.

'Have the police been in touch?' Alicia asks, but Frida shakes her head.

'I've decided to go round there after I've had this,' Frida says, tucking into the open sandwich.

'That's a good idea. They just want to find out when

you last saw Daniel and that kind of stuff. If you want, I can come with you?'

Frida regards Alicia for a moment, but before she has time to reply Liam appears in the doorway, carrying a tray with coffee and a plate of *Ålands Pannkaka*.

He looks unshaven and dishevelled, with red eyes, but Alicia realizes she is glad to see him. She's glad to have his support with Frida.

Liam can't believe what he sees in front of him. He smiles at Alicia and nods to the girl, who seems to be wearing every color of the rainbow—including in her hair. And this person is supposed to have had a loving relationship —or a relationship at least—with his son? No way, he thinks, and sits down next to Alicia.

'This is Stefan's father, Liam,' Alicia says in English, and the girl stares at him. Her round face doesn't betray much, although perhaps there's mistrust around the corners of her eyes? Liam is amazed how somebody like that could have fooled Alicia. She is an astute journalist. Even if she hasn't been a full-time investigative journalist since Stefan's death, she's still very aware of what is going on in the world. How can she be so gullible? Thank goodness Liam came over before any more damage could be done, or any money has changed hands.

'So you knew our son?' Liam asks, trying to take the edge out of his voice.

'What's this?' Frida's English is only slightly broken. She doesn't look at either of them but lifts a canvas holdall from under the table and gets up. It's a difficult maneuver because of her extended belly, which has got trapped between the curved back velour sofa and the coffee table.

'Frida,' Alicia gets up too and tries to take the girl's hand. She speaks in Swedish, 'Don't go! Liam came over last night and I thought you two should meet.'

Frida wrangles her arm out of Alicia's grip and continues to make her way out of the café. Now a pair of young tourists have got wind of their situation, and the English being spoken, and are staring at Liam and Alicia. They say something in Swedish to the girl, but she shakes her head and almost runs out of the room.

'For goodness sake!' Alicia says to Liam and runs after the girl.

The two youngsters, two lads about Stefan's age, continue to stare at Liam, who sips his coffee and cuts a slice of the sickly pudding. He tries to smile at the boys reassuringly. 'Nothing to worry about.' They go back to their own conversation, and Liam puts down his fork. He bought the *Ålands Pannkaka* for Alicia's sake, to show her he remembered it was Stefan's favorite, but it's no use to him now. It's far too sweet for him. Like so many things in this place, he just doesn't get it. How could anyone think the milky desert, something between a rice pudding and a French clafoutis, but with a skin as thick as a rhino's, could be considered a delicacy?

Liam waits for ten minutes, aware of the glances from his young neighbors. It's embarrassing being left like that in a café, not eating his *pannkaka*, he thinks. After another five minutes, he decides to make a dignified exit.

FIFTY

Although the sun is blazing down from a cloudless sky, the wind has got up when Alicia comes out of the *Ålandsbladet* office that afternoon. 'Alicia!'

Squinting against the sun, Liam is standing a few paces away, across the small road, by the corner of Arkipelag Hotel. Is that where he is staying, Alicia wonders. He's still wearing the same chinos he had on that morning, and is holding the same jacket in his hand, but he's changed into a dark green T-shirt. The shirt shows off Liam's muscular arms, something she used to find attractive. It was Alicia's favorite shirt. Is that why he's wearing it now?

'What are you doing here?' Alicia asks when she reaches him.

They are standing facing each other. Alicia glances around; she's afraid Patrick will pop out from somewhere. He's been bombarding her with messages all day. She managed to reply evasively to one of them, while also fending off the editor's requests for news of the investigation into the Romanian boy's death. Harri also asked after Patrick, who didn't turn up at the paper that day. Alicia and the editor had been the only reporters there. Frida had called in sick again, and Alicia wondered if the girl had come clean about her situation, because Harri didn't seem to worry about her absence as much as he did about Patrick's. It was the strangest situation Alicia had come across: Patrick, who didn't even work for the paper seemed to be held more accountable than the permanent staff.

So much for my part-time post, Alicia thinks, but she doesn't say anything to Harri. She needs the job in Åland more than ever now, if she is to stay and support Frida with the baby on her own. Liam's performance in *Svarta Katten* that morning had been appalling. And infuriating.

'I would like to talk with you,' Liam says. He glances at his watch. It's just past 4pm. 'We could have a beer?'

Alicia looks up at Liam. She's forgotten how tall he is, and how comfortable she feels with him. Although she's still angry at the bloody man for frightening Frida. But she understands that Liam has a lot to cope with suddenly. And she feels guilty. She should have at least told him she was moving on with the job. And Patrick. Possibly.

As it is, he's had a completely wasted journey to the islands. Unless he wants to see Frida again, that is.

'I was planning to see if my mother can give me a lift home, and then call Frida,' Alicia says. After the morning's meeting with the girl, Alicia has decided against pressurizing her with messages during the day. But she needs to find out if Frida has been to see the police, and how she is feeling. And if she has told Harri about the baby.

'It's Frida I wanted to talk to you about,' Liam says. His voice is calm and he looks serious, but his expression is open and his eyes have lines of concern around them. He seems different from how he'd been that morning. Perhaps he's getting used to the idea of Stefan's baby?

'Ok, I'll message Hilda to say I don't need a lift.'

'It's already done, I spoke to her earlier in the shop,' Liam says, and he takes hold of Alicia's elbow to lead her across the little garden and down the steps toward the East Harbor. *As if she is one of his patients.*

'What, you saw my mum?' Alicia is flabbergasted. Liam and Hilda have always got on well, but seeing his mother-in-law without Alicia would have been awkward in the circumstances. Of course, neither Hilda nor Uffe knew about her involvement with Patrick, but at least Hilda was aware (and Alicia assumed she had told Uffe) that Liam had left the islands because of a row, and that their marriage was in trouble. But neither knew about the baby.

If there was one thing Liam hated more than anything else, it was an awkward situation. A face-to-face conversation with Hilda today would rank as very uncomfortable in Liam's mind, she's sure of it.

'Is that OK?' Liam asks, not answering Alicia's question and pointing toward the floating restaurant, *von Knorring*. Liam and Alicia had often gone for a drink in the pub on the top deck during their holidays here.

Alicia glances toward the jetties and spots Patrick's

boat. It seems to be empty and locked up. She lets out a sigh of relief. A confrontation between the two men is the last thing she needs now.

'Shall we go up to the top?' Liam is behaving very strangely, Alicia thinks, but she nods in agreement and they ascend the wooden steps to the upper deck of the old steamer. The ship is all shiny mahogany, with tilting wooden decks, round brass portholes, and tables made out of barrels. While Alicia selects a seat at the stern, which is covered and a little more private, Liam heads for the bar. Before he goes, he asks Alicia, 'What will you have? White wine or *Lonkero*?'

Alicia smiles. She's touched that Liam remembers the Finnish bitter lemon and gin drink.

'OK, I'll have a *Lonkero*,' she says and smiles.

'Cheers!' Liam says as he sits down. He is sounding far too cheerful for the circumstances. What on earth has got into him?

But Alicia doesn't want to say anything. She nods and pours her drink into a glass. She takes a sip of the drink. Boy, it tastes good. It's carbonated, bitter and sweet at the same time. She hasn't had a *Lonkero* since the first sauna evening. Usually Hilda buys cans and cans of it for her, but this year she seems to have forgotten. As has Alicia.

'How are you?' Liam asks. He looks deeply into Alicia's eyes in a way she cannot remember him doing for a long time. There's concern in his eyes again and suddenly Alicia wishes she could just lean her head on Liam's shoulder and tell him all her troubles. And share her excitement for Stefan's baby.

'You haven't asked me how I am—and meant it—for

a long time,' she says instead. She is speaking in a low voice, and Liam pushes his upper body over the solid wooden table to hear her better. Their eyes meet again, closer this time. Alicia can see Liam hasn't shaved. There are prickly dark hairs all over his chin and some on his neck. His lips look dry, but it's his eyes that have changed. Although she can see he's tired, there's an honesty, a clarity to the green pupils that she hasn't seen for months. He is really looking at Alicia, truly seeing her.

Alicia moves her face away. Guilt, which she thought she didn't possess, suddenly rises and she has an uncomfortable, constricting sensation in her chest. She can't breathe. *Don't think about Patrick. He's not important. Stefan's baby is.*

'You don't believe Frida, do you?' Alicia says when she lifts her eyes to Liam again.

Liam shifts on his seat and moves away from her. He takes a swig of his beer.

He's buying time.

'It is rather surprising, isn't it?' Liam says after a few moments have passed.

'I knew it,' Alicia says and feels a new anger rise inside her. It hits her head like a wave. 'But I don't care what you think.' Alicia gets up, but Liam takes her hand and pulls her gently back down.

'We need to talk about this, don't we?' he says equitably.

Alicia exhales. How can she not agree to his reasonableness? She sits down again, but folds her arms over her chest, refusing to look at her husband.

'C'mon.' Liam tries to calm her down by leaning into

her again and forcing her to look into his eyes. 'It's a shock, that's all,' he says in his reassuring doctor voice.

Alicia remembers how she used to love that confident, low tone that Liam used if Stefan was ill with a simple cold, or when he had chicken pox at the age of ten and Alicia had been beside herself with worry. When the rash first appeared, she'd been sure it was meningitis, but Liam convinced her that they should monitor him through the night, taking turns to take his temperature and peer into his eyes. The poor boy was exhausted the next day, when the first blisters developed and Liam could diagnose him with certainty. He'd also used that voice when he'd 'treated' her migraines when they first met, and many times since. That voice was one of the reasons Alicia fell in love with Liam.

'Just imagine if it had been the other way around? You would not have believed me if I said I'd found someone who was carrying our late son's baby without first looking into it properly? Your journalistic brain would want to analyse it and search for evidence first, right?'

Alicia knew Liam had a point.

'But we won't know the truth until the baby is born, and then we'd have to ask Frida to do a DNA test. I'm not convinced she'll be prepared to do that.'

Liam finishes his beer and nods at Alicia's bottle.

'One more?'

Alicia agrees to have another drink, and when she watches Liam at the bar, his familiar, muscular, shape leaning on the mahogany ledge, she wonders if he is right to be skeptical about Frida. He is, of course, right. Alicia had not looked for any evidence of Frida's claim. It *could* be a cruel con, of course. Perhaps the father was the Romanian boy, something impossible to prove without a test on the baby. The police will have Daniel's DNA, but could she convince Ebba to share that information with them? No, it would be better to compare the tests with her and Liam's DNA.

Suddenly Alicia remembers the envelope containing Stefan's hair that Liam had handed her the morning of Stefan's funeral. Alicia had spent that day in a daze, medicated up to her eyeballs with the pills Liam had prescribed her, but the one event she recalls clearly is when Liam came into their bedroom, dressed in a dark suit with a white shirt and black tie. The sight of him took Alicia's breath away. When he handed her the brown envelope and she looked inside and saw the blond strands of hair resting at the bottom of the envelope, she flung herself at him and they'd held each other close for a long time.

Alicia is brought back to the present by Liam sitting down in front of her. He places the drink on the table and takes Alicia's hand. 'Can we start again? My flight back to London isn't until next week, so I have a few days to sort things out.'

Alicia is surprised: Liam never takes time off at short notice. His foremost concern is his patients, often to the detriment of his family. Is that what Alicia has always felt? Second best to Liam's patients? Alicia shakes her head; no, she loves the passion he has for his profession. It is something she wishes she could have had too. An important career would have helped her after they lost Stefan.

'You staying at the Arkipelag?' Alicia asks.

Liam nods. He's looking down at his beer, still holding Alicia's fingers in his hand. His expression is serious when he lifts his head up. 'I want you back.' Liam looks deeply into Alicia's eyes. She can see he is holding his breath. Again she is taken aback by the new honesty, a fresh directness in his gaze.

'I'm not sure,' Alicia begins, but Liam interrupts her. 'I don't want you to make a decision now. I just wanted you to know how I feel.' Liam lets go of her hand and smiles at her.

'I don't know what to say.' Alicia takes a sip of her *Lonkero*.

Liam gives a little cough, and glancing at the silver Rolex watch he'd bought when he got his first consultant's job, says in a stronger, more practical voice, 'I thought we could eat here tonight? It'll give us some more time to talk?'

FIFTY-ONE

Patrick is standing on the jetty. The wind has turned to a northerly and he zips up his windbreaker. He scans the people walking on the wooden boardwalk, at the same time keeping an eye out for the steps that run down by the Arkipelag and the newspaper offices. He thinks about the meeting with his lawyers in Stockholm that day, but his mind goes back to Alicia and her body pressed against his.

There is something about her fragility when he touches her. The pale, soft skin on her belly, her inner thighs and her pert, small breasts. She reacts to him in a way that he's never experienced with a woman before. Patrick shifts position as he feels himself getting aroused. Where is she? He checks his watch and sees it's nearly quarter past. He pulls out his phone and checks WhatsApp. Alicia still hasn't answered his messages. He sent one on the ferry back from Stockholm, telling her how much he was looking forward to seeing her later. He didn't think the lack of a reply meant anything; he saw she'd read them and assumed she just didn't get a chance to message him back.

And then he sees them.

He spots Alicia first and then, just before he raises his hand to wave at her, very close behind, Liam emerges from the depths of the von Knorring restaurant. They are walking along the ship's dark wooden deck, side by side. They are laughing, and as they come to the small gangway connecting the boat to the old stone jetty Liam takes hold of Alicia's arm and helps her safely to the other side. On the jetty, he puts Alicia's hand in the crock of his arm. They proceed like this, like the married couple they are, toward Arkipelag Hotel and after a brief conversation at the door, go inside.

Patrick doesn't know what to do. Naturally, he knew Alicia would need to talk to Liam, after he turned up last night and saw them together. Earlier that evening, she'd told him how Liam had been unfaithful, just like Mia. She cried when she recounted how she had found out, through some woman working as a volunteer at the hospital. And that the affair had started after their son was so tragically killed. From how she behaved, and from her words, he assumed she would not want anything to do with the man. Yet here she was walking arm in arm, laughing—*laughing*—with him. Could she be that fickle? Or had he completely misread her?

Patrick starts to walk toward the hotel but is stopped by a sudden surge of traffic. He glances at his watch and realizes the last ferry of the day has arrived. He curses under his breath as he watches the cars speed along the coastal road. Most contain holidaymakers from Sweden, their vehicles laden with bags and luggage. Patrick thinks he's already sick of this bloody place after only a few weeks.

His thoughts return to his meeting in Stockholm that morning. Mia's family have offered him a handsome settlement, but they want him to leave the islands. He can keep his boat, and the flat in Mariehamn, but he's only to use it for eight weeks a year. They want him to stay in Stockholm, ideally. His lawyer, Harriet Wisktrand, told him that the settlement was very generous. But Patrick told the woman that he wanted to stay in Mariehamn. He wants shared custody of the girls.

Harriet had sighed at Patrick's comment. She'd told Patrick before that the Eriksson's counsel was a famous man, reputed to be one of the best divorce lawyers in Sweden.

'It's up to you, but I would say this is an unusually good offer,' she'd said, closing the file of papers. 'It depends how quickly you want this to be over, and how much you want to pay in legal fees,' she added.

That morning, leaving the lawyer's offices in Hammarby, a new area where high-rise offices overlooked the straits separating the southern part of Stockholm, Patrick went straight to see his boss at *Journalen*.

'I'm making it easy for you,' he told the balding editor.

'What?' he said, finally looking up from his computer screen. For the whole time Patrick had been standing in his office the man had been tapping at his keyboard. 'Sit down,' he said and he rolled his chair to face Patrick.

But his old editor had not managed to convince

Patrick to stay. Patrick would never get to write that prize-worthy article, so he might as well take the redundancy money and run. It was time he moved on.

FIFTY-TWO

Ebba stands in the doorway to the large newspaper office. She's leaning casually against the frame, looking at Alicia as if judging her. Alicia wonders how long she's been there, then gets up smartly and walks toward the police detective.

'So I hear you're going to be a grandmother,' Ebba says as she sits down at the round kitchen table.

'Coffee?' Alicia asks. She smiles at Ebba and nods, although having spent yesterday in Liam's company, she is less sure that the baby Frida is carrying is actually Stefan's.

'Any news on the Romanian boy, Daniel?' she asks Ebba as she sits down at the other side of the table from her old schoolfriend.

'Do you believe Frida is carrying your son's baby?' Ebba asks instead, and Alicia tries to suppress her annoyance at the woman's habit of answering a question with one of her own. And of interfering in her life.

'I guess so,' Alicia says, but seeing Ebba raise an

eyebrow, she adds, 'Yes, I do,' trying to sound more assertive.

'Hmm,' Ebba says. She regards Alicia and takes a sip from her mug of coffee. Her eyes do not leave Alicia's and once again Alicia feels she's the one under suspicion.

'The pregnancy and your son's fatherhood seem very convenient now you're back on the islands and your son no longer ...' Ebba stops mid-sentence as someone opens the door to the kitchen.

The policewoman, who's seated with her back to the window, facing the entrance to the small kitchen, raises her eyebrows, as if she is conducting an interview in her own office. But when she sees who it is, she says, rather gently after what Alicia thinks she's just inferred, 'Ah, Frida, how are you?'

Frida walks into the room. She nods, and says in a surly, teenage voice, 'OK.' She gives Alicia a glance, not catching her eye. Still pissed at me then, Alicia thinks and smiles. That tone reminds her so strongly of Stefan, but she's surprised at her overwhelming feeling of pleasure at the memory, rather than sadness. She recalls Stefan standing in their kitchen in London with his back to her, unwilling to accept something, or not wanting to show he agreed with her, or concede that she, his mother, had been right all along. The recollection is so strong and warm, that it catches her breath.

Ebba, as usual, notices something is going on. 'You OK there?'

Alicia nods and smiles at the policewoman, who's now gazing up at Frida. Alicia senses that the two have agreed on something, or that they have come to some kind of conclusion or resolution, but she doesn't wish to rock the boat with Frida by asking questions. Last night she made Liam promise that if she can convince Frida to meet with them before he leaves the islands, he will listen to Frida and not say a word.

Briefly, Alicia's thoughts go back to the previous night. It was good to spend time with Liam. He was attentive, listening to her talk about Stefan and Frida, and her worries about her mother's finances and rows with Uffe. And she'd been able to tell Liam about seeing the Romanian boy's body, and how it had brought back her grief, and her regret that she hadn't visited Stefan at the morgue.

'There was nothing to see,' Liam had said. His eyes had been sad and he'd taken Alicia's hands into his. They were in Liam's hotel room, sitting opposite each other in two armchairs. The room overlooked the East Harbor, where Alicia knew Patrick's boat was moored, but she didn't look toward the jetty where she knew Patrick would be waiting for her. She and Liam had decided to go upstairs when they saw the Arkipelag restaurant was hosting a karaoke evening. It was too loud for them to hear each other shout, let alone talk.

'I was protecting you,' Liam continued, leaning closer to Alicia.

Alicia lifted her eyes, which had been fixed on her fingers as they rested inside Liam's palms. How many times had they sat like this, but it had felt different, as if it was the first time Alicia had been held by Liam. She had examined his bony fingers, looking at the hairs growing on his hands. She had always loved his hands, the hands that had saved so many patients. The hands that had not, however, been able to save their son.

'But that was a decision I should have made myself,' Alicia whispered in a low tone. She wasn't going to cry even if talking about Stefan, with Liam particularly, brought a lump to her throat. But there were no tears. Perhaps she had finished crying and there was nothing left in her?

Liam's eyes were sad too, and Alicia could see there were tears welling up behind them.

'I'm sorry,' he had said, and for the first time in months, years, Alicia believed that he really, truly, was sorry.

All evening Liam had acted like the man she married all those years ago.

It was after 11pm when Liam put Alicia into a taxi outside the hotel. There had been a strong wind, and the riggings of the many boats in the harbor opposite had rattled against the masts. Alicia pushed away thoughts of Patrick's proximity. As she stood facing Liam, she wondered if he would try to kiss her goodbye; a gesture they had made hundreds, thousands of times during their marriage, but Liam had just squeezed her arms with his hands. When Alicia didn't resist his touch, he pulled her toward him and hugged her. She had promised to meet him for lunch at *Svarta Katten* the next day, today at one o'clock.

Suddenly the kettle comes to a boil, bringing Alicia back to the kitchen in the newspaper office. Nobody speaks a word while Frida prepares a herbal tea for herself. With a quick glance at Alicia and Ebba leaning over the small table, Frida then leaves the room.

Immediately after they hear the door close, Ebba turns to Alicia.

'We've solved the case, thought you might like to know.'

'Is this an official statement?'

'The police chief will give a press conference in about an hour,' Ebba glances at her watch, a large manly one that seems unnecessarily complicated for just time-keeping. Perhaps she's a diver, Alicia wonders.

'I might as well save you a trip to the HQ.'

Alicia scrambles to get her phone out; she didn't expect this. Everything is done so differently in Åland. She cannot imagine any police in London, or Stockholm for that matter, would permit an official press conference to be bypassed like this.

'Can I record you?' she asks when she has unlocked her phone.

Ebba nods. Alicia gazes at the policewoman's face, and realizes she looks triumphant.

'It was a simple accident.' The police woman says, crossing her arms over her chest.

After Ebba has left the newspaper office, Alicia puts her earphones in and listens to the policewoman's account of Daniel's accident. According to Ebba, the boy had been in a rowing boat on his own, fishing, when his rod had got stuck in the reeds around the little island where his body was found. They assumed he'd lost his balance and, with the weight of his cast, drowned. The breakthrough came when they found the rod floating above the line and discovered the deserted rowing boat in a cove a few kilometers away, where it had drifted. There was Daniel's DNA all over the vessel, and some marks from the cast on his leg. Frida had confirmed that the boy used to go fishing alone in the evenings, because he didn't have a local permit. According to Frida, he earned so little on Uffe's farm that he had to fish for food, but he also sold some of his catch to a few locals.

Alicia takes her headphones out and wonders if these locals included her stepfather. Poor lad, Alicia thinks, and wishes she could have helped him when he was still alive. She resolves to talk to Uffe; surely he must know he pays the boys too little?

At that moment Harri, the editor, walks past and seeing Alicia says, 'What are you doing here? There's a press conference at the police station!'

Alicia fills him in and plays Ebba's statement.

'This is the headline. On my desk in an hour?'

Alicia nods, replaces her headphones and starts transcribing Ebba's words.

FIFTY-THREE

Liam is sitting in the restaurant *Club Marin* overlooking the jetties of the East Harbor. He is scanning the boats, tied to the ten or so wooden piers, wondering which one belongs to Patrick. He's nursing a beer, at eleven o'clock in the morning. Stepping onto the decking of the sailing club, he had remembered the many times he'd come here with Alicia while Hilda babysat Stefan. He remembers the time when there was a live band, playing old Finnish classics and he had made a complete fool of himself trying to lead Alicia in a tango. She had laughed, pulling her head back, letting her long, blond curls fall down her back. Suddenly no longer minding his awkwardness on the dance floor, he'd taken hold of Alicia and spun her around the space.

Later, when Stefan was old enough, he and Stefan would come here together to admire the boats, leaving Alicia and Hilda to do their shopping. Those holidays had been good, and Liam knows he should have appreciated them more instead of complaining about the food, the rudeness of the locals, and the Finnish and Swedish tourists, or the high prices in the restaurants. He realizes that he didn't even notice how much his beer cost today.

His thoughts about the past come to a halt when he spots the man walking along the jetty. His gait is a confident one, reinforced by his tall and impressive stature. Patrick is slim, with wide shoulders and a rugged look that comes from his sun- and sea-bleached hair. Liam can see why any woman would fall for this guy. But Alicia? She is intelligent and Liam is surprised that she would go for looks alone. *Perhaps the bloke is an Einstein too, although looks and brains rarely go together,* Liam thinks, as he drowns the dregs of his beer.

Patrick doesn't spot Liam until he's standing next to him on the jetty. He can't help the sarcastic smile that forms on his lips; a jealous ex is just what he needs now!

'Can I talk to you?' Alicia's husband says in English. Patrick notices the man firming his foothold on the moving pier. He's standing with his feet artificially wide apart, with his chest pushed forward, as if he's preening for a fight.

Patrick nods and stretches out his hand, replying also in English, 'What about?'

The man ignores his hand and says, 'You know perfectly well.'

Patrick sighs.

'I want to talk to you about Alicia,' the man says after a short silence.

Patrick gestures toward his boat. They're standing

right by *Mirabella*. Patrick steps onboard and begins to uncover the cockpit seats. 'I promise we won't leave the jetty,' he says glancing back at Liam.

I can spot a non-sailor a mile off.

After a while Liam steps uncertainly onto the deck and resumes his legs-wide-apart stance. He goes to take hold of the gunwale, but sees him watching, so sits down instead. Patrick smiles and opens the fridge. He pulls out two cans of beer and hands one of them to the man. He opens the tin and takes a swig.

'So, what is it? You left your woman and now you want her back, that it?'

Liam holds the unopened can, looking down at his feet. He's wearing a pair of Dockers at least, Patrick thinks.

Trying to blend in and look the part. But anyone can see he's not from the islands by his tidy checked shirt tucked into his pristine chinos.

'We've been married for 18 years,' Liam says in a quiet, calm voice, looking directly at Patrick. When he doesn't reply, the man continues, 'And we were happy— very happy—until,' here he pauses for a moment. 'Until we lost Stefan.'

Patrick holds Liam's gaze. He can't but feel sorry for him. He read somewhere in a magazine article that *there are no words, not in English, Spanish, Arabic, or Hebrew, that have been invented to explain what it's like to lose a child.* How true, he thought, and the most overwhelming sense of gratitude, an almost spiritual experience, for having escaped that inexplicable grief, overwhelms him. He remembers how happy he and Mia had been at their luck. Of course, he now thinks bitterly, he didn't then know about their doomed future together. That reminds him of what he knows about Liam.

'So happy that you had have an affair?'

The expression on Liam's face tightens.

'You don't understand anything,' he says, getting up. His movement makes the boat shift, and he takes hold of the edge of the seat to keep his balance.

Patrick puts his can down and opens up his palms. 'Look, if Alicia had been happy, she wouldn't have turned to me,' he says. He has no desire to fight with the guy. 'She's her own woman.'

'That she certainly is,' Liam says and steps off onto the jetty. But instead of walking away, he turns back toward Patrick. 'She's been through a lot. I just don't want her to get hurt again. What I really wanted to ask you is how well do you know Frida Anttila?'

The sun is in Patrick's eyes and he lifts his hand to shade them in order to see the man's face. Liam is standing slightly above him.

'She's a good kid.'

'Would she lie about the baby's father?'

Patrick thinks for a moment, 'No, I don't think so. Why would she?'

Liam sighs and says, 'Money, of course.'

'She doesn't need money! Her dad is loaded.'

Liam stares at Patrick for a moment. 'Thank you for your time.'

'No worries,' Patrick says, but Liam doesn't hear him because he's already striding along the jetty toward the road and the low buildings in the center of Mariehamn.

FIFTY-FOUR

Hilda is shivering inside the shop in spite of the sun blazing down from a clear sky outside. It's one of those early July days when it was possible to imagine she was somewhere completely different, like Estepona in Spain, where Uffe had taken her during their first year together.

Hilda sighs. Before their marriage, when Uffe was attentive, booking the best table at the Arkipelag, they'd dance the night away. They would often be the last ones in their group of friends to go home.

Uffe has lived on the islands all his life, so knows almost everyone, and in those days they had a large social circle. Slowly, this circle had disappeared. One of the couples now lives in Spain half of the year, several have since divorced and moved to Finland or Sweden. The rest are such miserable company that Hilda refuses to go out with them. Uffe has the odd beer out with his old class-mates in town, but that's it.

The lack of a social life, however, is not the reason

Hilda is out of sorts this morning. Naturally the death of the Romanian boy has upset both of them, as has pressure to repay her loan to the Russians, which Uffe eventually agreed to foot. But it's the news that her son-in-law delivered yesterday afternoon that is playing on Hilda's mind. Hilda's English isn't as good as it used to be, but she got the main points of Liam's revelations, she's sure of that.

Hilda can't believe that her wonderful grandson would have associated himself with someone like Frida Anttila. She hasn't spoken to the girl much but has seen her around. She would be difficult to miss with her awful spiky hair and strange clothes. What is it with young women these days, Hilda wonders, and she shakes her head. She looks around her shop, at the beautiful things she has filled it with, none of which the girls in the town want to buy, it seems.

Uffe's ultimatum to shut the shop down at the end of the summer if her sales don't improve plays on her mind briefly, but the prospect of having a great-grandchild by that awful girl consumes her. She knows her mother of course.

Sirpa Anttila worked at Arkipelag as a waitress for years and years. She's from Finland like Hilda, but more than ten years younger. She had Frida at a late age and Hilda remembers the rumors about who the father was, fueled when she suddenly moved into one of the expensive new apartments in the center of town. A rich Russian oligarch, they said, but neither Hilda or Uffe ever saw her with anyone. She brought up Frida alone.

The poor woman became an alcoholic, although no

one knew until one day she had a stroke right in the middle of the Arkipelag restaurant. Uffe had taken Hilda for a rare night out just before Christmas a couple of years ago, when they heard the most awful noise. The tray of empty glasses and bottles that Sirpa had been carrying clattered to the floor and the woman fell down like a marionette whose strings had been cut. Frida, who had been in Stockholm Gymnasium studying for her Baccalaureate exams at the time, immediately came home to take care of her, but couldn't cope in the end. Sirpa Anttila was now in the old people's home in town. Hilda heard from one of Uffe's friends that the girl visits her mother every day and that the bills for the home are paid by an unknown benefactor.

Frida's Russian father?

Hilda pulls her sand-colored cashmere shawl tighter around her shoulders and thinks about the awful possibility that her great-grandchild may have Russian blood. And that's not all. Hilda is nowhere near old enough to become a great-grandmother! Alicia herself is only 38!

No, the whole affair cannot be true, Hilda thinks. Where is the evidence that Stefan had been with the girl? Hilda, nor Uffe, had ever seen them together. Plus, they were so young! Hilda suddenly remembers that she herself fell pregnant with Alicia at the age of seventeen. She gave birth two weeks after her eighteenth birthday.

But times were different then, she thinks. At least Alicia's father did the right thing and married her. That he then left when Alicia was only a baby is another matter. Good riddance, Hilda had thought at the time. He was a selfish pig of a man and Hilda is glad she kept him away from Alicia all these years. In the beginning, it hadn't been hard, but when Alicia began to grow up and start asking questions, Hilda had decided to tell her he was dead. It was as good as true, anyway. She had hidden all the letters that her old landlady in Finland had forwarded.

In those days it was so much easier, without all this internet activity. Luckily, in the end he gave up when she moved to Åland and married Uffe and was able to change her and Alicia's surname without him knowing.

But what to do about Frida and the baby? Liam had given Hilda quite a shock when he walked into the shop yesterday. She didn't know he'd come back to the islands, but she was glad. Alicia would be foolish to let such a good man go. A surgeon! But Liam hadn't wanted to talk about Alicia. No, he just said that there was no problem, that he and Alicia would be staying at the Arkipelag for a few days, to 'talk'. Imagine Hilda's surprise when she saw her daughter on Uffe's old bicycle in Sjoland, riding fast toward Mariehamn that same morning. She'd turned her nose up at that same bike only days before. She had a good mind to send a text to her daughter asking what an earth was going on, but Uffe convinced her not to interfere.

'Let them sort it out themselves,' he said over the rim of his breakfast coffee.

Uffe was a man of few words, so when he did speak, Hilda usually took notice, even if this particular dilemma had nothing to do with Uffe, strictly speaking.

In any case, when Liam had dropped the baby bomb in this same shop twenty-four hours earlier, she forgot all about her daughter's marital worries. She was so shocked she didn't ask many questions.

'Can you try to convince your daughter that this is not a cut and dried thing?' Liam said.

Hilda nodded, 'You think Frida's lying?'

Her son-in-law nodded, 'Most certainly.'

'But why?' Hilda had spluttered. Even if she isn't particularly fond of the idea, she couldn't for the life of her think why Frida Anttila would feel the need to lie about it.

'I don't know.' Liam had crossed his arms over his chest. He'd been wearing nice clothes, Hilda had noticed. *To impress Alicia?* His striped shirt looked expensive, as had the dark brown chinos. On his feet he'd been wearing his brown Dockers.

A thought now enters Hilda's mind. There was something very different about Liam yesterday. He seemed more confident, more approachable. Not happier, but more settled in himself and more assertive.

Perhaps he's got another woman already?

As the owner of a fashion shop, Hilda knew that the first thing a woman changes in a man is his appearance. Perhaps that's why he is staying at the Arkipelag rather than in the sauna cottage with Alicia? Hilda puts her hand over her mouth and decides she must do something. Whatever Uffe said last night. Neither of them understood the severity of the situation then. She goes over to the door to turn the 'Sorry, we're shut' sign on. She glances at her watch and sees that it is nearly 10am. She locks the door of the shop behind her, and with a determined gait, crosses the road and heads toward the *Ålands-bladet* offices.

Alicia is typing furiously at her computer when Liam enters the newspaper office.

'What are you doing here,' she says before she has time to think how rude this sounds. *I'm already going back to being a Finn,* she thinks, and adds, 'Sorry.'

She gets up and steps closer to Liam. Out of old habit she slips her hand around his waist and brushes her lips over his.

Liam stands as if frozen into place. He touches his lips and says, 'Can you talk?' He glances sideways at the other two people working in the open-plan office. One of them is Frida, who is pretending she didn't see Liam enter, and isn't covertly watching him and Alicia. But Alicia notices the glance and says, 'Frida, would you join us for a coffee?'

'Let's go into the kitchen,' Alicia adds and stretches her hand toward the door at the side. Frida rolls her eyes but gets up and walks into the kitchen. She's wearing a bright yellow dress over a pair of see-through black leggings and her red Doc Martens. Her tummy is very visible now, and as Alicia glances toward the editor in his glass cubicle, she wonders if Frida has finally told their boss about her condition. Alicia sees that Harri is watching them. 'I'll just have a word here,' she says in a quiet voice to Liam, nodding toward the glass office. 'Be nice!' she adds, widening her eyes at Liam.

Liam nods and follows Frida.

FIFTY-FIVE

Patrick has been sitting in his boat for the last half-hour, thinking about why Liam came to see him. He's decided it wasn't to do with Alicia, but with Frida and the baby. The man seemed fairly confident about his relationship with Alicia. Is the baby the only reason, or has he managed to worm his way back into Alicia's good books? What happened to her the other day? Did she sleep with her husband?

Patrick doesn't understand how Alicia could possibly forgive Liam for his affair. He knows how it hurts to think about someone you love—loved—with another person. The images of Mia with someone else keep flashing in front of his eyes. He hasn't met the guy yet, but he knows exactly who it is from his internet searches. Good-looking, muscular, a little shorter than Patrick, but a successful property developer. Patrick doesn't care about Mia any longer, but he knows how he felt when he first found out about the affair. Even now, twelve months later, it sometimes hurts when she doesn't look at him the way she used to.

Patrick sighs. Just as he thought he had found someone else, the ex comes flying in (literally). Well, this time he isn't going to give up without a fight. Patrick gets up, locks the cabin door in the boat and steps onto the jetty. He knows Alicia cannot resist him if he gets her on his own. It's worth a try at least, he thinks.

When Alicia opens the door to the kitchen, she is faced with a silence. Frida is standing by the window, looking at the boats bobbing gently up and down in the East Harbor. The wind had been strong last night, before a band of rain swept through the islands in the small hours. Alicia had been up worrying about Liam and Frida and the baby. Now the sun is out and the temperature is in the twenties. Alicia looks at Liam, who's sitting down. The only sound is the burbling of the percolator on the kitchen top.

Alicia takes a deep breath, but just as she is about to speak, the door opens and Hilda bursts in.

'Here you are!' she says looking from Alicia to Liam. When she spots Frida, who's turned away from the window, she opens her mouth and blurts out, 'Ah, Frida.' Even just saying her name, Hilda sounds disapproving and formal. Alicia doesn't know what to do. Should she ask her mother to leave?

'This is nice—the whole family together!' Frida says with such sarcasm in her voice that Alicia feels the heavy weight of the difficult conversation they are about to have. She sits down at the table. She might as well let her mother weigh in too; they will all have to get used being one family.

Frida remains standing, with her arms crossed over her now quite considerable belly, as does Hilda, who seems to be unable to move.

Liam is the first one to speak.

'Look, Frida, you must understand our shock over your news. We are all delighted, of course, if ...' Liam looks from Frida to Alicia to Hilda.

Alicia notices that he's chosen his words carefully, so that he is understood in English.

'Why don't you sit down, Hilda. And Frida?' Alicia says in Swedish.

The older woman sits down first, next to Alicia, taking her hand and squeezing it, as if Alicia is ill. Alicia gives her mother a 'be nice' look, and Hilda smiles and nods at her. Alicia returns the smile and takes her hand away.

'Please, Frida, can we now talk about this?' she says, pleading with the girl. Alicia has switched to English. 'Liam — and I — would very much like to know about you and our son.'

Frida pauses, looks at them and shrugs. Dropping her arms by her side, she walks to the round table and sits on the other side of Alicia.

Liam places his arms on the table and knits his fingers together. Again he speaks.

'Thank you, Frida. As you know, Alicia and I—and the whole family—were devastated when we lost Stefan.'

'As was I!' Frida says. Her voice is loud, but shaky, and Alicia sees she's near to breaking down. She puts her arm around the girl and is surprised when she doesn't shrug it away. 'It's OK. We just want to help and understand, you know?'

Frida nods. She lowers her eyes and leans in toward Alicia.

Both Hilda and Liam are looking at Alicia and Frida. Alicia raises her eyebrows at them. She wants her mother to remain calm and to make Liam understand that Hilda's involvement will only make matters worse.

'OK, Frida, you have no idea what wonderful news it is that you are having our son's baby,' Liam says, at which Frida lifts her eyes toward him.

Alicia watches her mother.

So she already knows!

'But,' Liam continues, and Frida says, 'I knew it!' But she stays seated, letting Alicia hold her.

'You must understand that we are puzzled. We never saw you together, and nor did Hilda,' Liam nods to Alicia's mother and continues, 'So to hear that you were, hmm, that close, is a surprise to us. A wonderful surprise, but perhaps you could tell us more about what—and how —well, perhaps not how, but when did you meet, and where, and that sort of thing?'

Frida is fiddling with a ring on her finger and mutters, 'I already told Alicia.'

'Yes, but we need to hear it too. Hilda will be a great-grandmother and I will be a grandfather.' At the last word Liam suddenly stops. Alicia sees that the news has finally hit him.

He's beginning to believe it.

'And we will have something of what we lost with our

dear son,' he continues, more quietly now. Alicia stretches out her other hand and puts it over Liam's fingers, which are still laced together on the table. He gives her a grateful smile and continues in a more steady tone.

'I would love to hear all of it.'

Liam looks around the table and adds, 'As I am sure we all would.'

FIFTY-SIX

'At first we were just friends, but then we fell in love.'

When Frida begins to talk, it's in a low, barely audible voice at first, but slowly she begins to gain confidence. Alicia can hear the joy and love she shared with Stefan. Frida tells them how she first met Stefan at a summer camp years ago, and then fell in love at the reunion last summer. How Stefan had made her laugh, and how they'd agreed to see each other again. The day after the reunion they met in Mariehamn, mostly in the English Park, just talking until Alicia came to collect Stefan.

'He was going home the next day but we kept in touch online,' Frida says and looks at Liam, whose face is now softer. He nods and Frida continues her story.

'We were desperate to see each other again, I was able to come over to England last year, and we spent the rest of the summer together.'

Alicia is fighting tears, because she recognizes her son,

her gentle, loving son. But also because she wishes Stefan had been able to confide in her and bring Frida home to meet her and Liam. Frida's eyes shine as she tells them how, once she returned home, Stefan messaged her several times a day and how they talked every night.

'He wouldn't let me go to sleep until I told him I loved him,' Frida says, and tears begin to run down her face. 'I miss him so much.'

Alicia puts her arms around Frida and wipes her make-up smeared cheeks with a tissue. The girl's body is at last non-resistant in her embrace and her shoulders have lost their stiffness.

Liam is staring at Frida, not saying a word, and Hilda is looking down at her hands.

'Well, this is wonderful news,' Hilda says suddenly, in Swedish, and everyone around the table turns to look at the older woman. Alicia notices that her mother's eyes are dampened by tears, but she is smiling. 'We will have something of Stefan in our lives again.'

Even though Liam doesn't understand Swedish, Alicia can see he gets what Hilda is saying. That her mother has accepted the news and believes Frida's side of the story.

Suddenly everyone's faces brighten up with smiles; even Liam's has a wide grin. That's when the door to the kitchen opens and Patrick walks in.

'Well, isn't this cozy,' Patrick says. 'A family reunion, is it?'

Alicia is surprised at the sarcasm in his voice. He's speaking in English, with a very Swedish accent. She can feel her face getting hot with embarrassment. Her mother doesn't know anything about her affair with Patrick, and neither does Frida. The last thing she wants is for this delicate relationship between her and the mother of her grandson to be pushed off balance so quickly.

Alicia gets up and faces Patrick. With her back to everyone, she searches Patrick's eyes and in a low voice in Swedish says, 'Can I talk with you outside?'

'Sure, wouldn't want to disturb this little gathering,' Patrick replies, his eyes dark with anger. Alicia takes the few steps past him and opens the door, but Patrick isn't moving.

'So, Liam, all onboard with the baby now, are we?' He's still facing the room, rather than Alicia, who says, quietly, 'Patrick.'

Hilda's eyes dart from Alicia to Patrick and Alicia sees she's putting one and one together. *Damn, you, Patrick!*

Alicia glances at Frida, but the girl is still wiping her eyes, and hasn't noticed the changed atmosphere in the room. Now Liam, too, gets up and says, 'I should be going. Let you get back to work. He places a hand over Frida's elbow and says, 'Are you going to be OK?'

Frida nods and they exchange smiles.

Liam turns to Hilda, who's still staring at Alicia and Patrick in turn. 'Shall we?'

'Oh, yes,' Hilda says and she too gets up.

After Liam and Hilda have left the room, Alicia repeats Patrick's name once more, and finally the man turns around and follows Alicia out of the kitchen.

'Frida, take a minute, OK?' Alicia says as she closes the door behind her.

'I'll see you later at home,' she says to her mother and hugs her.

Liam faces Alicia and, taking her hand, says, 'We need to talk.'

Alicia nods. She's aware of Patrick's eyes boring into her.

'See you at the hotel later?'

'I don't know ...' Alicia says.

Liam gives Alicia a hug, which she responds to, holding onto her husband for a moment longer than she intended. She can see Patrick over Liam's shoulder and closes her eyes. She doesn't want to see his expression.

'I'll be waiting,' Liam says, and taking Hilda's arm, he leaves the newspaper office.

Patrick and Alicia are standing alone in the middle of the open-plan office.

'Alicia, where are my words?' Harri shouts through the open door to his glass office.

'Nearly there,' Alicia shouts back and she looks up to Patrick. His blue eyes are fixed on hers and she has to swallow in order to speak.

'It's all got very complicated,' she says.

'Has it?' Patrick says. His voice is gentle now. He lifts his hand as if to touch Alicia's cheek, but notices Harri is staring at them, so drops his hand. 'It doesn't need to be.'

'No?' Alicia says. Her heart is racing, beating so hard against her summer dress that she has difficulty breathing.

But this is wrong.

Patrick shakes his head and lifts one side of his mouth. 'Meet me later on the boat. When you finish here.'

Alicia doesn't reply. She glances at the door to the

kitchen. If Frida comes out now, she will see them together and guess what Hilda has already worked out.

'Is this an editorial meeting?' Harry is suddenly standing next to them.

'Sort of,' Patrick replies. 'But it's finished now.' He nods to Alicia and turns. She watches his long, lean body disappear out of the door and down the staircase. Just before he is out of sight, he turns and smiles at Alicia.

FIFTY-SEVEN

Alicia just makes the deadline for her story about Daniel's accident, which gets her a 'Well done,' from Harri. As she's about to leave his office, he asks her to sit down.

'I don't wish to interfere in your affairs, and I know you're a big girl, but take it from someone who knows. The Erikssons are a powerful family in this town.'

Alicia shifts in her seat and looks straight at Harri. 'I know that.'

'And you know Patrick is on his way out of that family. He will be what some might call "a persona non-grata" soon?'

Stunned by these words, Alicia stares at the editor. *How does he know about Patrick's impending divorce?*

Harri gives a short chuckle at Alicia's expression. 'Oh, my dear, I know everything that goes on around here. Plus Kurt is a good friend of mine, as well as the owner of this paper. So, if you want to be part of this little set up here, I'd keep my nose clean vis à vis the Erikssons. Kurt and his lovely daughter in particular.'

For the second time in two days, Patrick is standing on the jetty, waiting for Alicia. It's a pleasant afternoon, with very little wind, and just a few persistent clouds. The harbor is busy, with boats arriving in batches as they're let through the Sjoland canal. It's the height of the tourist season and Patrick smiles as he watches families, mainly Finnish, emerge from their boats, windswept and tanned. Some men are sporting jaunty navy caps, with bright shorts and worn-out Docker shoes.

Patrick thinks back to when he bought the boat (OK, when Mia bought the boat for him) and his plans for trips out to the archipelago with Mia and the girls. Foolishly, he thought he could cure Mia of her dislike of boating; the woman was born on the islands, for goodness sake. He envisaged all of them taking a long trip past the outer islands like Kumlinge and Brändö all the way to Kustavi, and even perhaps visiting Turku before turning back. They would dock at all the harbors on the way, overnighting onboard but eating in the marina restaurants. What could be better? Instead, Mia had refused to step onboard *Mirabella*, calling it his 'toy'. Their mother's reluctance had led the girls to reject the idea too, so Patrick had been left to take a few day trips here and there on his own.

As Patrick watches a slim, attractive woman competently deal with the rigging of one of the larger sailing boats that has just arrived in the harbor, exchanging shouted instructions with a man at the tiller, his thoughts turn back to Alicia.

As soon as he stood close to her in the newspaper office, he regretted his earlier sarcasm in the kitchen. But walking into that happy family scene made his temper flare. How could she want to be back with Liam now? What had changed? Frida's baby? Surely that is not enough to wipe out past hurts? Patrick needs to see her to convince her that she has already moved on from her husband, that he is no good, that he has been unfaithful to her. That he has betrayed her just like Mia has betrayed him.

Patrick has read Alicia's article on the Romanian boy's death online on his phone, so he knows her work is done. She should be emerging from the newspaper office at any moment. He wants to go and stand outside the office, to catch Alicia as she comes out but he can't bring himself to appear that desperate. He's certain she will turn up to see him this time. The way she looked at him, with her eyes soft and loving, she definitely still feels something for him.

Alicia wants him, there's no doubt about it. But would the pull of a safe future with Liam, now they are both going to be grandparents, be enough to make her go back to him? The way the two of them looked the previous night was as though they had never been apart. But appearances can be misleading, as Patrick knows all too well. He's been keeping up appearances with Mia for twelve months now, and as far as he knows no one apart from Mia's parents, Mia and the lawyers are aware of their marital problems even now.

Patrick imagines how wonderful it will be to spend the

rest of the summer with Alicia. He will look after her. After he left Alicia, he went over to the ALKO store and bought a bottle of pink champagne to celebrate the news of the baby again. He hopes the baby is what they were all discussing in the *Ålandsbladet* kitchen, and not Liam's return to the marital bed. Patrick pulls out his phone and begins tapping on it.

Alicia sits at her desk and stares at the article she has just posted online. It has a catchy title, it's well-written, and with just a few edits by Harri, most of her own work. She sees that the post has already received ten shares after just a few minutes. She has a sense of achievement that she hasn't really experienced since Stefan's death. She had more or less given up chasing commissions from *The Financial Times*. She's forgotten how good it feels to have something you have created read by others.

Alicia moves the mouse and closes the window and the computer. A black screen is facing her when her phone pings.

Are you coming over?

Alicia sighs and gets up. She waves to Harri, who's still sitting at his desk, staring at his screen. The man doesn't see her, so Alicia pops her head around his doorway and says goodbye.

'Good work,' he says and adds, 'And remember what I said. Don't want to lose you.'

Sounds very much like a threat, Alicia wants to reply. Instead, she just nods, 'Yes, thank you. See you tomorrow.'

She walks past Frida's desk, which is empty. Alicia

heard Frida tell Harri she wasn't feeling very well soon after their talk in the kitchen. When Alicia asked her if she was OK Frida smiled and said, 'Don't worry. I'm just taking care of myself.' She had her hand over her tummy and Alicia hugged her.

'Let me know if you need anything,' she said, to which Frida smiled and nodded.

Alicia walks slowly down the stairs and opens the glass-paneled door onto the street. She crosses the little garden and makes her way down toward the sea. The sun emerges from a thin white cloud, and the steel riggings and white hulls of boats in the harbor in front of her gleam in the bright sunshine.

Alicia doesn't know what to do.

If she turns left and walks along Strandvägen toward the entrance to Arkipelag, she is sure she is going to find Liam, and possibly Hilda, there. She will be welcomed into the old, safe family life that she knows. Although changed by the tragic loss of their son, there is hope that they can begin to support each other and accept life without Stefan, while they wait for the wonder of an unexpected grandchild. But has Liam really changed? And is the affair really over? And what about Patrick?

All she has to do is turn right, skirt the parking lot, and she will come to the harbor and Patrick, who is waiting to speak to her. But will he just want to speak? Can Alicia trust herself to tell Patrick face-to-face it's over? Does she want it to be over with him? If she goes to Patrick now, she will have to tell Liam. She doesn't want to see the same pain on his face that she witnessed when she opened the door of the sauna cottage to him. She wants to forget the way he looked, pale and drawn, like he had seen a ghost. Even though she was angry with him, she hated seeing him hurt. The more she thinks back to that night, the more shame she feels. The guilt about what she has been doing is suddenly so raw and real that she has to catch her breath.

She taps a message, 'Sorry,' on her phone and presses send.

She begins to walk, quickly placing one foot in front of another. She has made her decision, she doesn't want to linger and change her mind now.

FIFTY-EIGHT

After leaving the newspaper office, Liam managed to convince Hilda that she should go back to her shop. He and Alicia would talk soon, he said. They were standing in the middle of the busy Torggatan, having walked in silence through the *Sitkoff* shopping center.

'You go to her, yes?' Hilda had made him promise. He had taken hold of her arms and given her a reassuring squeeze. He then watched her walk over the road and enter her shop.

Now he is sitting in the outdoor café of the hotel, watching children messing around in the pool. Opposite him is the East Harbor, with its large yachts and the *von Knorring* steamer in the distance. He is keeping an eye on the road leading from Alicia's office, but he is glad that the *Club Marin* obstructs his view of the part of the jetty where Patrick's boat is moored. He wouldn't be able to stomach seeing Patrick with Alicia. Not again.

What if Alicia doesn't appear?

Liam is on his second beer when at last he sees his wife's blond hair appear on the pedestrian walkway between the hotel and the harbor. He holds his breath as he sees her walk determinedly, without smiling — such a Scandinavian trait of hers — toward the Hotel Arkipelag. He sighs with relief.

The first thing Liam asks her is if she's OK.

'I'm fine,' Alicia says and smiles. Now she's made her decision, the relief is palpable.

Liam reaches out and places his hand over hers on the table. 'That's good,' he says and returns her smile.

They both sit for a while, watching the children in the pool.

'Do you remember when we used to bring Stefan here and he never wanted to get out, even when his skin was wrinkled and his lips blue from the cold?' Alicia asks.

'Yes,' Liam nods.

'I hope we can bring the baby here too,' Alicia continues. She gazes at Liam. She needs to know he is fully onboard with Frida's pregnancy. He looked as if he accepted her story earlier, but she wants to make sure.

'I look forward to that,' he replies.

Alicia watches his face. It looks less drawn than it has done in the past two days. She wishes with all her heart that she hadn't brought such pain to him. But at least he seems to be happy about Frida's baby.

Alicia shifts on her seat and takes a sip out of her glass, removing her hand from under Liam's. It is only

4PM, but with the day she's had, it feels as if it should already be evening.

'I want to stay here,' Alicia says. Again, she is keeping an eye on Liam.

He lifts his head in surprise.

'I see.'

Now it's Alicia's turn to take hold of Liam's hand. The familiar feel of his slender, but strong, fingers under her own reminds her how much they have in common. The long marriage, Stefan, and now a future grandchild.

'But I also want to save our marriage,' she says.

Liam is quiet. He's not looking at her and suddenly Alicia feels cold. She shivers and brings her arms around her body.

What if he doesn't want me anymore?

'I can't give up my job. My patients rely on me,' he says quietly, lifting his now serious eyes to Alicia's.

Again she reaches out to him, this time taking his hands into hers.

'I know. And I don't want to give up seeing our grand-child being born and growing up. And I love my job at *Ålandsbladet.*'

'What do you want me to do?' Liam says.

'I don't know. But I do know that we can make it work. Until the baby is born, I'd like to stay here. You can see if you can get more holiday, and come and stay for long weekends, and then for a few more days when the baby is born? I can come over to London for weekends too. I know it's not going to be easy, but we often don't see each other for days even when I'm in London, not when you are working all hours. Especially not since ...'

Alicia lets go of Liam, but he pulls her back toward him.

'That's over, I told you. You must trust me,' he says and peers closely at Alicia. 'As I must trust you, if we are to live in two different countries from now on.'

Alicia nods. She pushes the feeling of guilt away. 'It won't be easy, but I can't leave Frida. You can see that, can't you? Her mother is not well enough to look after her and she has literally no one else now Daniel is gone.'

'I can see that,' Liam says and after a moment's hesitation continues, 'I love you Alicia. I never stopped loving you and I will do anything to make you happy. I am here until the end of the week, and when I go back I'll see how I can arrange my schedule to get more time off in longer blocks.'

Alicia is so relieved, she wants to jump up and shout out, 'Yes!' It's as if her old Liam, her loving husband, has come back to her.

At that moment, he leans over and whispers in Alicia's ear, 'Can I kiss you now?'

She nods and Liam places his hands on either side of her face, and gently, so gently, presses his lips onto Alicia's.

The effect of his touch, so familiar, yet so exciting, pulses through Alicia's body. Yet, she thinks, it's too soon, so she pulls herself away from Liam and takes another sip of her wine.

'You will be the sexiest grandmother in the world,' he says in a low voice.

Alicia laughs. They both silent for a moment, gazing at each other. Alicia can't quite believe how far they have come and how much has changed in just a matter of weeks and days. Suddenly she remembers her mother.

'I think we should go over to Sjoland for dinner. Hilda will be driving Uffe mad otherwise.'

'OK,' Liam says and smiles.

EPILOGUE

Little Anne Sofie is born at the Mariehamn Hospital at twenty minutes past midnight on September 1st. Alicia and Liam are in attendance. Liam had flown in from London the week before, while Alicia had been staying in Frida's flat for the previous two weeks. Several selfies are taken, and when the baby is asleep in the cot beside her mother, and Frida closes her eyes, Alicia and Liam tiptoe out of the room and hug each other for a long time in the hospital corridor.

As they walk arm in arm into the empty parking lot, the cold fall air hits Alicia. There's a harsh northerly wind and leaves are swirling beside the tarmac, where a line of birches dips down toward the sea.

'You're not going to work today, are you?' Liam asks as they reach Alicia's new car. She had bought a used Volvo a couple of weeks ago, so that she had transportation when the time came for the birth.

'No!' Alicia says and turns to Liam, smiling.

'Well, in that case, perhaps we should wet the baby's head?'

Alicia nods and they drive the short distance to the Hotel Arkipelag parking lot. 'You go on and order, I'm just going to let others know the good news,' she says.

Liam stays in the passenger seat for a moment, looking down at his hands. Alicia can guess Liam wonders if Patrick is one of the people she will contact, but she doesn't want to discuss him with Liam. Not today when her heart is filled with love for the wonderful new little person in her life. Alicia hasn't seen anything as beautiful as Anne Sofie. Her tiny fists tightly closed against her little body and the show of determination in her rosy little mouth. When Alicia first held her, tears began running down her cheeks and they all laughed. She cannot remember being so happy.

'Don't be long,' Liam says eventually, brushing his lips against her cheek.

As Alicia watches Liam walk toward the hotel entrance, shielding himself against the wind with his hand, she thinks how happy she was to see him when he stepped off the plane at Mariehamn airport. He'd decided to fly, to save time. He had to go via Helsinki, but he still arrived about half a day earlier than he would have done by sea.

Their relationship is in a good place now.

Alicia is still living in the sauna cottage and Liam in London, but they have plans for Liam to move to the islands. Alicia keeps in touch with Patrick too, but only as a friend. In the small town of Mariehamn, with the tourists gone, it would be impossible not to see each other.

Besides, now Patrick's divorce is official, Alicia is happy to help him by simply listening. As she has got to know him better, her attraction toward him has begun to diminish. Perhaps because she has moved on with her life? Frida and the baby have been Alicia's priority for months now, and she guesses it will be the case for months, perhaps years, to come. And that is exactly how it should be.

THE NORDIC HEART BOOKS 1-4

She has her life planned out. He lets the wind guide his sails. As the Cold War heats up, can they keep love alive on either side of the iron curtain?

Finland, 1980. Kaisa has never been a risk taker. After graduation, she plans to marry the dependable older man who helped to pay for her classes and kept a roof over her head. But when she accepts an invitation to a party at the British Embassy, a handsome naval officer makes her want to throw caution to the wind. She surprises herself when they share a passionate kiss under the stars and promise to see each other again. But how could she possibly give up her sure-thing relationship for a man she barely knows?

When Peter Williams pictured his future, he saw a

rising in the ranks and an endless trip around the world. Though when he meets the strong-willed Kaisa in Helsinki, his passion for the sea takes a serious turn. Not even the excitement of hunting down Russian submarines can compare to the thrill of his lips on hers. But despite his growing feelings, his commanding officers won't tolerate him pursuing a woman from a Soviet-friendly nation.

Both torn between impossible choices, Kaisa and Peter must search their souls for the right answer. With the Cold War heating up between them, can two star-crossed lovers find their courage or will their relationship sink on the high seas?

The Nordic Heart Series is a breathtaking contemporary women's fiction series with an undercurrent of romance. If you like vivid historical details, star-crossed chemistry, and complex characters, then you'll love Helena Halme's tale of a Cold War romance.

- Prequel *The Young Heart*
- **Book 1 *The English Heart***
- **Book 2 *The Faithful Heart***
- **Book 3 *The Good Heart***
- **Book 4 *The True Heart***
- Book 5 *The Christmas Heart*

Buy *The Nordic Heart Books 1-4* to experience a vibrant tale of courage and love in the face of war today!

ABOUT THE AUTHOR

Helena Halme grew up in Tampere, central Finland, and moved to the UK via Stockholm and Helsinki at the age of 22. She is a former BBC journalist and has also worked as a magazine editor, a bookseller and, until recently, ran a Finnish/British cultural association in London.

Since gaining an MA in Creative Writing at Bath Spa University, Helena has published eight fiction titles, including five in *The Nordic Heart* Romance Series.

Helena lives in North London with her ex-Navy husband and an old stubborn terrier, called Jerry. She loves Nordic Noir and sings along to Abba songs when no one is around.

You can read Helena's blog at www.helenahalme.com, where you can also sign up for her *Readers' Group* and receive an exclusive, free short story, *The Day We Met*.

Find Helena Halme online
www.helenahalme.com
hello@helenahalme.com

A NOTE FROM THE AUTHOR

I hope you enjoyed *The Island Affair!*

You may have heard authors talk about reviews and the effect they have on the success of the title.

Having a bunch of good reviews attached to your book has been likened to a scene in a new town when you're looking for somewhere to eat. The restaurant you've read about has a queue outside. You notice another place opposite with the same kind of food on offer. But this restaurant is nearly empty, with only a couple of tables occupied, and no queue outside. Which place do you choose? Most people join the queue, because why wouldn't you go for a restaurant that is so popular that people are willing to *wait* to eat there? The other place opposite must serve really bad food if only a handful of diners are inside, right? Perhaps it's had a case of food poisoning or something.

So please form a virtual queue outside my book in your favourite online store and write a review.

Thank you.

Lightning Source UK Ltd.
Milton Keynes UK
UKHW010725190519
342927UK00001B/34/P